Some Like It Hot

A-List novels by Zoey Dean:

THE A-LIST

GIRLS ON FILM

BLONDE AMBITION

TALL COOL ONE

BACK IN BLACK

SOME LIKE IT HOT

Some Like It Hot

An A-List Novel

by
Zoey Dean

LITTLE, BROWN AND COMPANY
New York ❧ Boston ❧ London

Little, Brown and Company

Time Warner Book Group
1271 Avenue of the Americas, New York, NY 10020
Visit our Web site at www.lb-teens.com

First Edition: April 2006

 Produced by Alloy Entertainment
151 West 26th Street, New York, NY 10001

Cover photography copyright © Getty Images

ISBN 0-316-01093-6

10 9 8 7 6 5 4 3 2 1

CWO

Printed in the United States of America

For Francois at the Hôtel du Cap.
Merci pour une nuit inoubliable.

Fasten your seat belts, it's going to be a bumpy night!

—Bette Davis, *All About Eve*

THE PROM COMMITTEE OF THE GRADUATING
CLASS OF BEVERLY HILLS HIGH SCHOOL, 2006
INVITES YOU TO THE 50TH ANNIVERSARY
SENIOR PROM

8:00 P.M.

MAY 16, 2006

GRAND BALLROOM
BEL AIR GRAND HOTEL

BLACK TIE

PER COUPLE *(Same-Sex Couples Welcome)*: $1,250

RSVP CARD ENCLOSED

Skirt So Short It Looked
Like a Loincloth

"Prom, Anna?" Cammie Sheppard asked disdainfully, shaking her trademark strawberry-blond curls off her forehead with a swift motion made perfect by experience. "Seriously, you want to go to the Beverly Hills High School *prom*?"

Anna Percy—an inch taller than Cammie at five foot eight, with the classic features of a girl whose ancestors had come over on the *Mayflower* (they practically had) and the razor-cut shiny straight blond hair of girls who'd been done personally by Raymond at his new salon on Rodeo Drive—glanced up from the small brown vial of an amber essential oil she'd been holding beneath her nose. "We're seniors. Why not?"

Cammie flashed Anna a look of pure scorn. "Because compared to the parties I have already been to and/or given, a high school *prom* is about as exciting as a square dance in Sacramento."

"I'll second that," Sam Sharpe agreed, as she

uncorked a small vial of essence of English rose that the well-coiffed and just as well-face-lifted saleswoman had suggested she try. "We can do something else that weekend. How about we take my father's jet to his house in Maui?"

Though Anna's family was easily as well off as her friend Sam's, and probably richer than Sam's and Cammie's combined, she still hadn't gotten completely used to how easily the two of them were willing to be extravagant. Back in New York City, before she'd moved to Los Angeles, Anna had certainly gone on lavish vacations, lived in a coveted Upper East Side town house, had a spacious walk-in closet full of great clothes, and been well aware of how fortunate she was to have been born to this life. But the conspicuous consumption of Los Angeles was somehow . . . different.

Anna, Sam, and Sam's friend Cammie had stopped at the Scent Bar in the Hancock Park neighborhood of Los Angeles as part of a project to help raise money for DIS—Drama in Schools, an after-school drama program in the least fortunate L.A. neighborhoods. Everyone in Hollywood had a cause, either because they were truly philanthropic or because it made them look like they were. DIS was the pet project of a former raven-haired child actress now in her twenties, who'd recently exploded from flat-chested to Pamela Anderson territory—the tabloids cried, "Implants!" but she claimed a late adolescence. That actress had asked Sam's father, Jackson Sharpe—"America's Most Beloved Action Hero"—to be part of her new campaign. The idea was that a star would create a limited edition of a scent with his or her name on it; the perfume or cologne would be auctioned on eBay, and all proceeds would go to DIS.

The blossoming—in more ways than one—young actress had asked her young showbiz friends to participate. As "Action Jackson" Sharpe was staring down middle age and the very real possibility of post hipdom loomed on the horizon, he'd readily agreed to participate. But since he was on location for his newest movie, *Ben-Hur* (a remake of the often-remade classic set in the Roman Empire—Jackson was not just starring in it, he was directing it), he'd asked his assistant Kiki to do the honors for him.

Sam, though, had decreed that she'd do it instead. She'd wanted to check out Scent Bar. Plus, as she explained to Anna, if she smelled the actress Jena Malone's signature scent on one more girl at Beverly Hills High School, she was personally going to spray her with some vile Jungle Gardenia knockoff you could buy from a street vendor near the Staples Center.

Anna had been curious to come, even if Cammie had been invited too (they didn't get along, to put it mildly). Scent Bar was a one-of-a-kind boutique, where you couldn't get through the door without an appointment, and to get a good appointment, it definitely helped to be the daughter of America's top action hero. The place looked more like a well-appointed living room than a store. It had white upholstered chairs that circled a central, low-slung metal table, and a spare white counter for the resident saleswoman/perfume expert; there was even a sound system for which the clientele could choose from thousands of MP3s. Sam had allowed Anna to choose, and she'd selected some piano variations by the French composer and pianist Erik Satie.

"Ugh." Sam recoiled from the pungent odor wafting from yet another bottle of essential oil. "I had a nanny who wore this shit." She passed the vial to Cammie. "Remember?"

Cammie sniffed and grimaced. "She was from Sweden or something. We were what, eleven? She hooked up with that actor who did all those guest spots on *Friends*."

"And lived in that asshole producer's guesthouse— the one who jumped from ICM to CAA and then to your dad's agency," Sam added, nodding.

Anna barely followed this Hollywood shorthand. Unlike Sam and Cammie, Anna had neither been born in Beverly Hills nor had show business in her blood. In fact, she'd been in Los Angeles for barely five months, having moved from the Upper East Side of Manhattan to live with her father and finish her senior year at Beverly Hills High School before going back east to Yale the next year.

There were a lot of reasons that she'd made this huge change in her life, but the biggest one was that she wanted to reinvent herself. The box into which Anna had been born and bred was a confining one of old money and privilege. She wanted to push boundaries, to have new experiences, to stop being the proverbial literature-devouring, well-mannered—and worst of all, predictable—*good girl.*

Anna caught sight of her reflection in the stark, mirrored wall at the rear of the perfumery. She was slender, with the carriage of a girl who had spent many hours toiling in ballet classes. Her wheat-blond hair fell straight to her shoulders, brushing the white eyelet of her Valentino halter top. With it she wore ancient khakis—she couldn't remember when or where she'd purchased them—and Chanel leather cutout ballet flats. Five-karat antique diamond studs inherited from her great-grandmother adorned her ears. She wore a touch of Stila lip gloss and some brown Yves Saint Laurent mascara but was otherwise makeup-free. She'd heard others say she resembled Gwyneth Paltrow, but that wasn't what Anna saw. All she saw was a traditional-looking girl who screamed, "I'm safe!"

Her gaze slid to Sam, who had the pampered air of the semifamous teen daughter of a very famous movie star who made the most of her better-than-average—but by Beverly Hills standards less-than-average—looks. Her perfectly made-up brown eyes were the color of rich chocolate and sparkled with intelligence; her glossy, shoulder-length chestnut hair was perfectly streaked with varying shades of butterscotch highlights. Her golden tan, sprayed on weekly at B2V Salon, was flawless. Her outfit, a citron Follies tank top with a braided leather neckline and high-rise Joe's Muse jeans (because low-risers were *so* last year—and thank God, because she was sure her ass looked like a relief map of Colorado in them) were as expensive as they looked. Sam's jeans were two sizes larger than her tank top. In her Beverly Hills neighborhood, this fact alone could have been the kiss of death. Her perceived bodily deficits colored everything she said, did, and thought—no one was harder on Sam's appearance than Sam. That said, Sam was by far the smartest person Anna had met since she'd come to California. Anna liked her a lot.

Then there was Cammie, aka Walking Sex. Cammie was thin but also curvy in every right place ever dreamed up by mankind. Her hair fell in strawberry blond ringlets past her shoulders. Luminous honey-colored eyes were lined with Shiseido black eyeliner and mascara, her pouty lips slicked with Nars lipstick in Masai. Cammie always showed as much creamy skin as possible. At the moment, she wore a sequined Purp7e Agua bikini under a transparent pale pink silk Pia Hallstrom peasant top, plus a pair of Joe's jeans. The jeans were how-low-can-you-go (and screw the fact that the fashion rags were saying low rise was over—Cammie didn't follow fashion, she created it).

In Anna's experience, whenever she was anywhere with Cammie, the eyes of every male in the vicinity gravitated to Cammie like tourists to the Hollywood Walk of Fame. Even Ben used to—

Anna winced. She *definitely* did not want to think about Cammie with her boyfriend, Ben Birnbaum. They'd been a couple the year before. Mental pictures of the two of them together made the normally sane and dependable Anna a little bit crazy. Sane and dependable, she feared, could not compete with luscious. And Cammie was luscious.

Ben and Cammie had been together before Anna had first come to California. Today, she'd be seeing him again for the first time in three months; he was *finally* home from Princeton for the summer.

Her stomach did a loop-the-loop in anticipation. There had been such a strange but powerful connection between the two of them right from the very start. They'd actually met on Anna's airline flight to Los Angeles; Ben had impetuously invited her to Jackson Sharpe's wedding that very evening—her first in Los Angeles—at the Griffith Observatory. The night had been so wonderful, until Ben basically abandoned her at a marina after a midnight cruise. He'd later offered an excuse, but Anna had been slow to forgive. Only when Ben had shown up in Las Vegas a couple of months ago when he knew Anna would be there did their relationship get back on track, and only then when they'd vowed to be honest with each other.

"How's it going, ladies?" the saleswoman asked. She had gorgeous red hair and a thick Irish accent—Anna guessed that she was in her late thirties, though in L.A. it was impossible to tell anyone's real age, because nearly everyone had work done. If you hadn't had work done, people assumed you had anyway, which meant that if you were in your late thirties and *looked* like you were late-thirties, everyone assumed you were really forty-five. She was petite in black capris and a sleeveless turtleneck; she had doe eyes, thin lips, and wore her lovely long mane in a retro French twist.

"We want to create something better than Clive Christian No. 1," Cammie announced, crossing her legs for emphasis.

"Ah, what could be better than Clive Christian?" the saleswoman rhapsodized. "Two thousand dollars an ounce. Spicy citrus top notes, bergamot, orris root, cardamom—"

"Excuse me," Cammie interrupted, getting up from her white chair to put her hands on Sam's shoulders. "Talk to them, because I'm meeting my boyfriend in, like, five minutes. Don't forget, you're dealing with Jackson Sharpe's daughter." She kissed Sam's cheek. "It was real." With an emotionless wave at Anna, she took off, a slew of boutique shopping bags in hand.

"Don't say it," Sam warned Anna, even as the saleswoman stood by. "She gives new meaning to the term *self-centered*."

Anna smiled. "You took the words right out of my mouth."

She couldn't be mad at Sam for inviting Cammie, because she understood about their friendship. It went back to their childhoods. Anna's best friend from New York, Cynthia Baltres, sometimes rubbed people the wrong way too. Yet there was something deeply important about their history—something special and precious about having a friend who knew you since before you could even write your own name.

Whether it was Anna and Cyn or Sam and Cammie, it was the same timeless thing.

A half hour later, with the assistance of Miss Ireland, 1985, Sam and Anna had created the Jackson Sharpe signature scent—lavender, lemon, and marzipan. Miss Ireland, 1985, explained that Scent Bar's favorite lab would mix some samples, send them over to the Sharpe estate for Jackson's final approval, and then create a limited batch for the charity auction.

"I like it a lot," Anna told her. She sniffed the back of her wrist again. "Are you going to save a vial for Eduardo?"

"The guy's halfway around the world," Sam reminded Anna, as she signed a few papers that the saleswoman had given her. "He doesn't need me to give him cologne."

Sam had recently returned from a long weekend in Paris, visiting Eduardo Muñoz at the Sorbonne. She'd first met him on a winter vacation with Anna to Mexico; Eduardo had been taken with Sam immediately. She'd been wary, though, assuming that any hot guy who paid attention to her had an angle—that he either wanted a role in a Jackson Sharpe movie or had just written the perfect Jackson Sharpe vehicle.

As it turned out, Eduardo was from Peru and neither knew nor cared who Sam was; he'd simply found her beautiful and charming. He loved her ample curves as much as she hated them, which was really, really hard for Sam to accept.

"Didn't you have a good time in France?" Anna asked, as they pushed out of Scent Bar and turned south on La Brea, a broad boulevard that twenty years ago had been gritty and industrial but now was well into gentrification, with pricey boutiques and just-as-pricey restaurants in between the hardware stores and restaurant-supply dealers.

Sam stopped to inspect a turquoise Elegantly Waisted leather belt by Selma Blair in a shop window. "Would that belt give me hippo hips?"

"I take it you don't want to discuss it."

"Selma is married to Ahmet Zappa, did you know that? Fifty-fifty they'll be divorced by Christmas."

"I don't know who either of those people are, Sam."

"Sam! Oh, Sammy!"

Across the street, Anna saw two brunette girls frantically waving in their direction. One of them was actually jumping up and down to get Sam's attention. When the light changed, they ran across La Brea like a pair of Olympic sprinters.

"*Merde.*" Sam reached in her bag for her new Maui Jim polarized sunglasses and slipped them on as the light changed and the two girls trotted across the street and up onto the sidewalk. "Jasmine Eckels and Ophelia Berman. Battle stations, battle stations. Prepare for the attack of the prom weenies."

"Attack of the *what*?"

"Sam!" The shorter of the two girls squealed and threw her arms around Sam as if Sam were her long lost sister; then she shook Anna's hand. "Hi, I'm Jazz— short for Jasmine. And this is Fee—short for Ophelia."

"My parents met doing *Hamlet* at the Utah Shakespearean Festival," Fee explained to Anna, rolling her eyes. "I always have to explain my name. Anyway, it's better than 'Oaf.' I've seen you around school."

Anna smiled politely. She'd seen them, too, but they weren't in any of her classes. They were both cute but plump. Jazz's eyes were quite close together—it seemed like she'd spackled on a fair amount of makeup to compensate. Her clothes, too, pushed the outer limits of good taste—a short plaid Catholic-schoolgirl skirt fastened with an oversize silver safety pin, a shrunken sleeveless Cardin cashmere shell, and white thigh-high boots. Fee, on the other hand, was quite tall and angular. She wore a red silk shirt unbuttoned and knotted under her bust, about two dozen beaded necklaces, ditto on the bracelets, and a skirt so short it was approaching a loincloth.

"It's so cool running into you, Sam!" Jazz gushed. "Because I was going to call you tonight. About prom! Did you hear that Fee and I are co-chairmen?"

"You betcha." Sam shifted the strap of her white-with-gold-grommets Hermès bag to her other shoulder and didn't even try to muster false enthusiasm.

"This prom is going to be the most amazing ever," Fee cried. "We're doing it at the Bel Air Grand Hotel. Isn't that totally awesome?"

"No, it's totally *old*," Sam replied.

Jazz nodded eagerly. "Old *Hollywood*. Sinatra, Clark Gable, Jane Fonda—"

"Exactly," Sam interrupted. "No one under the age of, like, *death* goes there."

Both girls laughed heartily as if Sam had just cracked the world's funniest joke. Then they all had to wait a moment as a dozen noisy Harleys, all piloted by bare-chested gay guys with pierced nipples, roared past. The pause apparently gave Jazz and Fee the chance to recharge their "perky" batteries.

"It's going to be so cool, I swear," Jazz insisted. She grabbed Sam's hand and held on for dear life. "You're coming, right?"

Sam stared pointedly at Jazz's viselike grip; the girl hastily withdrew her hand.

"Sorry," Jazz apologized, then geared up for her next frontal assault. "This is our high school's fiftieth prom since 1946—they didn't have them during Vietnam—and I'm sure you wouldn't miss it. Neither would Cammie or your other friends, like Parker and Krishna and Blu—"

"And Dee Young of course, if she becomes more mentally healthy," Fee put in. "I heard about what happened in Las Vegas. Yikes! I am *so* planning on visiting her."

Dee Young was Sam's other longtime best friend. Dee had always been a bit . . . off, and then when they'd all been in Vegas, she had a nervous breakdown. Currently she was an in-patient at the Ojai Psychiatric Institute, diagnosed as bipolar. Sam had told Anna that Dee was improving, but her release date was uncertain.

"How about you cut the bullshit, Fee," Sam suggested coldly. "You barely know her."

"You *had* to bring up Dee, didn't you?" Jazz hissed at Fee. "I *told* you not to." She took a deep breath and fixed her gaze on Sam. "So, prom?"

Sam shrugged. "I'll get back to you."

Fee looked as if she'd just gotten word that a close relative had died in a plane crash. "You have to come," she muttered, eyes on the pavement. "You can't *not* come."

"Why not?"

The two girls traded an intense look; then Jazz seemed to steel herself. "I'll level with you, Sam. If the coolest girls in the school don't come, then the coolest guys in the school won't come. And if *none* of the coolest kids at school come—"

"We're screwed," Fee concluded, throwing her hands wide. "Only the losers will show up. We'll go down in history as the pathetic girls that gave the lame-ass fiftieth-anniversary prom."

"I think prom sounds like fun," Anna put in.

"Thank you, Anna! See, Sam? She's coming." Fee looked ready to embrace Anna.

"She didn't say that," Sam corrected. "She said it sounded like fun."

"Well . . . what if we do it for charity?" Jazz offered. "Any charity you want."

"We did charity last year," Sam reminded her. "That's why Cammie and I went."

"Please?" Fee begged. "Pleasepleaseplease? We need you."

Sam raised her sunglasses to better make eye contact. "You know, Fee, since my friend Anna really was thinking about going, I was starting to think about going. You almost had me. But bringing up Dee and saying that you guys were going to visit her? Come on. You guys wouldn't visit her if I gave you comp tickets to the opening of *Ben-Hur*. That was a low blow. Even for this town. Better luck next time. Have a great prom."

The Anti-Anna

They ducked into the Insomnia Café on Beverly Boulevard, with its square white front and blocky black INSOMNIA lettering; Sam said it was the best dessert and coffee place close to La Brea. The décor was comfortable—a brown and mustard yellow interior, with framed watercolors for sale on the walls and early Beatles music playing in the background. There were square burgundy couches and maybe twenty-five wooden tables with chairs. At most of these tables sat screen-writer types—baseball caps and two days of beard growth for the guys, dark sweatshirts and black jeans for the girls. The laptop of choice was either an Apple or a Sony Vaio, with nary an Averatec in sight.

Even better than the creative décor was the delicious aroma. The place smelled heavenly, of almond cookies and fresh potato bread. Anna's mouth literally watered as they found the last open table. Meanwhile, Sam kept glancing toward the front door. "What are you doing?" Anna asked.

"Looking to see if the prom weenies followed me."

A bone-thin out-of-work-actress type with a pierced eyebrow, dreads, and matte red lipstick took their order—espressos and chocolate croissants—and immediately brought them two bottles of spring water.

"You still want to go," Sam declared with a grin. "I see it in your nauseatingly perfect face."

"I do," Anna conceded.

"Why?"

"Well . . . I'm curious."

"They don't have proms back in New York?" Sam challenged.

"Of course we do. I think I thought . . . this might be interesting."

Sam grinned. "It might be, if you were a cultural anthropologist. You know, they were fine until they brought up Dee."

Dee had basically had a psychotic breakdown on the same Las Vegas trip where Anna had reunited with Ben. It had been a sign of Fee and Jazz's desperation that they'd tried to wheedle their way into Sam's graces by playing the Dee card. Anna understood how that made Sam feel: used and manipulated. If she knew anything at all about Sam, it was that her friend detested being used.

On the other hand, Anna still thought the idea of the Beverly Hills High School prom was entertaining.

"Let me explain to you why our prom is a joke," Sam opined. "It's the same shit every year—B-list girls in charge. If they don't get the A-list to come, then their lives are utter and abject failures forevermore. You really want to be part of that tawdry little scene?"

"That's not exactly an embracing attitude," Anna jibed. "A-list, B-list . . ."

"You told me you have proms in New York," Sam scoffed. "Tell me it's not the same thing. I dare you."

Okay, Anna had to admit that was true. On the West Coast, you were A-list either because you were so hot that you couldn't be anything else or because your parents were movie stars, had their own TV series or talent agency, or ran a studio. Sam was automatically A-list because of her father. Cammie was double-barrel A-list, qualifying both because of her looks *and* because her father was one of the most powerful agents in Hollywood. Dee was A-list because her father was a famous music producer.

The East Coast version of the A-list was demarcated differently, along the lines of old money, relationship to royalty, and/or the arts. You could be A-list if you could trace your lineage back to Peter Stuyvesant; you could be A-list if you were the kid of the first-name partner at a Wall Street law firm; you could be A-list if you were well-reviewed in the *New York Review of Books*.

There was one other big difference, now that Anna thought about it. Looks were far less important in New York. You could be ugly as a horned toad in New York and still be on the A-list, if there were other qualifications in your favor. Here in La-La Land, there was a minimum standard of attractiveness.

The whole thing struck her as bordering on the insane. Eduardo had fallen for Sam without caring what list she was on.

Anna sighed. "I was actually thinking that Eduardo and Ben would get along great."

Sam leaned back in her chair. "You don't *really* think Ben wants to go to prom?"

Excellent question. Would her boyfriend, who had just finished his freshman year at Princeton, find the high school prom unbearable?

"Maybe he would," Anna ventured.

"And maybe he wouldn't," Sam insisted. She craned around, looking for the waitress. "Where is she? Probably in the break room reading *Variety*."

"Come on, Sam," Anna coaxed. "I think you should reconsider. I bet you could get Eduardo to fly in, and the four of us could go together."

Anna couldn't gauge Sam's reaction because Sam had turned completely around. There was a small bulletin board on the wall directly behind them, one of the informal ones that you found in coffeehouses all over Los Angeles for people who were not ready to turn their self-marketing efforts over to Craigslist. This one was run-of-the-mill, overflowing with hand-scrawled file cards advertising for roommates, cleaning services, and cars for sale.

"I mean it. Ben and Eduardo would really like each other," Anna prompted, trying to get her friend's attention.

Suddenly, Sam's right arm shot out and ripped a notice off the board. "This is perfect. I can do this!"

"Prom?"

"No, *this*." She thrust the yellow flyer at Anna.

INTERNATIONAL COMPETITION
DOCUMENTARY FILMS BY YOUNG FILMMAKERS
Middle-grade and High school divisions
Winning documentaries of no more than twenty
minutes will be screened at a variety of
festivals, including the Greater Atlanta Film
Festival, the Tennessee Film Festival, the
Brussels Fête du Cinéma, and the Los Angeles
Independent Festival of Moving Picture Arts
Submission deadline: June 30, 2006
Sponsored by Cahiers du Cinéma, the National
Institute of Film (Canada), the National
Institute of Film (USA), and the British
Documentarians Association.

There was a ton of fine print at the bottom, specifying length, format, how to enter, and a host of other rules. The most interesting rule that Anna saw was that the judging would be blind. That is, filmmakers would be assigned a number, and only their number could go in the credits.

Anna looked up at Sam, perplexed. "You don't do documentaries."

"So? I could learn. Look, this is great. It's international. And it's totally fair. No one would know that I'm my father's daughter. I'll be judged on my talent alone. How not Beverly Hills is *that*?"

The skinny waitress finally bought them their croissants and espressos; Sam sipped hers thoughtfully as she perused the flyer again.

"Well, what would you make a film about?" Anna asked. She stirred a lump of real sugar into her espresso.

"The muse hasn't hit yet." Sam bit into her croissant. "Oh my God, is this good. You've got to taste yours."

Anna took a bite; it was heavenly. "So, what do you think? You, me, Eduardo, Ben?"

"I am *not* asking Eduardo to my high-school prom."

"Why not?"

Sam wiped crumbs from her lips with her black INSOMNIA napkin. "Fine, you wanna know? Because a film about the *amours* of Eduardo would be longer than all three *Godfather* films put together."

Bingo.

Finally, it all made sense, which made Anna feel terrible. "Eduardo is seeing other girls?"

Sam shrugged and stared into her dark espresso. "Other girls are definitely seeing him, that's for sure."

Anna was confused. "Wait, is he or isn't he?"

"Allegedly he isn't. But he showed me around the Latin Quarter last Saturday. It was a freaking parade of gorgeous, skinny girls. *'Bonjour, Eduardo. Salut, Eduardo, Comment vas-tu mon chebran, Eduardo?'*"

"*That's* your evidence that he's cheating on you? That girls were saying *hello* to him?"

"*French* girls, Anna. Gorgeous, skinny, *French* girls. French girls who aren't afraid to get naked in his presence."

"You're obsessing over imagined negatives that don't exist."

Sam shook her head and giggled. "Every once in a while, you remind me why I like you so much. No one actually says, 'You are obsessing over imagined negatives that don't exist.'"

"I do, and don't change the subject." Anna wagged a finger at Sam. "This isn't really about how much you hate prom. It's about Eduardo."

"Of course it's about Eduardo. He has a fabulous pied-à-terre in the sixth arrondissement, for God's sake. Have you ever *seen* the girls in the sixth arrondissement who go to the Sorbonne?"

Anna, who had been to Europe many times, nodded. "Of course I have, but—"

"Then you know what I'm talking about. And not just French girls, Anna. Polish girls. Czech girls! Do you have any idea how beautiful Czech girls are? A coke 'ho could cut lines with their cheekbones. Eduardo's there. With them. And I'm here. With you. Eating eight thousand calories of chocolate croissant."

"But he wants *you*," Anna reminded her.

"When he's with me. How do I know that there isn't a United Nations of girls swinging through his bedroom when I'm not around?"

Anna frowned. "What did he tell you?"

Sam waved a dismissive hand. "He only wants me, blah, blah, blah. Who would buy that crock of shit?"

Whoa. Paranoia. Then Anna had a sudden thought, one that she tried to banish without success.

How do I know that Ben didn't have a different girl every night while he was at Princeton?

No. That was ridiculous. Ben called her often and e-mailed her more than that. The only reason that thought had popped into her mind was because of Sam's rant. Evidently, boyfriend doubts could be contagious.

"You're feeling insecure," Anna translated, doing her best to erase the notion of Ben with someone else from her mind.

Sam pointed at her. "You'll go far with that astute brain of yours, Anna."

Anna took a bite of her croissant. Sam's sarcasm didn't bother her. She knew Sam well. When Sam got insecure, her wit got acidic. Even acidic, Sam was the funniest person Anna knew.

"Like I'd ever invite Eduardo to prom," Sam muttered, savagely stirring the contents of another Equal into her espresso. "Then he could, like, *weigh* offers. Let's see, mack in the Tuileries with sex kitten Ekaterina from Latvia who wears a size nothing and has breasts the size of Estonia, or go to American prom with Sam and her thunder thighs?"

Anna tried to reassure her. "If Eduardo wanted to be with one of those other girls, he would be. He'd be honest about it, too."

Sam put her head in her hands. "It makes me nuts, okay? I mean, the whole long-distance thing sucked to begin with, and that was *before* I saw the babe parade in Paris. You never felt insecure about Ben while he was at Princeton?"

Anna gulped. How about thirty seconds ago?

"Yeah," she admitted softly. "But he's coming home

this afternoon." She checked her new Locman Nuovo watch, which featured pavé diamonds set in brushed aluminum. Undoubtedly overly expensive, it had been a recent present from her father after he'd closed a deal on the hotel property in Mexico. It made him happy when she wore it, which was pretty much the only reason that she did. She was making an effort to get along with him these days.

"In fact," Anna continued, "I'm meeting him in an hour at his place. We'll . . . talk."

There was certainly plenty to talk about. When they'd gotten back together in Las Vegas, in their new spirit of honesty, Ben had told her about a girl named Blythe he'd been seeing at school. Allegedly, it wasn't serious. Anna recalled that the information hadn't fazed her—the rest of their time together for those few days in Las Vegas had been wonderful. They'd made love until dawn in Ben's room at the Palms, taken a tour out to Lake Powell, and even rented a boat for an afternoon on the lake. It had been open, romantic, and unforgettable.

After Ben returned to Princeton, she'd talked with him by phone every few days—the usual about school and family, since Anna was never one for intimate long-distance conversations—it was strange enough to muster an "I love you" before she said good-bye. Neither of them had ever mentioned Blythe. So how could she be totally sure that he'd dropped her? What if Blythe was the anti-Anna—someone earthy, uninhibited, a party girl with lush curves?

"Hel-lew?" Sam teased, nudging Anna in the ribs.

"Are we mentally doing our significant other, or are we sharing like sisters?"

"I was thinking about the girl Ben had been seeing at Princeton," Anna admitted.

"Aha! If Anna Percy, a girl so regal she apparently has no bodily functions, feels insecure in a long-distance relationship, how do you think *I* feel?"

"It's hard sometimes," Anna acknowledged, shifting in her seat.

Sam polished off the rest of her croissant. "It's this town. This town is insane. It's like you're never good enough, gorgeous enough . . . *enough* enough. There's always some other bitch who has it going on more than you do." Sam crumpled up her napkin and threw it on the table. "Paris was that, squared."

Anna thought for a moment, running a slender ballet-pink-polished fingernail over the rim of her espresso cup. "It has to be about your relationship, Sam. It can't be about a certain town or . . . or comparing yourself to other girls."

"You are so full of it," Sam insisted smugly. "Cammie gets to you. When you think about her with Ben, it makes you insane. Admit it."

Anna flushed. "I just tell myself that was before I knew him."

The knowing look on Sam's face didn't change.

"Besides, I'm going to do everything right with Ben this summer," Anna continued. "We're both going to be completely honest—that's what we agreed on. In the past, it's been dishonesty that always messed us up."

"Do tell."

"Well, Ben wasn't honest with me about what happened on the boat, and that hurt us. And then I wasn't honest with him about some of the other guys I was seeing after he went back to Princeton, and that hurt us, too. And then he wasn't honest with me about his feelings for me, and . . . well, you know. So that's why you need to be honest with Eduardo."

"That may be the least articulate thing you've ever said." Sam stood. "I'll be back in a sec. Excuse me."

As Sam headed for the ladies' room, Anna drained the last of her espresso. Sam was right; she was in no position to lecture anyone about relationships. The truth was, she was woefully inexperienced. Love was something she knew so little about. Her feelings for Ben felt . . . overwhelming sometimes.

She sat alone for several moments, watching the scene in Insomnia. Most of the writers were either reading newspapers, chatting with friends or on their cell phones, or checking their e-mail via Wi-Fi. There was little actual writing getting done. It made Anna remember something that her seventh-grade teacher at Trinity used to say: Luck is the residue of determination. If only—

"Omigod, I'm so brilliant." Sam slid back into her seat, brown eyes shining. "I've got it. *The B-List.*"

"Sorry?"

"Keep up with me here, Anna. The documentary. The Beverly Hills High School B-list. The pathetic B-list, for whom prom is the defining moment of their lives. I'll do my documentary about that. It's perfect.

A documentarian has to know her subject matter. What do I know better than the Hollywood social structure?"

Anna shook her head. "Think about it, Sam. Jazz and Fee are not about to agree to you filming them as 'the pathetic B-List.'"

"That won't be the title. I'll think of something else. *It Happened One Night*. Naw. Already taken . . . I just have to figure out a way. . . ." Sam snapped her fingers. "I've got it! I tell the prom weenies that I'm making a documentary called *Beverly Hills Prom*." She used her hand to mime a marquee. "They'll be the stars. We'll all go to prom. I'll even invite Eduardo, because I'll have an excuse—my movie. It's brilliant!"

"Why do you think you need an excuse to—?"

Sam raised a hand to silence Anna. "Please, I'm on a roll. I can see it now. I'll take the audience step by step through prom. The shopping, the makeovers, the food, the prep, the makeup. Maybe I'll even contrast it with some proms in the valley, so the audience can see how the other half lives. What if I focus on a girl at a prom in Sylmar who has to buy her dress secondhand, and on the weenies who have an unlimited budget? The weenies will *weep* with gratitude at their good fortune. I'll win the contest; they'll show my movie at all these festivals; no one will know its me until after I win—maybe I'll even make it under a pseudonym!—and everyone can take their assumptions about Jackson Sharpe's daughter and shove them you-know-where. And then my brilliant career begins. I've got only one question."

"What's that?" Anna asked warily. She wasn't thrilled with this notion of Sam's documentary. Some of it sounded good, but some of it sounded . . . mean.

"What time is it in Paris? I've got to call Eduardo."

An hour later, Anna pulled her silver Lexus into the circular driveway of Ben's family home—a mansion, really—on Foothill Drive in Beverly Hills, five blocks from her father's estate. It was a huge and imposing two-story structure, painted brown and white, intelligently made out of a wooden frame so it would bend and not break when the Big One struck the San Andreas fault line. The front of the house featured picture windows that covered both floors. Ben's parents had recently had it repainted and reroofed—the roof was now covered in terra-cotta shingles that gleamed in the afternoon sun. The grounds had been redone, too, with the lush grass replaced by rock gardens and cacti, and a sandstone walkway replacing the old gravel one from the driveway to the imposing redwood front door.

Anna sat behind the wheel for a moment, Sam's words about Eduardo in Paris echoing in her head. Ben supposedly had been a bit of a player in high school. Had he changed, really? She eyed the front door anxiously. What about Blythe? What about other girls whose names Anna didn't even know? Could she really expect a guy as hot as Ben to live like a monk because he was pining for the high-school girl back home? She didn't know what Blythe looked like, but she imagined her to be the anti-Anna in looks as well as attitude. *Hmm.* Flaming red hair down to her ass, with eyes a few shades darker than her hair. Maybe five-foot-four, with a voluptuous body and large breasts that didn't need a bra, the kind of lips most girls only got via injections of some kind of filler, that practically begged to be kissed. . .

Anna inhaled deeply to settle her nerves. Thinking like that was crazy. It wasn't her. She was *never* this insecure. Well, hardly ever.

She looked at the front door again.

"Blythe who?" she said aloud to steel her confidence, then stepped down the new stone path to the door. When she pressed the recessed doorbell, she heard chimes go off in the grand foyer. The door opened a few moments later.

It wasn't Ben. It was a girl Anna had never seen before. *Oh God.* She was clad in nothing but a white silk robe that showed off the curves of her lush body, and she had a towel wrapped around her hair. Obviously, she'd just stepped out of the shower. Anna had to look up at her eyes—she was easily five-nine or ten. Damp, thick waves of inky dark hair fell, Rapunzel-like, well past her shoulders. She had very pale skin, with a splash of freckles across the bridge of her nose. By Hollywood standards she was a long way from thin, but the whole thing definitely worked.

She really *was* the anti-Anna.

Blythe. It had to be Blythe. Anna felt blood rush to her head; so much so that she actually felt woozy.

Meanwhile, the espresso she'd had at Insomia welled up uncomfortably in her stomach. How could Ben do this to her? She'd thought she was just being paranoid, letting Sam's anxiety get to her. But no, this was real. This girl was really here. Yet Anna had been raised according to the *This Is How We Do Things* Big Book, (East Coast WASP edition). Rule number seven: control at all times.

"Is Ben here?" she asked, her voice even.

"Oh, sure," the girl replied breezily, casually ruffling her wet hair with the towel. Then she smiled. "I hope you don't mind waiting. He's still in the shower."

A Biiig Shocker

Anna followed the girl into the grand foyer, feeling numb.

Bitch slap.

The term flew into her mind. Anna, who only ever cursed mentally because she'd been raised by a mother who wouldn't say "damn" if her right foot got caught in a paper shredder. She wasn't even exactly sure what a bitch slap was, but wanted to bitch-slap Blythe anyway. Or maybe she should reserve the bitch slap for herself. Why, why, why hadn't she spelled it out for Ben: If you don't end your relationship with Blythe, we're through? She was filled with remorse, because she knew *exactly* why she hadn't done it. There was a whole chapter in the apocryphal Big Book that drew distinctions between what was couth and uncouth to talk about. Couth: skiing in Gstaad, the best Parisian hotels, arts and culture, clothes, charities, and four-star restaurants. Uncouth: white shoes after Labor Day, ice cubes in wine, the Lower East Side of Manhattan, spelling out to on-again-off-again-on-again boyfriends that they had to dump anyone else they were seeing.

Anna felt her throat tighten, but she lifted her well-sculpted chin with new resolve. As much as she wanted Ben, if he was going to be a first-class *dick*, she was not about to shrivel up like a dead aspidistra.

They took seats in the living room. Just like the exterior, this room had been remodeled since Anna had been in it, in a Southwestern theme with charcoal-sketched cowboy art and classic rodeo posters. Low-slung buff leather couches held Indian-print blankets while a hand-woven Navajo rug adorned the hardwood, rough-beam floor. Anna was on one of the leather couches, the girl on the other.

She calmly cleared her throat. "I'm Anna Percy. I imagine you must be Blythe."

The girl looked puzzled. "*Who?*"

"*Blythe.*"

"My name isn't Blythe."

Her name wasn't . . .

Wait a *petit moment*. If this *wasn't* Blythe, it made things even worse. Ben was cheating on *both* of them.

"Would you mind telling me who you are?"

The girl grinned. "I got it. You think I'm Ben's girlfriend."

Anna brushed some hair behind her right ear. "Actually, I assumed *I* was Ben's girlfriend until about two minutes ago, when you opened the door in your robe."

The girl, whoever she was, cracked up. "That is sooo funny!"

"I fail to see the humor."

"Okay, okay, okay." The girl waved a hand as if to fan herself into the end of her laughing fit. "I'm sorry. Really. Seriously. *Really* really. My name is Madeleine, but you can call me Maddy. Everyone does whether I like it or not, so I've convinced myself that I like it, even if I don't."

Anna wasn't sure what to feel. Shock? Embarrassment that she'd leaped to such a hasty judgment? Anger at herself, for not having the confidence in Ben that she knew she should have? She felt all these things and more.

"You're not a friend of Ben's from Princeton?"

Maddy shook her head. "I wish. I'm not a brainiac like *Ben*." The emphasis in the sentence was on the word *Ben*, with reverence. "He's totally super smart—brilliant, really—don't you think? I'm a junior at Pacific Palisades High School and I'm living here. And you've got to be Anna. Ben told me all about you. You are so lucky to be with him. Does it make sense now?"

Only marginally, Anna thought, though she could feel her muscles begin to unclench.

"Oh golly, I really messed this up," Maddy lamented. "See, I'm actually from Michigan—Pellston, ever been there? If you haven't, don't go, except in the summer, which is, like, two days in July, if we're lucky—and I came from there to live with my aunt and uncle in Pacific Palisades and go to school at PP high school. Do you know any kids who go there?"

"I don't think so." Anna let the four words linger,

just so she could process what Maddy was saying. The girl was *definitely* not terse.

"Oh well, some of them are nice, but some of them are *sooo* mean. Anyway, my uncle works for the State Department and he had to go to Singapore in March, which was bad, except that my aunt and uncle and the Birnbaums are friends, you know? So Mrs. Birnbaum said I could stay here through the end of the school year. And that's why I'm here. Whew." She drew the back of her hand dramatically across her forehead. "Glad that's out of the way. Hey, want to see what I used to look like?" She reached for a red photo album on the side table, flipped open the cover, and passed it to Anna. "Get ready for a biiig shocker—and I do mean *big.*"

Anna peered at the photograph on the open page closely. Same girl, hair, and face as across the living room. She was standing on a lakeshore on a bright summer day, wearing Bermuda shorts and a brown T-shirt that flowed over what Anna estimated to be approximately three hundred pounds of Maddy.

"This is really you?" Anna was astonished.

"A hundred and fifty-five pounds ago," Maddy hooted. "I *love* showing people that photo." She nodded toward the album. "It was taken the day before I came to Los Angeles. I had my stomach stapled last August, which was gross but not as gross as I thought it would be, even though they make you pee out of a tube for a while, did you know that? Anyway, big difference, huh?"

"I'll say," Anna agreed as politely as she could, handing the photograph back to Maddy, who held it in both hands and stared at herself in wonder. Anna couldn't imagine what it would be like to walk around in a body that large. People could be cruel and ruthless. She thought of how Cammie Sheppard might have reacted to the "before" Maddy and shuddered. Maddy was lucky that she'd chosen Pacific Palisades High School.

"You're a brave person," Anna told her admiringly.

Maddy shrugged. "I was fat my whole life. My whole family is fat. We could have a contest for fat, fatter, and fattest. Anyhoo, when I go back to Michigan for senior year, I'm going back totally skinny, which will be so cool and amazing, and all the guys who used to tease me will be, like, drooling, and I'll tell them to go screw themselves."

She bounced up and spun around like a fashion model on the runway, turning sideways and pulling her robe taut against her body—the lush, curvaceous body that was living in Ben's house.

"I'm losing twenty-five more pounds, and then— watch out, world!" Maddy crowed. "Except I'm kind of inexperienced in the guy department. That worries me a little."

Anna smiled. "It'll come naturally to you; you'll see."

Maddy's face lit up. "You think? Because I really have to make up for lost time."

"Anna Percy."

The voice was male and deep, but it didn't belong to Ben. It wasn't Ben. Anna turned to see a college-age guy in an oversize blue bowling shirt, jeans, and white Converse All Star high-tops. He was tall and skinny, with gelled rust-colored hair that stood straight up. Old-fashioned black tortoiseshell glasses framed his dark eyes. There was an insouciant smile stretched across his quirky-cute face. Anna rose automatically, thinking what a strange few minutes these had been— how people she didn't know kept appearing, while Ben was still nowhere in sight. At least this guy, whoever he was, wasn't female and dripping wet from a shower.

No way she'd mistake *him* for Blythe.

"Hi," she responded, grinning at her own thought. "You're right, I'm Anna. And you are . . . ?"

"I'm Jack. Jack Walker. Think Jack Daniels meets Johnny Walker and you'll remember my name; friend of Ben's from Princeton." He winked at her. "You're Ben's lady?"

Anna had lived in New York City long enough to be able to pick out Jack's accent. New Jersey. More specifically, northern Jersey. Not one of the affluent suburbs like Tenafly or Alpine, either. More like Jersey City or Union City. She realized that if this guy had gotten into Princeton, it wasn't because his grandparents had donated a building or because his father was a member of the Federal Reserve Bank board of governors. He had to be smart. Independently smart. She wouldn't be surprised if he'd earned a full ride to Princeton.

"Lady?" Anna responded wryly. "I'll go with *girlfriend*."

Jack laughed. "Me too. Sorry for the Jerseyism.

Anyway. I'm out here for the summer. Got a killer internship at Fox TV in the reality-programming department. Living in this exec's guesthouse in Santa Monica, drivin' his second car, which just happens to be a Beemer. Sweet."

"Hey, wow, maybe the four of us could go on a double date," Maddy interjected. "Well, I mean, not really a date date, but just, you know, hang out?"

She sounded so needy; Anna wanted to reassure her. "We could do that, maybe. Right, Jack?"

"Who's with who?" Jack winked at Anna again. The winking thing was getting a wee bit repetitive.

"I'm with Ben, that's for sure," Maddy chirped.

Jack raised his eyebrows at her. At least he wasn't winking. "I don't think Ben would—"

"Joking!" Maddy added hastily, then grew solemn. "Anna, you are so, so, so, so lucky to have him as your boyfriend. I hope you know—"

"Hey. It's *great* to see you."

Anna's heart jumped at the sound of Ben's voice; it was finally really and truly *him*. She whirled, and there he was. Six feet tall, he'd let his short brown hair grow out longer than Anna had ever seen it; it gave him a sexy, shaggy look. He wore jeans and was just buttoning his plain white oxford shirt over his tanned, hard-body six-pack.

He walked over to her, a huge grin on his face. Those eyes of his, electric blue, had the same effect they'd had on her the very first time she'd seen him on the airplane; she couldn't look away.

"Hi," she breathed.

"I took forever, sorry," Ben apologized. "I got a phone call."

"No problem," Anna forced herself to sound easy, though her mind was already running through the list of people who Ben might have been talking to. Damn Sam for talking about how jealous she was of Eduardo. It was *contagious*. "I was getting to know your friends."

"Hey, Maddy, go throw on some clothes and let's blow this pop stand," Jack suggested. "Leave these two to reunite."

He winked yet again, but Maddy didn't seem to mind. "Oh, sure!" she giggled, then threw her arms around Ben. "I just want to thank you again. For everything."

Ben gently extricated himself. "Thank my mom and dad. I didn't really do anything, Maddy."

"I'll wait for you in the Beemer," Jack told her.

"I'll just be a sec!" She practically flew out of the room. Meanwhile, Jack shook Anna's hand—this time without a wink—and told Ben he'd call him, making the sign of a phone with his hand.

Finally, they were alone.

Something was wrong; Anna could sense it immediately. He wasn't kissing her, he wasn't hugging her. She'd been through enough with Ben to know when—

"Anna," he whispered. Then she was in his arms, his lips on hers, and thankfully, her endlessly babbling inner voice finally shut the hell up.

"Took you long enough," Anna murmured into his neck when their lips parted.

His only answer was to kiss her again.

They lay on the couch, Anna nestled against Ben's chest. Somewhere amid their torrid kisses Ben had whispered that his parents were in Hawaii and weren't coming home until Sunday, but Anna had been in no hurry. Just when the kisses had started to turn into more, she'd asked Ben to find them something to eat. That gave her about two minutes to cool down before he showed up with a quart of Cherry Garcia ice cream and a single spoon. Immediately Anna thought about licking the ice cream off Ben, but she settled for actually swapping spoonfuls with him. They had the whole summer ahead. There was no reason to rush things. It was not just going to be about sex, either. They would finally have the chance to get to know each other in a way that they'd never been able to before.

"It's only May," Anna murmured. The prospect of the summer made her lightheaded with happiness.

Ben kissed her forehead. "Um-hmm."

"May, June, July, August," Anna ticked off the months on her fingers. "We'll have four months together, and no school."

"I have to work, though. I told you that on the phone, right?"

He had. "At the Riviera place?" He'd mentioned that he'd possibly be working in the pro shop at the Riviera Country Club.

"Got a better offer. Have you heard about this new club in Hollywood, Trieste?"

Amused, Anna craned around to look at him. "This is me we're talking about."

Ben chuckled. "Right. You're club-challenged. Golf club *and* nightclub."

"I have, however, read all the classics," she teased. "In three languages."

He laughed again. "Let me fill you in, Miss Trilingual. Trieste is the hip place of the moment; fashionistas, young Hollywood wanna-be suck-ups, very *Day of the Locust*. Dad got me a job there." He paused. "Correction: Dad's skills in the OR in the form of an extremely successful tummy tuck got me a job there. Kind of a management-trainee thing. To see if I like the business."

Ben's father was the foremost plastic surgeon in Beverly Hills, known to one and all as the "Plastic Surgeon to the Stars." He likely earned more in a week than many Americans earned in a decade. However, Dr. Birnbaum had recently joined a twelve-step program to deal with his gambling addiction, and Anna hoped that maybe while Ben was home, he and his dad would have a chance to repair their strained relationship. She knew all about parental estrangement; she'd lived with it her whole life.

"Maddy will want you to sneak her in," Anna joked.

"Believe me, she already asked." He shook his head. "Poor kid. She's this innocent girl with a new body; she doesn't know how to deal. Her mom and my mom are friends from high school; I've watched her grow up—and out. The kid suffered. It really sucked."

"She showed me her 'before' picture."

"Pretty shocking, huh?" Ben kissed her forehead again. "I'd ask you to be nice to her, but I know you will be. Because that's just . . . you."

"Yep, that's me. Anna of Sunnybrook Farm," she quipped.

"To the world maybe. But with me, alone . . . definitely not."

He kissed her again—the kind of kiss that proved how well he knew her, the secret her who didn't overanalyze or worry or . . . or anything. She adored it.

The B-List

The Bel Air Grand Hotel was located in a private
wooded eucalyptus and palm grove just to the
north of Sunset Boulevard, not far from UCLA. The
exterior of the place was beautifully designed in the style
of the Spanish and Italian Renaissance, with eight huge
ivory columns sweeping up from the ground to support
an arched entryway nearly fifty feet above the valet area.

"You're going to love this, Sam, I swear," Fee gushed
as they sat in the front of Fee's cherry-red Audi, waiting
for the valet to open their doors. Jazz sat in the backseat.

An Audi. Trust Fee to have a B-list car, too.

Sam had a plan: Let the weenies talk her into a tour of
the prom site; play it cool so they thought there was no
way that she and her A-list friends would attend the
prom; then turn the tables on them so that she could not
just make her documentary but also have some artistic
control over the party. Once everything was set, she'd tell
Cammie and the others. Loyalty counted for something
in Hollywood—she was confident they'd participate.

Who knew when they might need favors of their own? As for Anna, there was definitely a bit of a rift—Anna thought that the idea of *The B-List* was mean. Sam, though, knew Anna wanted to go to prom. Ultimately, the idea of a double date of her and Ben with Sam and Eduardo would certainly prove too enticing to pass up.

The obvious thing for her to do, of course, was just to tell the prom weenies that she would come and ask them to be in her movie. If she did that, though, Fee and Jazz would instantly be suspicious of her intentions. That was not the way the Beverly Hills High School elite operated.

"Good afternoon," the two uniformed valets—both college age, both sporting crew cuts (they looked like Mormon missionaries in their starched white shirts and dark trousers)—said simultaneously, as they opened the Audi doors and helped the girls out. "Are you checking in?" the shorter blond one asked.

"Gawd, no." Sam was aghast. "Does anyone actually *stay* here anymore?"

Jazz blushed. "We're here to meet with—"

Before Jazz could finish her sentence, a toady little man in his late fifties with black hair swirled atop his head like soft-serve ice cream, to cover an orbital-size bald spot, burst through the glass front doors, arms open wide. He wore a black suit, white dress shirt, and yellow power tie, circa 1985 which, Sam figured, was the last year anyone actually *breathing* had held a hip event at this hotel.

"Welcome, welcome, welcome to the Bel Air Grand

Hotel. I'm Donald Plummage, hotel manager." He nodded vigorously to the valets. "These lovely ladies are my special guests."

"Yes sir," the taller, skinnier valet said dutifully, and slipped into Fee's car to park it.

"You are the lovely Miss Samantha Sharpe, are you not?" the Donald inquired. "I've seen your photo in various publications and might I say that you're even lovelier in person. I am a great fan of your father's work."

Fee and Jazz beamed—clearly, they'd hoped for just such a reaction when they'd cajoled Sam into taking the tour.

"How fresh," Sam chirped. "You and twenty million other people."

The Donald bellowed as if Sam had just said the funniest thing on record. She was used to this kind of sucking up. Sometimes she said or did the most horrid things just to see how far a suck-up would go in pretending that she was scintillating or sweet or sexy. It was a fascinating exercise, in a sick kind of way. The really crazy thing was, Fee and Jazz had stumbled onto a decent idea in thinking this would be a cool prom location. A new place could become hip, but then the tourists and wanna-bes would hear about it and flock to it, rendering the death knell of post hip, and then it was on to the next. The idea that a famous locale gone to seed could be made hip again by a soon-to-be-A-list event was . . . well, near genius. Not that Sam was about to let on to that logic.

"Welcome to our lobby, ladies," Donald intoned, as they entered the cavernous hall.

The lobby walls were dark mahogany, the lighting provided by antique crystal chandeliers. Ornate red velvet furniture was arranged in various conversation areas, flanked by priceless hand-tied Oriental rugs. Black marble pedestals held massive white vases filled with long-stemmed blossoms. Though the furniture was ancient and the carpets showed some shiny spots, the lobby had a certain *Casablanca* air to it, a whiff of the grandeur of days past.

"Isn't it fabulous?" Jazz gushed. She pointed to the couches nestled near a giant stone fireplace. "Right over there, Mae West got drunk and did a striptease for Montgomery Clift by firelight—or at least, that's what Donald told us."

"True, true, it's all true," Donald assured them. He closed his eyes and breathed deeply, putting fingertips on both his eyelids. "When I do this, I can still feel her presence."

"It's empty in here," Sam sniffed. There were perhaps a dozen extremely low-key guests scattered about the lobby. "Why is that, Donald?"

"It's two in the afternoon," Fee pointed out nervously. "I'm sure it'll be more crowded later."

"Doubtful," Sam declared, playing her snotty role for all it was worth. "All the biggest clients are busy pushing up daisies at Forest Lawn Cemetery."

The Donald laughed his hysterical laugh anew. "Aren't you witty, Miss Sharpe! Actually, it's a little-known fact that Swifty Lazar gave his first post-Oscar party here."

"He's *so* twentieth century," Sam intoned, and then shook her head. "You know, I just don't think my friends are going to get behind this. Where's your valet ticket, Fee?"

Fee grasped Sam's arm. "Let us show you around, at least."

"Right, I mean, this is just the lobby!" Jazz added, a half-octave higher than normal.

Sam feigned reluctance, but the hotel manager cajoled her. For the next fifteen minutes or so, the Donald, Jasmine, and Fee led her on a tour. They took her to the grand suite on the tenth floor, which would be reserved as part of their prom package. Though Sam sniffed, it was quaintly lovely. There were two spacious bedrooms with white, eggshell-and-ochre quilts from Marks & Spencer on the beds; a large, long bathroom with a charming blue porcelain tub perched on claw feet; and a cozy living room with a faux-bearskin rug before a red flagstone fireplace. The balcony just off the living room facing south and west was airy and elegant, with marble railings and comfortable rattan furniture.

"It's the original marble from 1919, Miss Sharpe," the Donald explained, his voice just so proud. "We've tried to retain as much of its historicity as possible and still make it modern and luxurious for our guests."

The elevator to the Grand Ballroom was claustro-phobic and slow—two facts Sam delighted in pointing out—but the banquet room itself was massive: it could easily hold five hundred people. Sam found as much fault with it as possible, from the yellow-toned color scheme to the Italian and Spanish coats of arms in the corner, and especially the priceless knights' metal suits in Plexiglas display cases in the rear.

"We're going to go with a renaissance theme," Jazz blurted. "In keeping with the surroundings."

"It's going to be so fabulous!" Fee rushed to join her. "We contacted those people who do those renaissance fair thingies? We've hired them for jousting and Tarot readings, and, um, wenches, you know?"

"Right," Jazz agreed. "Total debauchery."

Sam folded her arms. Not bad at all. But if you were going to have those kinds of out-of-the-ordinary entertainers, you needed to hire an actual party planner, like Fleur Abra, who had done her father's wedding.

"Let me ask you girls something. Have you ever gone to one of those lame ren fairs?"

"No," Fee admitted, shifting uncomfortably, "but my cousin works for the one in Santa Fe Springs. That's how I knew who to contact."

"I think you can do better."

Both girls were silent. For a nanosecond, Sam wondered if she'd carried her act too far. She changed the subject. "What about the band?"

"The stage will go up over there." The Donald pointed to the far corner of the room.

"The band?" Sam asked.

Jasmine and Fee exchanged a fearful look.

"We've got the Roadsters," Fee offered tentatively.

Sam threw them a bone. "Good choice."

The wattage in the girls' grins could have powered a third-world nation for a year.

"Ladies?" The ever-jovial Donald got their attention. "Time for the pièce de résistance—the food. A table has been set up for you ladies in the main dining room."

"Sam, you're going to like this," Fee declared. "I know it."

The dining room's décor leaned heavily toward its Old Hollywood connection—the walls were adorned with posters of classic films from the thirties and forties, ranging from *Mrs. Miniver* to *The Third Man* to *How Green Was My Valley?* The tables had white tablecloths, the lights were kept dim, and the waiters all apparently had been working since the Bel Air's heyday judging by their age. The sound of old show tunes from movie musicals trickled in from the grand piano next door.

The Donald led the three girls to their table and held Sam's chair for her. "Bon appétit, ladies," he wished, with a little bow. "I leave you to dine."

Sam read the white card at the center of the table as the Donald departed. "Beverly Hills High School Anniversary Prom Menu," she read aloud. "Bagaduce oysters and osetra caviar. Fresh Mendocino champignons with truffles, marlin niçoise, and whole roasted lobster. *Délice au chocolat et caramel*, or homemade Cold Stone Creamery ice cream hand-mixed on the premises. Accompanied by assorted beverages."

Sam's mouth was watering just reading the menu; she

hadn't eaten lunch. But she shook her head. "Not good."

"You haven't even tasted it yet!" Jazz protested.

"We—you—need a vegetarian alternative." Oops. Almost a slip.

"You're so right," Jazz agreed. "We need to talk to the kitchen."

Great. She had them where she wanted them. Time to shift gears.

"I was thinking about some other things that could make this prom special," Sam mused.

Both girls' faces lit up as if Orlando Bloom had just asked them to dance. "We'd love to hear them," Fee exulted.

"Here's my thought." Sam tapped a forefinger against her lips. "I help *refine* your prom concept, all of my nearest and dearest friends come to prom, and . . . what say I film the transformation? Sort of a . . . prom makeover movie. What do you two think?"

Fee and Jazz turned into happy bobble-head dolls.

"Excellent." Sam shook Fee's hand, then Jazz's. "It's settled, then. We have a lot of work to do while we eat. Someone make a list. By the way, once we've got a vegetarian option, the menu will be outstanding."

Fee beamed and instantly whipped a small notebook out of her purse.

Sam smiled. In the end, it had been as easy as giving candy to Kirstie Alley.

So. . .Curvy

As Ben piloted his parents' yacht, the new *Nip 'n' Tuck*, out of the harbor—at forty feet, it was longer than its predecessor, with brass fixtures gleaming and the scent of new paint mixing with the glorious smell of the ocean—Anna stood at the bow and flashed back to a moment when she'd been in seventh grade.

She and her best friend, Cynthia Baltres, had let themselves into Cyn's brownstone one afternoon after school. Cyn had gone to the kitchen to find some chips and Cokes, and Anna had wandered into her father's home office, a small room off the library that held a black steel desk and chair, a laptop, stacks of papers, and several shelves of books. Cyn's father, though a businessman, was at work on a novel. Right by the computer was a copy of a book that Anna had never heard of before, Kahlil Gibran's *The Prophet*. Anna idly flipped it open and began to read one of the short poems.

"Love gives naught but itself and takes naught but from itself. Love possesses not nor would it be possessed. For love is sufficient unto love."

The words had struck her in their simple profundity. Not only had she memorized the verse, but she'd also hand-lettered the words on an index card and put the card inside the top desk drawer in her private study. (That year, her mother's designer had redone Anna's bedroom and adjoining study suite in Chinese antiques from the late Ming and early Qing dynasties. Anna's new desk had been made from priceless huanghuali hardwood whose hand-carved pieces fit together without glue or nails.)

By the time Anna was in ninth grade, everyone at Trinity was jaded or at least pretending to be. Ragging on *The Prophet* was party blood sport. No one believed that love existed and everyone pointed to the off-the-charts divorce rates of their parents as empirical proof.

Anna had tossed away the index card but had kept the words emblazoned in her memory. Yes, she'd temporarily jettisoned them when she'd been so certain in the autumn that she was in love with young writer Scott Spencer—a crush she hadn't mentioned to Cyn—and then Cyn had hooked up with Scott. Now that Cyn and Scott were history and Anna didn't want Scott at all, Gibran's words had come roaring back. Could those words apply to a guy who, the last time she'd been on a boat with him, had abandoned her in the middle of the night and then made up some absurd excuse about it?

"Ah. My Selkie maiden longing to return to the sea," Ben intoned, coming up behind Anna. She was in her ancient gray cashmere sweater and faded jeans—she'd worn her Ralph Lauren deck shoes because it sometimes got slippery. He was in khakis and a faded Princeton sweatshirt. He lifted her ponytail and kissed the back of her neck.

She half-smiled. "The sea is not what I'm longing for. Who's steering the ship of state?"

"It's on autopilot. Kind of like the government." He put his hands on Anna's shoulders and turned her toward him. "Care to elaborate on what you're longing for?"

For a moment she was ready to fib, but she decided to hold to her honesty policy. When he'd lied about why he'd abandoned her, when she'd not been up-front about the guys she'd been seeing in Los Angeles, when he'd hidden the fact that he had to return to Princeton or that the school would kick him out, it had hurt them. She didn't want that to happen again.

"The truth? I wasn't longing for anything. I was thinking about the first time you brought me out here. New Year's Eve."

Ben winced and shook his head. "Don't."

The *Nip 'n' Tuck* cut across the wake of a larger vessel and pitched forward and backward. Ben put his hands on Anna's hips to steady her.

"I was so sure you had used me. But you'd gone off to play the knight in shining armor to your dad."

"You had no way of knowing that," Ben reminded her. Anna saw the flush of shame in his cheeks. "I don't blame you for jumping to the wrong conclusion."

"That's the whole point." She traced the line of his jaw with her forefinger and gazed over his shoulder at the California coastline. The further they went from the harbor, the more beautiful it became. To the north she could see the Santa Monica Pier, with its famous Ferris wheel. To the south, planes were roaring into the sky from LAX. "Why was I so quick to think the worst of you instead of the best?"

"Because men are dogs?" Ben ventured.

She smiled. "Because I was afraid of . . . of everything. Being hurt. Wanting you." She ducked her head self-consciously. "I should shut up now."

He cupped her chin until she lifted her head to face him again, and turned his body slightly to shield her from the fine spray as the bow of the yacht cut through some choppy water. "Hey, don't do that. I'm just as sick of all the bullshit out there as you are. You can tell me anything." His hand traced a line from her chin down her neck; then he gently brushed his knuckles against her collarbone. "Man, I missed you."

"Me too." Her eyes searched his. "I really think . . . if we're honest with each other, we can be . . ." She searched for the right words. "Far from the madding crowd."

He pointed at her playfully. "Thomas Hardy. You thought I wouldn't know."

"'*The sky was clear—remarkably clear—and the twinkling of all the stars seemed to be but throbs of one body, timed by a common pulse,*'" Anna half-whispered. "Isn't that amazing, that one man could write something like that?"

Ben's strong hands circled her slender waist. "I think *you're* amazing."

Anna rested her check against his strong chest and shut her eyes, letting the perfection of the moment wash over her. Then she opened them again. Honest. She had to be honest.

"I wanted to ask you. About Blythe." She cleared her throat.

"Blythe-at-Princeton Blythe?"

"Is there another one?" she asked archly.

He laughed. "Yeah, somewhere in the universe, I guess. It's just that I haven't even thought about her in three months."

Anna wanted to make absolutely certain she had this right. "You broke up with her?"

"There wasn't anything to break up. We hung out a few times; that's pretty much it."

"That's not how it sounded when you first told me about her. You're really not 'hanging out' anymore?"

"No, Anna," he replied as if humoring her. "We are not 'hanging out' anymore. I have no female hang-out partners under the age of eighty, I swear."

"Well, then." She smiled. That was that. "You need to kiss me."

He did, over and over, until Anna couldn't think at all. Then he lifted her up in his arms and carried her down the steps to the main cabin. It was bigger than the one that had been on the original *Nip 'n' Tuck*, more lavishly appointed, with actual portholes, a white Berber rug, and an Adriatic desk. The light brown teak king-size bed was built into a darker teak headboard-bookshelf combination—recessed track lighting plus twin reading lamps provided all the illumination one could desire. The bed frame was hand-carved with Moorish designs and inlays so new that Anna could smell the faint aroma of the wood.

The big brown and white pillows on the bed, though, were the same. So was the down comforter with the gold-inlaid comforter cover. So were the light gold silk sheets, his arms, his body—the him that she remembered so well.

Anna opened her eyes to the gentle rocking of the yacht. She was nestled in Ben's arms, the silk sheets crumpled beneath them. His eyes were still closed. She thought about everything they'd shared before falling asleep and shivered deliciously. Whoever had invented sex was a genius.

"You're thinking again," Ben accused, but there was a smile on his lips.

She gazed at his peaceful face and ran the tips of her fingers down his hard chest. "Your eyes aren't even open; how would you know?"

"I can *feel* it."

"I had no idea you were so sensitive," she teased.

"Oh yes you did." He opened his eyes and pulled her closer. "I think the past hour or two proved that."

She kissed one of the ridges of his abdominal six-pack. "I have problems with short-term memory. I might need an instant replay to remind me."

"Oh, really?"

"Yes, really."

"Or maybe you need . . . *this*!"

He picked up a pillow and bopped her with it. She whacked him with another one. She thought she was on the verge of vanquishing him, until Ben held her down and made her say, "Ben is the king!" three times in French. She was laughing so hard she could hardly get the breath to say it.

"*Ben est le roi! Trois fois!*" she teased.

Who knew she could be this happy, this carefree? He rolled over next to her, a big, dopey grin on his face. Could it be possible that he was just as happy as she was? Yes, it was. She could feel it.

It was the perfect time to ask him.

"Ben?"

"Anna?"

"How would you feel about going to prom?"

He pretended to muse for a moment. "Prom. You're talking the Beverly Hills High School prom?"

"Is there another kind?"

"I went last year," Ben remembered. "But that was only because it was for charity. You *really* want to go?"

Anna nodded, conscious of a real lack of enthusiasm in his voice.

"Are Sam and Cammie going?"

"I think so." For a moment, she was tempted to tell Ben about Sam's movie idea and about how irritated it made her, but she decided she'd wait until she knew if the movie was actually happening. It could, after all, fall through.

"There's just one problem." He frowned. "If I decide to go, who should I take?"

She laughed. "Don't start or I'll smack you with another pillow and this time I'll win."

He kissed her tenderly. "Yes, Anna. Of course I'll take you to prom."

Ben pulled on his jeans and went up top to restart the engine and take them back to shore. There'd been a coastal storm forecast to arrive sometime after midnight; he didn't want them to be caught in it out at sea, even though there was no real danger other than seasickness. Meanwhile, Anna lay under the silk sheets grinning like a fool. It had been so simple. It seemed ludicrous that she'd ever stressed about it, about him.

She dozed off for a while as Ben was piloting them back, and awakened only when the engines reversed as they were pulling into the slip at Marina del Rey—a quick look through one of the cabin's portholes confirmed that this was what was happening: the huge, floodlit marina spread out before her, row upon row of docks and boat slips, literally hundreds of white sailboats and cabin cruisers awaiting their next journey to the high seas. Per the marina regulations, Ben cut the power to no-wake so that the moored vessels wouldn't get sloshed, which gave Anna time to find her clothes, get dressed, and rejoin him on the bridge. She even helped him tie the *Nip 'n' Tuck* to the slip moorings and swab the decks as the first gusts of wind from the incoming storm blew through. They were just finished getting the vessel shipshape for her next outing when they noticed someone bounding up the wooden dock toward them, footfalls echoing in the still night.

Maddy.

What was she doing here?

"Hey, you guys! Hi!" Maddy shouted. She wore an oversized wheat-colored fisherman's sweater and baggy jeans. The rising wind had whipped her dark, wavy hair onto her face. "You know there's a storm coming?"

Ben nodded. "That's why we're back. You didn't have to come down here."

"I got worried because you forgot your cell phone." Maddy held up Ben's Samsung D600. "So I called Jack, and he drove me."

"Sweet of you, Mad, but not necessary," Ben told her.

"No problem." She eyed the *Nip 'n' Tuck*. "Wow, that is awesome. I'd love to see it from the inside—hint, hint."

"Sure, Mad, but some other time—this puppy is coming in sooner than I thought it would." He gave her a cockeyed look. "Is that . . . my sweater?"

Maddy looked down at herself. "Oh, yeah. I just grabbed the first thing I saw. You left it in the den." She made a move as if she were about to remove it. "You can have it back if you want. I only have a really thin little T-shirt on underneath, though."

I only have a really thin little T-shirt on underneath?

Anna felt heat creep up the back of her neck. She would not let her angst level over this girl spiral out of control again, but there was no mistaking the flirtatiousness of that remark or the unnecessary gesture of Maddy's coming to the marina.

Crush, Anna realized. Well, of course, that had to be

it. Maddy had a crush on Ben. It was sweet, really. Sort of. Kind of. It would have been a lot sweeter if Maddy wasn't quite so . . . curvy. And if those curves hadn't been living in Ben's house.

Ridiculous. I am being ridiculous.

"So where's Jack?" Anna asked brightly.

"He went into that place, Joe's Clams." She tilted her head toward the rectangular wooden restaurant/tavern at the far end of the marina parking lot. "I just wanted to bring this to you, then I'm gonna meet him. We're going to a late movie."

A movie? Anna felt like a fool. She'd jumped to conclusions yet again. So much for the crush-on-Ben theory. She was with Jack. How could Anna possibly be so happy and so in love and yet feel so easily threatened? That was not who she was. Not at all. In fact, she was ashamed of herself.

As if to prove the point, she gave Maddy a big, spontaneous hug. "This was so thoughtful of you."

"Gee, thanks." Maddy beamed. "Do you guys want to hang out with us for a little while? I can't eat much—that's what happens when your stomach is stapled—but I'll have a few raw oysters and watch you guys. Okay?"

"Sure," Anna told her, nodding. "Let's go."

She hooked her arm in Ben's, sure she had nothing to worry about. Nothing at all.

Some French Sex Kitten

The door to Joes's Clams opened; Jack saw Ben, Ben's young friend Maddy, and Ben's girlfriend, Anna, step inside and look around for him. He waved and headed in their direction from where he'd been waiting at the bar. The place had a nautical theme—stuffed marlins and tuna on the walls, heavy nautical rope crisscrossing the ceiling, life preservers lashed to the backs of many of the seats, portholes in the walls instead of conventional windows—and served the young, single crowd that lived in Marina del Rey, whether they were boat owners, aspiring boat owners, or were allergic to water. At eleven o'clock, weekend or weeknight, Joe's Clams was always jammed—tonight easily a hundred and fifty people were drinking, shooting pool, or throwing darts; some even danced to eighties rock 'n' roll from an old-fashioned Seeburg jukebox.

He joined them at a table for four by the darts area of the club. "Having fun?" he asked Ben as he smoothly held a chair out for Maddy. She looked dazzled by the old-fashioned gesture.

"For sure," Ben replied as he and Anna sat down. He gave her a meaningful look.

She smiled at him. "Yeah."

Jack knew that look. The two of them had just screwed their brains out. Well, cool; he was happy for Ben. By any objective standards, Ben was a richie. He didn't have a richie 'tude, though. Maybe that was why he was Jack's best bud at Princeton.

"Did you eat already?" Maddy asked him eagerly. "Not that it matters, because I can only eat, like, one shrimp. Seafood kind of yucks me out anyway. Fish go to the bathroom in that water; think about it."

Jack grinned at her. Her long dark hair had frizzed up from the humidity, she wasn't wearing any makeup, and she was very pale. Her clothes were clueless, too—baggy carpenter pants with an even baggier sweater, those curves of hers completely hidden. That was kind of sexy, in a way. The way she looked right now, other guys would walk right past her. Jack could imagine how a smart guy, a guy with a discerning eye, could go for that.

"What can I get you from the bar?" Jack asked Maddy. "It'll take forever for a waitress. Believe me, I've been watching."

"Just a Diet Coke."

"Coming right up," Jack promised. "Anna? Ben?"

He got their drink orders—a beer for Ben, a cranberry juice for Anna—and cut through the crowd back toward the bar again. Someone had put Roll Deep's "Let It Out" on the jukebox, causing a surge of dancers to make their way to the tiny dance floor.

You'd like it here, Margie.

He was thinking about his little sister, Margie. She loved to dance.

Margie's real name was Marguerite, after some long-dead relative. Jack had been six when they brought her home from the hospital, bundled up in a pink blanket with yellow elephants on it—funny how he remembered that—and his ma had insisted they all call the new baby by her full name. Jack immediately told his two little brothers that they should call her Margie, and Margie it was.

Jack was the oldest. Everyone in his family listened to him. In fact, people in general listened to him. He was smart, savvy, and a born leader who, when the situation called for it, knew exactly how to manipulate pretty much anybody and make them like it at the same time. Maybe that was why he loved reality TV; it was the star-fuck of manipulation.

Jack intuitively understood how reality TV worked by setting people against each other. He got how producers chose footage that would invent a story arc—a villain to hate, a hero to root for, influencing viewers into giving enough of a shit to tune in week after week. It was the same thing for every show. *American Idol. Big Brother. The Amazing Race. Survivor.*

Jack sucked down some of his brew; the TV mounted over the bar caught his eye. The sound was off so it wouldn't compete with the jukebox, but it was a *Survivor* rerun marathon from the Australian Outback season. They were up to the movie-star-looks-Texan-aww-shucks-sure-I'll-let-the-little-lady-have-my-million finale. Margie loved the movie-star-looks Texan and would kiss the TV whenever he was on. Two things she loved: dancing and reality TV. No, three things. Jack. She loved Jack.

It really pissed him off when people called her mentally retarded. Brain-damaged was a totally different thing. Margie was now thirteen, but usually she acted like a three-year-old and only talked baby talk. Other times, though, she could read a simple book or even add numbers. There were tests to figure the whole thing out, for sure, but Jack's parents couldn't afford to get her those tests. Instead, his mom went to Our Mother of Mercy three times a week and burned candles for her daughter, as if the good Lord was going to suddenly undo what had happened to her.

Shit. His family was worthy of its own reality-TV show.

Margie went to a special school paid for by the state of New Jersey, but in Jack's opinion, the school sucked ass. His parents couldn't afford one of those private schools where the privileged sent their brain-damaged kids so they could actually learn something and do things for themselves and have some kind of decent life that didn't sitting in a living room watching reality TV all the time.

If not for him, Margie would have been very lonely. His brothers were always studying or playing video games or running around with their friends. His parents were always working. But Jack could always do his homework inside of an hour and ace every test; he didn't really give a shit about running around with other kids, and video games bored the hell out of him because they were pointless. Plus, the sight of Margie sitting there, rocking herself, glued to *America's Next Top Model* or whatever, made his chest ache. He'd watched with her, and he'd gotten hooked, too.

He glanced around. No one else cared about what was on TV. They were too busy being richies, with their Bass Weejuns and Sperry Topsiders and jeans they paid double for if they were pre-ripped at the knee; faded Lacoste shirts, English tropical worsted jackets, London-made silk rep and club ties.

Not that he had anything against money. He loved to daydream about just what he'd do when he was finally making his own show and making the chip. Move his parents out of their Jersey City row house that needed a new paint job, for damn sure. Dad could quit his job at the Newark freight yards; no more coming home dog tired and covered in soot, dirt caked under his finger-nails, with nothing more to look forward to than the same damn thing the next day. His ma would quit, too. No more overnights with that old buzzard she worked for, Mr. Millar, with his emphysema and his diabetes. He owned half the tenement blocks in Jersey City but lived in a mansion in upper Montclair. No matter what, Jack vowed, no matter how much money he made in "the industry" (as they called it out here), he'd always remember where he came from.

He got the drinks and a tray and carried them through the crowded bar back to the table. Everyone thanked him profusely. He sat down, but then Maddy ducked her head under her own arms like she was shielding herself from flying shrapnel.

"What?" Anna put a hand on Maddy's forearm. "Are you okay?"

"Uh-huh," the girl muttered. "It's just that my—"

"Madeleine? Is that you?"

Jack watched Maddy cautiously lift her head as a man in his twenties—dressed in the worn jeans/faded tennis shirt combo of most of the patrons, with blond hair parted on the side, a strong nose, and round rimless glasses—bounded over to the table. Jack thought the guy looked like Trent Reznor of Nine Inch Nails, if Reznor had worn glasses and had blond hair.

"Hey, how's it going?" the guy asked.

Maddy muttered something and looked as if she were trying to shrink inside the collar of her sweater.

"I'm Brian Tarantella," the guy introduced himself. "Maddy's math teacher at Pacific Palisades High School—the kids call me Mr. T. Madeleine's one of my best students."

Maddy half-smiled but didn't speak. Jack gazed at the math teacher intently, wondering what he would do or say next. He remembered how weird it was to run into one of your teachers outside of school—it was almost as though you couldn't believe that your teacher had an actual life.

"So, what are you and your friends up to tonight, Maddy?" Mr. T asked.

"Oh, you know . . ." Maddy studied the floor as if searching for the Holy Grail among the oyster cracker crumbs.

"Okay, well, I just wanted to stop over and say hello, Madeleine. See you in class, okay?"

"Uh-huh."

The teacher took off to rejoin a group of people who were just leaving.

"I never had any teachers who were that handsome," Anna told Maddy, who still looked wildly uncomfortable.

"You think?" Maddy wondered aloud. "He's . . . okay. And I still can't do trigonometry."

Sam lay on her new California king bed with its silver-poled, lattice canopy and stared at the far wall. It was after midnight. She was wearing a set of old sweats from Harvard-Westlake, where she'd gone to junior high school, her most comfortable clothes for thinking and writing. Down the hall, she could hear one of the night nurses cooing in Russian and realized it had to be time for a Ruby Hummingbird feeding. God forbid that her young and annoying stepmother, Poppy, would get up and feed her own kid herself. Instead, there was a round-the-clock battalion of wet nurses to do it for her.

The far wall was Sam's normal workspace, where her antique Italian desk and classic Eames chair would usually be flanked by contemporary artwork that had been given to her father by movie studios and agents but that Jackson didn't want in his personal gallery. Sam loved the Alex Katz paintings especially—so disaffected and removed.

But now the artwork was gone, along with all the furnishings. In their place she'd had Kiki bring in four enormous Corrasable whiteboards, which Luis the handyman (he'd worked for the Sharpes for years and drove a Mercedes CL500 coupe to prove it) had fastened to the wall five feet off the ground. Sam had already taped dozens of colored index cards—blue for ideas, green for production notes, and plain white for shot sequences—to the whiteboards.

Only an idiot would make a serious movie without figuring out the sequences in advance; Sam had grown up so steeped in moviemaking that she would not let herself make that rookie mistake, no matter how much of a pain in the ass it was to do the index-card thing. *Hate it, but do it anyway.*

An idea struck her; she got up and filled out one more blue index card, then taped it to one of the whiteboards:

FIND HOME MOVIES OF OLD BHH PROMS FOR CONTRAST?

Hmm. That could be good. But she didn't get the usual rush that came with a great creative idea. Instead, she just felt depressed. And her stomach growled. A hot fudge sundae would be heavenly. However, it would not make picking out a prom dress a hap-hap-happy moment.

Maybe gum would help. She reached for the pack of Trident cinnamon sugarless on her nightstand and accidentally knocked over the small framed photo that Eduardo had given her in Paris—the two of them at the Eiffel Tower. She righted the picture and sat on the new white silk-and-lace quilt that adorned her bed. The facts of her life stared at her as clearly as any index card on the wall, resulting in her current funk: Eduardo had not called since she'd returned from Paris. Five days had passed. Anna could say whatever she wanted to say about how much Eduardo liked/loved/adored her; he evidently didn't like her well enough to pick up the goddamn phone.

Her stomach growled again. Why did she get the hungriest when she was feeling like crap? Visions of Porcelana chocolate from Amedei, the most expensive chocolate in the world, danced in her head. Her father had mentioned in an interview with Diane Sawyer that he loved the stuff, and fans sent it by the truckload. Sam knew exactly where he kept his copious stash. Her shrink, Dr. Fred, would say, "Sam, when you're feeling bad, does it *really* make you feel better to stuff your face with sweets?"

Hell, yeah, it made her feel better.

She glanced at the clock. Twelve-fifteen. Eight-fifteen in the morning in Paris. Eduardo was awake for his international relations class. Was there some French sex kitten named Françoise in his loft bed next to him? Sandrine? Frederique? Valerie? Corinne? Chantal? Mariel—?

The phone on her nightstand rang. *Crap.* Had to be

a wrong number. Everyone knew to reach her on her cell. She answered, barking into the phone. "What?"

"I woke you up, I can tell from your voice."

Sam bolted upright.

"Eduardo?" she asked cautiously, heart pounding.

"Go back to sleep, Samantha, I can call you tomorrow—"

"No, no, don't hang up! I mean, I wasn't asleep, I just didn't expect you to call on this line."

"Yesterday, I left my backpack on the Metro. My cell, my Palm Pilot. Laptop. It made me crazy. Then I recalled that in Mexico, you wrote all your phone numbers for me on a napkin. So . . . I found the napkin."

Fact: Eduardo had wanted to call her, but he hadn't been able to. Fact: He'd actually *kept* the napkin from Mexico.

"I'm glad you found it," Sam said. It was an insipid comment, but she was too ecstatic to worry about it.

"I missed the sound of your voice very much," Eduardo murmured. "I miss you even more."

She felt like doing a happy dance around her room. His voice sent chills up and down her spine. And his accent was pure velvet. "I miss you, too."

"So, tell me everything," Eduardo prompted. "How are you?"

Sam launched into a monologue of what she'd done since returning from Paris. Then Eduardo talked about his classes, a dinner with his cousins from Barcelona at Le Taillevent, a wonderful French film she should see.

Sam was only half-listening, because she was figuring out exactly how she wanted to ask him to prom.

"And the love scene was so intense," he concluded, "I thought of you."

The love scene made him think of me? For chrissake, just ask *already.*

"So Eduardo, I was wondering," she began, hands suddenly sweaty. "In America, we have this stupid thing called 'prom,' which is—"

"A formal party for high school students," he filled in; there was a smile in his voice. "I live in a different country, Samantha. Not on a different planet."

"Right. Of course. Silly. So . . ." She took a deep breath. "The Beverly Hills High School prom is Friday night. I know that isn't much notice, but I'll be there making a documentary, which you might find interesting, and I'll totally understand if you can't come because it's too little no—"

"Tell me about your film."

Sam couldn't help noticing a distinct lack of the words *prom, yes,* and *love to* in that request. Still, she gave him a two-minute rundown on the documentary, putting it in the best possible light. She even managed to sneak in a couple of her hottest ideas, like how she'd have an assistant film the prom weenies—she didn't call them that; she called them the prom organizers—as they went through their pre-prom-day routine and that she was planning to give walkie-talkies to some of the professional hotel staff so that she could be summoned instantly in the event of a meltdown. What the hell. Maybe he'd be dazzled by her creative genius.

"Impressive," he remarked. "So, will I be in it?"

Wait, did that mean he was going to be at prom? As in, *be with her* at prom?

"You mean . . . you'll come to my prom?" she asked cautiously.

"Yes, of course."

"I'm so happy!" Sam gushed into the phone, unable to contain herself.

"But I would have to leave right after your prom, because Saturday night is my parents' twenty-fifth anniversary and we are having a surprise party for them in northern Mexico, at my cousin's estate. My family will disown me if I miss it."

"That is so no problem. I'm sure you can take my dad's jet there. I'll ask him."

"Samantha?"

Sam lay back on her bed. "Yeah?"

"I'll be coming on *my* father's jet."

She heard the smile in his voice. Then he told her he'd e-mail her the information about when he was arriving, but that it would probably be Thursday—two days away. A moment or two later they hung up, and Sam lay back against her pillows, stunned with happiness. The whole world looked wonderful. Eduardo was taking her to prom. This call changed everything. If he weren't really and truly into her, he wouldn't come halfway across the world just to spend a few nights with her.

This was it. She'd get him to stay until dawn on Saturday, at least. They would finally make love.

Unlike her other sexual experiences, which had almost always involved 420 or alcohol and had had nothing to do with an actual human connection, she would find out what it was like to really *make love*.

All that plus making an award-winning documentary. Did her life fucking rock or what?

The World's Tiniest Leopard-Print Thong

Cammie pulled her jeweled and beaded emerald green Emanuel Ungaro peasant shirt over her head as slowly as possible, knowing that her boyfriend Adam's eyes were glued to her full breasts, perched inside the top of her white matte microfiber Gottex bikini top. While said breasts had been, pre–surgical intervention, three cup sizes smaller, it was a matter of personal pride to Cammie that no guy had ever commented nor any girl inquired in the locker room at the country club as to the identity of her plastic surgeon.

Shirt tossed on the bed, she hitched her fingers under the waistband—well, more like *hipband,* since the skirt's top fell several inches below her waist—of her 7 for All Mankind ruffled white cotton miniskirt and slid it down. She'd renewed her SunFX spray-on tan at Christophe's salon earlier that morning—the only tech she'd allow to touch her body, Marina from Moldova, had come in on her day off just to do Cammie—and knew her artificially golden skin glowed against the stark white of the Gottex.

A slender rose gold belly chain loosely encircled her waist, with two tiny charms hanging from it: the letters *A* and *F* in platinum, taken from her boyfriend Adam Flood's initials. She'd had the charm specially manufactured by Rone Prinz, the famous jewelry maker who lived for some godforsaken reason in Woodland Hills. Cammie was utterly confident that she was about to kick off yet another new trend—two months from now the Bel Air Country Club pool would be overflowing with girls wearing their boyfriend-initialed belly chains. Of course, Cammie would have jettisoned hers weeks before. Honestly, most girls were just sheep—it didn't matter how much money daddy and mommy made.

Cammie had arranged for this private little picnic to take place early in the morning, because she was supposed to go up to Ojai with Sam in the late afternoon to visit Dee at her inpatient facility. (Sam, unlike her and Adam, was going to school that day. Cammie and Adam were taking "senior" days; in other words, cutting school. By the end of the school year, senior attendance at Beverly Hills High School dropped precipitously.)

The drive up the coast to Malibu had taken an hour, but it was worth it. No sense going to the public beach at Zuma or Will Rogers State Park, where the sand was full of cigarette butts and you ran the risk of encountering the entire graduating class of Reseda High School on senior-cut day. Better to have a cozy getaway for two on the semiprivate beach in Malibu, where the sand was ostensibly open to the public but you had to know someone whose house had beach access to actually get there. She and Adam had been having a scratchy time of it lately. This outing seemed like the perfect remedy.

That Cammie cared as much as she did about Adam surprised her on a daily basis. He was cute and appealing, with his lanky basketball player's build and spiked dark brown hair short enough to show off a small star tattoo behind his left ear, yet he wasn't nearly as hot as Ben Birnbaum, for example. In her eighteen years, Cammie had enjoyed countless boyfriends and even more flirtations—usually she was in it for the game, the tease, or the sex; her heart was never involved.

Ben had been different, though she hadn't really let him know that. He was different, too, in that he was the first guy Cammie had ever been with who had been the one to end the relationship. She was used to being the dropper, not the droppee.

The end had broken her heart. And then, adding insult to injury, Ben had hooked up with the New York ice princess goody-two-shoes Anna Goddamn Percy. It still made Cammie insane.

Her relationship with Adam was sweeter, kinder, even nicer than the one with Ben had been, because Adam was so essentially decent. He'd only been in Beverly Hills for two years, having moved here from Michigan with his lawyer parents. Though he was accepted by the school's A-list, he was also accepted by everyone else. That he was the starting point guard on the school basketball team didn't hurt, but Adam couldn't have cared less about the social pecking order. That was weird, because everyone Cammie knew could pinpoint his or her own place on that pecking order with cruise-missile accuracy. Not Adam. He was sincere, smart, and always his own person. He didn't care where he was in that social pecking order, for example. As for the sex, it had started out south of zero but had improved rapidly once he got over his initial nervousness.

Plus, he treated Cammie like a jewel . . . which was a bit of an issue. Cammie knew she could be a stone-cold bitch, and she preferred to be treated like one at least some of the time. Sure, she knew that was twisted, but if a good man was hard to find but easy to hold on to, a bad boy was easy to find and impossible to hold onto. She admired badness. In fact, she often craved it. Whoever said that your boyfriend had to have the sensitivity of Dr. Drew? It wasn't like *he* was hot.

Cammie gazed up and down the pristine beach, cut off from the Pacific Coast Highway by an endless stretch of mansions that appeared nondescript from the highway but were in fact spectacular from the beach side. Azure waves lapped against the diamond-white sand. Terns wheeled and dove at a school of baitfish driven to the surface by hungry albacore. Off in the distance, a luxury liner lumbered north, maybe to San Francisco, maybe to Alaska. It was a perfect setting for peace and serenity, which she needed today, for reasons she hadn't shared with Adam.

Her gaze followed a bikini-clad redhead who was

running her golden cocker spaniel down the beach; Cammie vaguely recognized her from a long-running, now-deceased sitcom set in the seventies. Coming in the opposite direction was an older world-famous singer who had married a second-tier television actor; they were hand-in-hand, strolling on the packed wet sand left by the receding tide. She had a long paisley scarf wrapped around her head that trailed behind her in the light breeze, and wore baggy white linen clothing that covered her completely and sported oversize black Chanel sunglasses—but still, that *nose* made her instantly recognizable.

The actress lived just up the beach, three houses away from a diminutive female rap artist who had just switched representation to Apex, the new agency co-owned by Cammie's father. It was courtesy of this singer that Adam and Cammie were here—Cammie and the singer had bonded when a crucial strap on the rap artist's metallic dress had snapped at an Apex party, exposing perhaps the world's tiniest hot-pink leopard-print thong. The omnipresent photographers had done their thing, as other party guests offered safety pins. Cammie had done two things. One, in the bathroom, she showed the artist that she was wearing an identical thong. Two, she figured that the rap artist had done it completely on purpose, as a publicity stunt. The suspicion was confirmed when the artist made the cover of *Star* magazine just in time to coincide with the release of her latest CD, *Your Mama Ain't in Kansas Anymore, Neither*.

Cammie had called her new friend to ask if she and

her boyfriend could hang on her beach. The rap artist said sure, but she'd be lounging by her swimming pool since she hated the beach, as it was full of fucking sand.

Now Cammie stretched, the better to show off her curves, and smiled down at Adam, who sat on the large Indian blanket he'd brought along, looking extremely cute in blue-and-white surfer jams. She knelt so that he could see his initials dangling near her right hipbone.

"I thought about getting a tattoo," she told him, shaking her strawberry curls out of her eyes. "But those are so Cher–Angelina Jolie–mall-girl-in-the-'burbs now. Every chick in the valley has a tattoo just above her butt. And it's not like those girls can afford laser removal."

He fingered the charms. "I'm flattered."

"You should be. Plus, I got up early for you; I never get up early for anybody." She leaned over to kiss him gently, concentrating on his lower lip. "Nice here, huh?"

"Very. You have friends in high places."

Yes, she did.

Adam reached for Cammie and tugged her down next to him on the blanket. She landed artfully, her head on his chest. "Did I tell you how hot you look in that?" he asked.

"That's called stating the obvious, Adam. The real question is, How did you ever hook up with such a babe?"

"Brat." He reached for a giant white chocolate–dipped strawberry that nestled on a special cold plate he'd brought in their cooler and dangled the berry near Cammie's lips. She flicked her tongue out and licked it, eyeing him slyly.

"Don't do that in public, Cam. It gives me a very private reaction."

"Good." She took the strawberry and bit into it. When they'd first been getting together, she'd tried to seduce Adam on a beach and it definitely had not worked out. Adam was a private-sex kind of guy, while Cammie adored an audience. He kissed her gently, and she felt it down to her flame-red pedicure.

"Hey, you think we should rent a limo for prom, or should I drive?" he asked, then kissed her collarbone.

She made a face. "Everyone has prom on the brain; Sam and Anna were talking about it yesterday. It's so desperately high school."

"We're *in* high school."

"Please. Prom makes me think of clueless fat valley girls stuffed into mall gowns like huge pastel sausages. Then their dates rent some hideous purple tux and buy every rubber in Rite Aid in case they get pathetically lucky."

"You're such a snob, Cammie." He reached for her hand and helped her to her feet.

"Thank you."

"Come on, you. You're about to get wet." He spanked her ass once and started jogging toward the water. Cammie sighed. When she'd planned this private, serene picnic, actual swimming had not been part of her plan. She couldn't even remember if the MAC mascara she'd put on was waterproof, but since she was in dutiful-girlfriend mode, she trotted after him. When they reached the edge of the surf, they goofed around for a while, kicking water at each other with each gentle breaker that rolled up the beach. Then they waded into the cold water, up to their thighs.

Adam pointed. "Nice boat. Gotta get me one like that."

A white cabin cruiser, maybe thirty-five-feet long, was cutting slowly through the water from north to south about four hundred yards offshore. Cammie could see two fishing rods in the stern.

She wasn't fond of small watercraft, hadn't been ever since her mother had mysteriously drowned at sea. Every New Year's, Cammie made a secret, private, and very drunken pilgrimage to her mother's gravesite at Forest Lawn Cemetery in the valley, where she wondered if her mom's death ten years ago was really what it had been reported to be: an accident.

That night, her parents had been guests on the yacht of their friends the Strikers. They'd been cruising near Santa Barbara Island. Cammie had spent that night at the Strikers' second home in Montecito. She was friends with their son Brock, and they'd had a live-in Irish nanny. It was strange: Cammie remembered nothing of that evening other than a game of Scrabble for Children with Brock and the nanny.

At that point in his brilliant career, Clark Sheppard had yet to make his fortune as a talent agent and the Sheppards had not been living large, so Cammie had been wowed by the place. It was a French château that had been brought to America stone by stone and then painstakingly reassembled on a hillside with a perfect view of the Pacific.

Cammie had been eight at the time; she remembered hearing her parents argue a lot. Her father, who had always been very ambitious, was frustrated that his career hadn't yet gotten on track. Cammie's mother was an elementary school teacher who couldn't have cared less about the whole upwardly mobile show-business thing. She taught at the Crossroads School in Santa Monica, where the most liberal Los Angeles families who could afford the tuition sent their kids. Cammie had gone there for a while—until her mom died, in fact. Donna had been quiet, introspective, soft-spoken—the exact opposite of Cammie's father. In fact, she'd been perfect. At least that's how Cammie remembered her.

If one parent *had* to die, why couldn't it have been her son-of-a-bitch father? Of course, she understood full well how if that had happened she'd have been one of those valley girls buying a prom dress at Proms R Us in Sylmar, because that's all they would have been able to afford on her mother's schoolteacher salary.

That terrible night ten years ago, her father had awakened to find her mother missing. He'd immediately called the Coast Guard on the Strikers' ship-to-shore. When he was interviewed by the police, he claimed he'd taken a sleeping pill and hadn't realized she had never come to bed—he'd been out like a light since ten o'clock. The Strikers' story was that everything had been lovely on the yacht that night. No fighting, and only a single bottle of Cristal shared four ways. They'd been as surprised as Clark Sheppard to awaken and find Donna gone without a trace.

But that made no sense to Cammie. For one thing, her father would never share a bottle of Cristal with three other people, if only on principle. Plus, she remembered, even after all these years, how her parents and the Strikers would get sloshed together. She recalled, on one occasion, walking in to see Mrs. Striker sitting on her father's lap. That memory made her feel like puking; she quickly banished it from her brain.

Cammie gritted her teeth to keep herself from tearing up. The hardest thing was that her mother's body had never been recovered. At the Forest Lawn Cemetery, the headstone was merely symbolic, though she gave it the same respect as if her mother were actually buried there.

Mom. Mommy. How could you leave me?

Once when Cammie was about twelve, a bird had managed to fly into the chimney of one of the six fireplaces in their new mansion, and the bird had headed straight for Cammie's room. It was a small yellow finch, and it perched on the silver headboard of Cammie's bed as if it belonged there. Yellow had been Cammie's mother's favorite color. She'd wanted the bird to stay, hadn't even called anyone to tell them it was there. But then she went off to school, and when she returned, the bird was gone.

Though Cammie had never told anyone, she always wondered if that bird had been . . . more than a bird.

"Where'd you go?" Adam asked softly. His voice pulled her out of her musings; he put his large hands on her hips.

"Just thinking." She nudged her chin toward the distant yacht. Adam knew all about her mother. She'd told him everything. Except this: "Today is her birthday."

"Your mom's?"

Cammie nodded.

Adam turned her around and held her fast as a bigger-than-average wave rolled by.

"That's tough." He kissed her lightly. "Want dry land?"

She nodded, not trusting herself to speak. They waded back to the beach and padded to their blanket, using two oversize black towels to dry off.

"Remember in Vegas, Cam? When you asked me if I'd help you find out what really happened to your mom that night?"

Cammie nodded. She *had* asked him.

"Well, I asked my parents to see what they could find out. I mean, they're lawyers. They can get access to all kinds of stuff that we can't."

Cammie felt her throat close. Yes, she'd mentioned it to him, but she hadn't expected he would do anything about it. The idea that he'd actually followed through made her feel . . . what? Threatened. Scared. Closed down.

"Why did you do that?" She struggled to keep her voice steady.

He looked bewildered. "You asked me to."

She tossed her towel on the blanket, allowing anger, which covered her fear, to percolate. "No, I didn't. I mean, we talked about it, but I never told you to tell your parents and you know it."

"Wait. You're *mad*?"

Cammie stared past him down the beach. "I don't want to talk about it."

He touched her arm. "Come on, look at me."

Her eyes narrowed. "What?"

"You told me you wanted to find out the truth, right?"

She had. So why did she feel so . . . invaded by what he had done? She couldn't answer him, because she didn't know.

"Maybe you're—I dunno—afraid of what they might find out," he guessed. He reached for her again, but she stiffened. "Cammie, I'm sorry. I didn't think this would upset you so much—"

"I'm not upset, okay?" she snapped. "I'm pissed that you did this shit behind my back, Adam." She simply couldn't stop herself from venting at him—if she didn't, she felt as if she might explode.

He shook his head. "You are not making any sense."

"Ask me if I care. On second thought, don't ask me anything. I'm out of here."

She padded through the sand toward the stairs that led up to her friend's house, leaving everything behind— clothes, towels, food, Adam. He wanted to do some- thing useful? He could clean up after them. The worst part, though, was the one thing Cammie couldn't leave behind: her fear about the truth regarding her mother's death.

Lately, in the darkest part of the night when she would awaken and be unable to get back to sleep, she wondered, why was it that she could never be satisfied with anything? Things that used to make her happy— spending massive amounts of money on new clothes, for example, or being the hottest girl in any room, wherever she went—weren't making her happy anymore. It was almost like looking at someone else's life. It *should* have been wonderful, but it wasn't. Because her mother wasn't there to share it with her.

Sometimes it made Cammie so sad that silent tears trailed down her cheeks. She'd hug her pillow and wonder about a horrible, unthinkable thing: Had her mother killed herself? Had she wanted to be dead more than she wanted to be Cammie's mother?

Maybe that was why she wasn't satisfied with a wonderful guy like Adam. If her mother didn't love her enough to stick around, she must be utterly unworthy of love. Love made you weak, vulnerable, gave people power over you.

Love, Cammie knew, could destroy your heart.

Mr. I'm-So-Talented-But-I'm-All-Fucked-Up

"Next exit, Ojai." Cammie read the highway sign from the back of Sam's black Hummer. "Thank God. I hate long car trips."

"Two and a half hours isn't a long car trip," Sam pointed out. She turned to Anna, who sat next to her. "Wait until you see this place. More famous people have freaked out there than at the Ivy."

"You'd think rich people could have breakdowns closer to Los Angeles," Cammie groused. She held the window button down, then stretched out in the backseat, thrusting her orange Nars Boccacio–polished toes out on the driver's-side window.

"The air-conditioning won't work with the window open," Sam said.

Cammie ignored her.

"How is Dee doing, anyway?" Anna asked.

"So much better," Sam replied, peering at Cammie in her rearview mirror. "Which Cammie would know if she'd managed to get her ass out here more than twice since Dee got admitted."

"I'm impervious to guilt, jerks," Cammie sang out. "According to daddy dearest, some of the biggest deals in Hollywood get made at Dee's new home away from home. He's threatened to check himself in just to close a film thing he's doing with Mr. I'm-So-Talented-but-I'm-All-Fucked-Up, and we all know who *that* is."

Sam smirked at Cammie in the rearview mirror. "*You* definitely do, anyway. You made out with him at Nicole Richie's birthday party at House of Blues."

"I did not *make out* with him," Cammie corrected. "He may have semi–made out with *me,* but only because I was so pissed off at Ben." She pretended the comment had been unintentional and clapped a hand over her mouth. "Oops. Sorry, Anna."

Anna didn't bother to respond. She'd vowed that Cammie would not get to her during this trip to visit Dee. Ben, she told herself, had been with Cammie when he'd been much less mature. It had nothing to do with what he and Anna shared now.

But her eyes slid to Cammie anyway: her endless, tanned, perfectly toned legs, which led to her low-slung purple-and-silver paisley miniskirt, which revealed a belly chain with Adam's initials dangling from it, topped off with a flirty white lace Gianfranco Ferre blouse that was unbuttoned enough to show the lacy top of her La Perla lavender-and-silver bra and miles of cleavage. Cammie was not known for her subtlety. Ever.

Sexual attraction was biological, Anna reasoned. Either you were attracted to someone or you weren't, and no amount of liking someone, or knowing intellectually that they were right for you, could change that. Well, Ben was male; therefore, Ben had been attracted to Cammie. So why wouldn't he be attracted to her now? Or to some other girl who was everything that Anna was not?

" . . . these jeans, Anna?" Sam asked.

"Sorry, what?"

"I said, my so-called stepmumsy told me the Allen B. by Allen Schwartz jeans I'm wearing were being hawked on the Home Shopping Network."

Anna frowned. "So?"

"So what woman with a shred of self-decency even watches Home Shopping Network?"

Anna shrugged. "Don't know."

"It sucks," Sam groused. "I'll see my jeans on some fat-assed tourist shopping on Montana Avenue. Gawd."

"Isn't imitation supposed to be the sincerest form of flattery?" Anna asked.

Sam shot her a look. "I *know* you're kidding." She fingered the lacy shoulder seam of the scarlet Sandy Duftler camisole that crossed over her bust. "See this cami? I bought it two weeks ago. So I go to this party last week and Kirsten Dunst is wearing it. Now if she sees me in it, she'll think I'm copying her. She won't be flattered; she'll just think I'm pathetic. Which is why I can only wear it outside L.A."

Anna laughed. Sam's fashion obsession was hilarious, really. And it certainly pulled Anna out of her mental overtime on Ben and whomever he was attracted to when she wasn't around.

Cammie took her Prada eau de parfum perfume from her new pink, mint green, and aqua plaid canvas Antigua tote and spritzed it on—the Hummer was now filled with the fragrance. "I brought a bottle of this for Dee. It's her fave."

Anna craned around and smiled at Cammie. Regardless of Cammie's occasional rant, Anna knew she really did love Dee. "That was nice of you."

Dee had been transferred to the Ojai Institute shortly after her breakdown in Las Vegas, and she'd been there ever since. According to Sam, though, she had a release date three weeks hence.

"Cam?" Sam called from the front seat. "I've been meaning to ask you about something."

"Ask away."

"About prom. I know that prom is on the diabetic side of the too-sweet lifeline, but it could be hilarious. I mean, think about it," Sam rushed on. "Kevin Johnson and his middle linebacker man-boobs? What'll he wear, a sumo diaper or a tux? And what will his boyfriend, the crossdresser, wear? The entertainment possibilities are endless! You really ought to—"

"Yeah, okay," Cammie said, flipping her Stila lip gloss back into her tote bag.

Even Anna had to turn around at that one. Just two days ago, Cammie had insisted that she'd never, ever go to prom. And now the mere mention of one of the odder couples in their senior class had made her agree to go?

"Wait," Sam began, "did you just say *yes*?"

"What's the BFD?" Cammie asked. "Adam wants to go."

Oh, so *that* was it. Adam wanted to go. And Cammie wanted to make Adam happy. Well, Anna had always said that Adam brought out the best in Cammie.

"Damn, you're easy," Sam exclaimed.

"Only when I want to be"

Sam smiled. "It's sweet that you're willing to do it for Adam. Let's face it, no one expects sweet from you."

"Yeah." Cammie sighed. "We had an argument this morning."

"About what?"

"Forget it." She stared out the window, a shut-down look on her face.

Anna didn't mind that Cammie was upset about a fight with Adam, but she was glad the fight hadn't been enough to break them up. It meant that, theoretically at least, Anna would not be treated to the spectacle of Cammie rubbing herself all over Ben like a cat in heat on the dance floor.

She cringed at her own train of thought. How ridiculous was she being?

"It could be fun," Sam went on. "You and Adam, Anna and Ben, Eduardo with me."

"Eduardo said yes?" Anna asked, surprised that Sam hadn't told her.

"You need to read your e-mail, Anna," Sam replied. "I sent you one right after I talked to him. He's flying in on his father's plane."

Anna had a moment of true joy for her friend. "That's great. I'm so happy for you."

"Thanks," Sam replied. "I still have to work out the logistics of him and shooting the prom-weenies movie at the same time, but multitasking is my middle name."

Now that Eduardo was coming to prom, Anna wondered why Sam didn't just drop the movie idea altogether. Evidently, though, what had begun as an excuse to invite Eduardo to prom had turned into something Sam really wanted to do.

Ten minutes later, Sam pulled up to Ojai Psychiatric Institute's understated main gate, with its stone block-house guarding the entrance. They stopped there for visitors' badges; Sam explained that steel spike strips that could blow out her tires would have elevated from the driveway at the touch of a button if they hadn't. She'd visited Dee often and knew the whole drill.

"It looks like a resort," Anna noted as they drove past a series of classic gardens landscaped in the British style, lush lawns, a regulation basketball court, and two baseball diamonds. A hard right turn revealed a magnificent vista of the distant Pacific. There were picnic tables scattered about, two clay tennis courts, a volleyball court, a gazebo, and an actual concrete band shell appropriate for outdoor concerts. A cobblestone path paralleled the entry road, and every fifty yards or so Anna would see one or two people out for a stroll. Without fail, they waved politely to the Hummer. Anna found herself waving back.

"That wave will cost you a thousand bucks a day if you stay here," Sam declared. "Professional assessment, two grand a day. Treatment, a thou a day, for as long as you need your hand held and your brain fried. They don't accept insurance, either—and don't ask me how I know. If you're going to go crazy, it's a good idea to be rich."

The Hummer approached the main building—a low-slung structure of yellow sandstone with a circular drive that circumnavigated a lavish Italian-style fountain. Sam pulled up between a Porsche 917 and another Hummer in the visitors' parking lot. "My advice," she said, before she turned off the engine, "if you recognize a famous face, pretend you don't know them."

"That won't be difficult," Anna pointed out. "I'm bad at celebrity spotting."

It had been a difficult decision for her, whether or not to come to visit Dee. In the brief time Anna had known Dee, she'd found her . . . well . . . odd. Early on, she'd announced to Anna that she was pregnant with Ben's baby. Now *that* had been weird. It had also turned out to be a bald-faced lie. Dee had a habit of trying and discarding philosophies like plates of tapas at Meson G on Melrose Avenue—a bite of Jainism one day, a taste of Marianne Williamson New Age woo-woo the next, followed by a plate of Jewish kabbalah mysticism. Who the real girl was inside that delicate body, Anna didn't know, but the fact that she'd been in Vegas when Dee had had her Vegas breakdown made Anna feel somehow involved.

They climbed down from the vehicle—it was a magnificent spring day, with high, puffy clouds and temperatures in the low seventies—and strode across the parking lot to the main entrance. As they did, Anna saw Dee tear out of the front door to greet them.

"Hey, you guys!" Dee chirped in her high and breathy little voice. "I'm so glad you came! I've missed you sooo much!"

"I was here last week," Sam reminded her with a broad smile.

"Well, sure," Dee acknowledged. "I mean, since then." She embraced each of them in turn, including Anna, as they stood together under the canopy of the entrance. It was redolent with the scent of fresh roses, courtesy of dozens of well-kept bushes to either side of the glass front doors.

"You look great," Anna told her, and it really was true. Dee's shaggy, straight yellow-blond hair had been styled since the last time Anna had seen her, shaped into a pixie cut that that offset her huge, doll-like blue eyes. Her cheeks were flushed, eyes clear, smile bright. She wore white cotton twill shorts and a pale blue cotton ABS tank. In fact, Dee looked totally healthy. No stranger would have been able to guess which of the four of them was the patient.

Dee smiled serenely. "Thanks."

"So, how are you feeling?" Anna edged to the left to allow a middle-aged couple step out through the front door. Her jaw almost dropped as she recognized the Countess of Beaune and her husband, Count Guillemet. She'd met them on a ski trip she, her mother, and her sister had made to Les Deux Alpes several years earlier. She did the discreet thing, however, and pretended she didn't know them at all.

Dee had no such hesitation. "Hey, Count," she greeted the distinguished-looking gentleman in the black corduroy pants and white cotton dress shirt. "Pretty awful lunch today, huh?"

"Pretty *degoulasse* indeed," the count responded with a tender smile. "Not quite Bernard Morillon in Beaune. Perhaps our dinner will be better. We're off for a walk."

"See ya." Dee turned back to Anna as if bantering with the Count and Countess of Beaune at the inpatient psychiatric facility in California were the most normal thing in the world. "So, want to see the place?" she offered. "Sam's seen a lot of it, but not Cammie or Anna."

"What is there to see, Dee?" Cammie queried.

"If you don't want to come, you can wait for us here or in the lobby." Dee's tone was even. "I don't really care one way or the other."

Cammie's face actually reddened, and Sam whooped with laughter. "She *so* got you!"

"Bitch moment," Cammie admitted. "Sorry."

Dee led them all into the lobby that had been

decorated by the world-famous designer John Saladino in cool blues, with ultramodern furniture.

"I'm feeling so good," Dee chirped as they passed a white grand piano, on which perched an eggshell-blue vase of gardenias. "It took them a while to figure out my whole bipolar thing."

"I *hate* it when that happens," Cammie quipped.

Dee's eyes grew even wider. "It's not a joke to me, Cammie. It's my life."

She said this with such honesty and lack of flakiness that Anna could hardly believe it was the same girl. Evidently Cammie couldn't either, because she had no comeback and actually appeared chastised.

"Anyway, it turns out my brain chemicals aren't steady," Dee continued as they strolled along. "Lithium didn't work for me, so then they wanted to use valproate, but my mom freaked because she said I'd grow a beard or something. They finally settled on something else so new I don't even remember what it's called, and that's why I'm doing so great. I can't wait to go home."

Cammie hugged her. "This is like a whole new you."

"This is the real me," Dee explained. She opened a door to their right and led them into a giant dayroom that had every nearly video game known to man, three Xbox 360s, two billiards tables, and a high-definition big-screen television.

Then it was on to Dee's room in one of the three out-buildings. Each was connected to the main building by a canopied redbrick path. Dee's room was large, with a single bed covered in a blue-and-white Mark James silk quilt. A Swedish Modern wooden desk held Dee's silver HP laptop. There were several big potted plants, a mini-refrigerator, a large poster of Piet Mondrian's *Broadway Boogie Woogie*, and a colossal picture window that faced a huge lush garden, and, beyond that, the Pacific.

"It's really nice, Dee," Anna commented.

"It's hot in here." Cammie lifted her hair and fanned her neck. "It's just a *room*."

Sam gave Cammie a sly look. "You're being pissy because our little Dee is not quaking in your shadow."

Anna waited for Cammie's comeback, but there wasn't one. How refreshing. Sam had spoken the truth, and they all knew it.

"It wouldn't be such a shock to you if you had come to visit me more often."

"I came."

"Twice," Dee pointed out.

"You know hospitals get me all weird." Cammie pushed her spiraling curls off her face. "What is it, Beat Up on Cammie Day? First Adam and now you?"

Anna was surprised to see actual tears in the corners of Cammie's eyes. *Tears*. Something must be upsetting her deeply that had nothing to do with their trip to visit Dee. It had to be the fight with Adam.

"It's okay to *feel*, Cammie." Dee's voice was soothing; she put her arm around her friend. "Let it out. Just breathe. Why don't we go to the juice bar? Everything's free."

A few minutes later, they were sitting on comfortable upholstered chairs around a round wooden table in the clinic's juice bar, which had been decorated like a 1950s beatnik coffeehouse, filled with mismatched furniture, posters of Buddy Holly and the Big Bopper, and stacks of board games to play and books to read. Except for the four of them, and the prim barista who'd mixed their Jamba Juice–style raspberry-and-mango concoctions, the place was deserted.

"Dee, there's something I wanted to talk to you about." Sam stirred her juice with a pin-striped straw that bent in the middle. "It's . . . prom. It's Friday night."

"It was fun last year," Dee recalled wistfully. "What was that charity thingie we raised money for? MS?"

"I think it was AIDS," Cammie mused, apparently over her pique.

Dee nibbled on a fingernail. "No. Was it global warming? Or maybe the African drought?"

"The point is," Sam interrupted, "we're going this year, Dee. All of us."

"Yeah, but what charity?" Dee asked.

"None," Cammie replied. "That's what's great about it."

Dee pointed at Anna. "You and Ben?"

Anna nodded.

"There was a time when I was jealous of the two of you," Dee admitted. "Wow, I was such a toxic bitch."

"It's okay," Anna assured her.

Dee pointed at Cammie. "And you're going with Adam. And . . . Sam?"

Sam grinned. "Eduardo called. He's flying in from Paris."

"How fun." Dee's tiny shoulders sagged. "I'll still be stuck here." She polished off the last of her juice. "Unless . . ."

Anna could almost see the wheels turn in Dee's head. She excused herself and dashed out the door to parts unknown.

Five minutes later, Dee was back.

"I'm sprung!" she sang out.

"You're shitting me," Cammie marveled. "Just like that?"

"Not sprung-for-good sprung. I mean I asked Dr. Verheiden if I could get a day pass for prom—actually, a night pass—and he said yes!"

Anna grinned, remembering how out of it Dee had been in that Vegas hospital room, how she'd claimed to hear voices in her head. Anyone who had seen this girl then would have had a hard time imagining that she would ever recover. Yet here Dee was, more normal than Anna had ever seen her. Not only was it an incredibly inspiring story, but she could *like* this girl, she decided.

Suddenly, Dee's face clouded.

"What is it—are you okay?" Sam asked, instinctively moving toward her friend.

"I'm fine," Dee answered. "But . . . what am I going to do? I don't have a date."

No date. Of course not. Why hadn't they thought of that before?

"Well, we'll all just kind of go as a group then," Anna suggested brightly.

Cammie shot Anna a withering look. "Are we acting out scenes from *Saved by the Bell*? This is *Beverly Hills*, Anna. Ignore the boring, tight-ass, beige girl to my right," she suggested to Dee. "I'm not only going to find you a date, I'm going to find you the hottest date in southern California."

Prom Means Sex

B en sat on his bed, sorting through a plastic box of CDs he'd brought home from Princeton. Jack had burned them for him—assorted bootlegged concerts, songs by some of the alt bands he loved that he'd downloaded from the Internet.

Being home was weird, because in some ways, Princeton now felt more like home. He could be completely himself there, not the dutiful son of the "Plastic Surgeon to the Stars." Whatever or whoever he was had no complicated psychological tethering to who he'd been as a kid, the mistakes he'd made, his mother's depression, or his father's gambling addiction. He was his own man.

The fact that his mother had gone on a redecorating spree in honor of his father's Gamblers Anonymous sobriety contributed to the weirdness of being back home. Without even mentioning it to him, his mother had changed everything, including his bedroom. Gone were his childhood dark maple furniture and his bulletin board covered with high school paraphernalia. In their place was a resort motif inspired by his parents' recent second honeymoon, at Round Hill in Jamaica. The new furniture was pale, sun-bleached wood; his new high-top bed boasted a white cotton quilt and various down pillows in white, eggshell, beige, putty, and cinnamon. Gone was the wall-to-wall carpeting. The natural wood floors had been stripped and sanded; atop them were various white cotton throw rugs. Bamboo baskets of various sizes held all the things that used to be on his bulletin board. The bulletin board itself resided someplace in a South Bay landfill. That his mother had done all this without asking him, or even telling him, made Ben quite pissed. Evidently you really *couldn't* go home again.

But okay, it was good that his dad wasn't gambling away the family fortune anymore; even better that his mother appeared to be coming out of her depression with the help of a great therapist and some well-chosen pharmaceuticals. Being around them this summer would be a hell of a lot easier than it had been during the nightmare of a summer that followed his high school graduation. Plus, his bud Jack was in town. Jack made Ben laugh. He was a dog with the ladies, but a charming dog. Ben knew more girls who referred to Jack as "the asshole" than girls who knew his last name, but most of them smiled when they said it. He had, however, also been known upon occasion to be quite the heartbreaker; Ben knew, because more than one girl had called to cry on his shoulder.

The best part of being home, of course, was Anna.

Ben tossed his green Princeton T-shirt into the

wicker basket that held his laundry, then lay back on his bed recalling everything he and Anna had done on his father's new yacht. That such heat came from a girl who seemed so pristine was just so damn sexy. When he'd gone away to school, he hadn't been looking for a heavy relationship; he had actually run away from them at Princeton. There were so many girls who were hot in so many different ways—why would he tie himself down to one at this point in his life? Freshman year, running around with Jack, sampling different girls who were up for a good time, had been a blast. There was no way he'd planned to give that up.

Then he'd met Anna on the plane on New Year's Eve. Everything had changed. Sure, he still had his issues with the whole monogamy thing, because that seemed a short step away from the we're-together-forever thing, and he *definitely* didn't want to go there at this point in his life.

Anna, though, had been irresistible; and the more he got to know her, the more irresistible she became. She was this fascinating combination of innocence and experience, and for all her wealth, she was totally unpretentious. Most of the girls he knew were so jaded. But Anna had no artifice, no faux cool to hide behind.

The idea of hooking up with other girls lost all appeal for him. The times he and Anna had fought had sucked; they were a black cloud hanging over his head. When they'd gotten back together, he'd been so afraid of screwing it up again that he'd held on too tight; he knew that now.

There was a soft knock on his door. Before he could ask who it was, it cracked open. Maddy stuck her head in.

Ben sat up. "Hey, what's up?"

"Oh gosh, I'm bothering you, you don't have a shirt on, you were getting undressed, I should have asked—"

"Maddy—take a breath." He motioned her in. "It's just a chest."

"A nice chest," she said, and padded in. She wore that silk robe she seemed to have on half the time, and, as far as Ben could see, nothing else. From the neck up, she still looked like dorky Maddy.

Ben carefully kept his gaze on her face as she sat in the new wicker chair at his new antique bleached wood desk. "Do you have to shave your chest to get it all hairless like that? Do lots of guys shave? Or do you wax?"

That was just such classic Maddy—clueless, but sweet, which made it a lot easier to have this girl with that body in that robe in this bedroom.

"You came in to ask me about hair removal, Mad?"

"Oh no. Actually, I came in to tell you about Jack."

"What about him?"

"Well, last night, after we met you guys at the marina, we took a drive."

Oh, shit. I should have seen this coming.

"Go on," Ben prompted.

"He's really nice and funny and everything," Maddy continued. "We went for ice cream at Bethanee. I couldn't get any but I had a lick of his: chocolate, with pecans and peanuts and little, tiny marshmallows—"

"What about the drive, Maddy?"

"Oh sure, right, sorry." She patted her stomach. "I love being thin—well, thin*ner*—but I kind of miss eating. So anyway, we ran into these girls I know from school; they were total bitches to me at the beginning of the year because I was so fat. And they still call me fat even though I'm so much smaller. I guess compared to them I still am fat, because they all wear size zero or something. Plus, you know my hair was, like, all frizzy from being near the ocean and everything? And I wish I knew how to do makeup, but I never wore any because I didn't want people to notice me. Which is stupid, because at three hundred pounds *everyone* noticed me. So, anyway, they walk by and one of them goes, 'Nice 'do, Porky.'"

"Bitches," Ben declared. "Ignore 'em."

"No, wait, I didn't get to the good part yet." Maddy leaned forward, eyes shining. "Jack leaned over, right in front of them, and he kissed me."

Ben couldn't decide what he felt. What Jack had done was cool. But Maddy was so clueless that she had probably misinterpreted it and now thought she and Jack were engaged or something.

"You should have seen the looks on their faces," Maddy went on. "Jack is a hottie, kinda. Not like *you*, but, you know, cute."

"*And?*"

"And, you know, it's almost prom, and . . . he said he'd go with me!"

Ben nearly groaned aloud. Everyone knew that prom meant sex. Especially Jack Walker.

Ben had known Maddy forever. She was the closest thing to a little sister that he was ever going to have. The idea of someone actually taking advantage of her innocence appalled him, even as he realized the temptation to stare at her in that robe. What the hell, maybe he was just a sucker for underdogs. The way Ben saw it there was more than enough cruelty in the world, and way too much every-man-for-himself. Beverly Hills was full of people like that; he'd grown up with them. It had helped him figure out what he *didn't* want to be.

"You guys are going as *friends*, right?"

"Oh, you!" Maddy laughed gleefully. "Anyway, I'm so excited! Jack has to be a great guy because he's your friend, so I know I can, like, totally trust him! I just wanted to say thank you."

She crossed the floor to his bed and hugged him hard. Was it his imagination, or did her hug linger just a little too long? He felt her huge breasts separated from his naked chest by the thinnest of silk. Way . . . weird.

He pulled away and tried to make it seem natural. "Hey, that's great, Maddy."

She didn't move.

"We'll talk about it more tomorrow, okay?" He hoped she'd get the hint that he wouldn't mind if she departed.

She did, waving a happy good-bye from the doorway before disappearing down the hall. Ben got up and shut the door.

Shit. Maddy thought Jack had to be a good guy because she trusted Ben. The truth was, when it came to girls, Jack was anything but trustworthy or good. Maddy was definitely not prepared for Jack Walker's moves, and Ben had no clue what to do about it.

Her Notorious New Playmate

Cammie sat across from her father at one of the round glass tables in the piano bar at the Bel Air Grand Hotel. Her dad was entertainment *über*-agent Clark Sheppard, who had come to meet his daughter straight from the office. He was dressed in one of his custom-made-in-Hong-Kong single-breasted gray vent-less suits, a light blue dress shirt, and an elegant lavender tie. The bar was close to full at this hour: tourists having post dinner cocktails, actors and Hollywood types stopping off after the day's shootings. Cammie recognized Vince Vaughn and a couple of his friends watching the Dodgers game on the bar TV.

Cammie was in a funk so deep it hadn't been repaired by the two Grey Goose cranberry martinis (all the rage on the west side of Los Angeles, these consisted of a Grey Goose martini into which exactly seven ripe cran-berries were added prior to the shaking process—the shaking bruised the cranberries but didn't crush them) she'd imbibed.

After her blowup with Adam on the beach, she'd

actually called him to apologize—not for her feelings, because she still thought he was out of line for having enlisted his parents' help without clearing it with her first, but for the way she'd handled it. She shouldn't have stormed off like she had.

Adam's response had been so *him*—understanding, accepting. He still thought that if his parents could find out anything about what had happened to her mom it would be a good thing. But that was her call, not his, so he wouldn't push it. They were still on for prom, right?

One part of her was pleased by his response. Another part of her wished that he had the balls to call her on being a total bitch and a half. One day, she really would push him too far. On purpose, maybe. God, what kind of a girl did something like that? What was it about her that made her want *bad* things to happen? Maybe danger and love and sex were all confused in her mind, some deep psychological shit like that.

She ragged on Sam for seeing Dr. Fred. Maybe she needed to see him herself.

She'd thought about her mom all day. Her father hadn't even acknowledged his dead wife's birthday when she'd seen him briefly that morning. So she called him at Apex on the way home from Ojai and asked if he'd join her for a drink later. She'd suggested the Grand, figuring she could see and book the biggest suite there for prom night and then meet her dad in the piano bar.

The suite she'd found barely met her minimum standards; it was the kind of place that was written about in

Zagat guidebooks as "quaint" and "venerable" and "charming," which actually meant that there was no bidet in the bathroom and that the shower had only one head. Still, the Mayer suite on the top floor was the nicest in the hotel, named for the movie mogul Louis Mayer, who'd had it decorated to match the grandest Art Deco suite in his film *Grand Hotel*, one of the all-time Hollywood classics. She and Adam could simply adjourn up here when they tired of the proceedings in the ballroom.

Drinks with her father? She'd expected him to disappoint her, and he wasn't letting her down. Clark's movie-actor cleft chin bobbed as he rattled on about his day, the various exciting projects that his agency was handling, and all the people in the business who had fucked him this week. Like she cared. Why couldn't he talk about anything personal?

"So this is sick," her dad was saying, oblivious to Cammie's disinterest. "There I am, with Harvey on one line and Renee's manager on the other, and I'm telling Harvey I can bring Renee in for five mil less than her quote, and I'm telling Renee's manager that Harvey will meet her quote plus a dresser and a makeup artist for her publicity tour, plus a private jet."

She drained her martini. "Don't tell me, Dad. You made them both happy."

Her father smirked and twirled the stem of his martini glass. "Nothing makes me happier than to dick Harvey. He's screwed me so many goddamn times—"

His sentence was interrupted by a discreet chiming tone from his cell phone. "Hold on a sec, babe." He checked the number. "Gotta take this."

Cammie shrugged and glanced around for the waiter—she wanted another drink. Meanwhile, her father launched into a conversation that quickly escalated into a heated negotiation. Three minutes later, he muttered good-bye to whomever was on the other end, snapped the phone shut with supreme anger, and stood up from her chair.

"Gotta go back to Apex for a conference call," he barked, angrily flinging a fifty-dollar bill on the table. "Harvey's dicking me again. I'll see you at home."

"No, you won't." Cammie kept her tone even and conversational.

"What's that supposed to mean?"

"Just that you won't get back till after midnight. I've seen this movie before."

He gave a snort of disgust. "Can you hit the guilt thing some other time, Camille?"

"Today was Mom's birthday."

A beat. He sat back down again abruptly. "*That's* what this is about?"

"You didn't remember, which doesn't surprise me."

"Shit." He ran a hand through his perfect silver hair. "I'm not big on birthdays of the living, Cam. Let alone the dead. You know that."

She looked away. "Right."

"What was I supposed to do, send her a card?" He leaned toward her. "I'll always care about your mom,

Cammie. But I'm married to someone else now. I've moved on with my life."

Cammie felt something clench in her stomach. "Gee, Dad, I guess I didn't get that 'moving on' memo."

"Look, I get that this is hard for you, okay?" He stood again. "If I get home at a decent hour, I'll knock. We'll talk. Okay?"

"Whatever."

"'Whatever,'" he echoed with disgust. "What are you, twelve? You can't come up with something better to convey your disgust with me than 'whatever'? "

Cammie raised cold eyes to him. "How about fuck you, then? That better?"

"Excuse me while I earn a living." He walked away.

Gosh, she sure loved these family-bonding moments. How dumb could she be, after all these years, still harboring a secret hope that he'd suddenly turn into a decent father? It was stupid for her to feel hurt.

The pretty, pug-nosed waitress with auburn hair razor cut to her chin set another cranberry martini in front of her. "From the gentleman at the bar," she announced, handing Cammie a napkin. "There's a note on this for you."

She unfolded the napkin: *You're the most gorgeous girl in this place. May I share a drink with you?*

Cammie always enjoyed the "you're the most gorgeous girl" thing; there was nothing that could lift a girl out of a funk than a hot guy telling her how cute she was. She had on a canary yellow eyelet lace Twelfth Street by Cynthia Vincent silk tunic with an uneven handkerchief hem. It was supposed to be a top, but it barely cleared the bottom of Cammie's yellow silk La Perla thong. She wore it with nothing but miles of tanned leg and Michael Kors cork sandals with gold braiding. She glanced lazily over at the bar. She vaguely recognized the twentyish actor at the bar—he'd been in that Orlando Bloom movie set in the desert. The guy sitting next to him gave Cammie a quick wave. She vaguely recognized him from a medical show on TV where he played the young rock 'n' roll rebel doctor. His sandy-colored hair was short and curly, and he wore a short-sleeved gray T-shirt over an olive-green long-sleeved T-shirt, with Levi's. Very Justin Timberlake.

She lifted the cranberry martini to her lips and gave him the smallest of smiles.

He took that as a yes, picked up his drink, and joined her. "Hey," he said easily as he slid into one of the purple upholstered chairs at the table. "I'm—"

"I know who you are," Cammie said, cutting him off. "Do you like playing doctor?" She gave the question a double meaning on purpose.

He flashed a lazy grin. "I'm good at it. And you're—?"

"Cammie Sheppard."

He nodded. "I recognized your dad. Figured you were a client." He took another sip of his drink—it looked like scotch on the rocks. "So. Clark Sheppard has a daughter."

"We've just established that."

He studied her a moment. "You really are, you know, incredible looking."

She sipped her martini and didn't respond. This was a game she knew and loved. The art of flirting. The thrill of feeling how much a guy wanted her. It had all the fun of cheating, with none of the guilty consequences.

They bantered back and forth for a while. He lived in the neighborhood and liked to hang out at the hotel bar; he liked the Old Hollywood vibe. When it was Cammie's turn, she lied and said she was a sophomore at USC, just for fun. Turned out he'd gone to school there and wanted to know if she knew any of his friends, which was monumentally boring. Like she gave a shit about his friends. Just when she was ready to draw the little flirtation to a close, he mentioned that he had some killer Thai stick; a friend had brought it back from a recent trip to Phuket. Was Cammie interested?

Cammie thought about it a moment, then decided why the hell not get fucked up? It wasn't like reality was so attractive. The guy suggested they torch up in one of the second-floor bathrooms. The floor was only used for conferences; there were no conferences at ten o'clock at night.

Rock 'n' Roll Doctor Actor was right. The dressing area that led in to the vintage black-and-white-tiled bathroom was deserted. They didn't bother to turn on the light; they could see well enough from the moon-light streaming in through the windows to sit together on a red velvet chaise and torch up the fat doobie he took out of his back pocket. He sucked in a huge hit and passed it to her. "Oh man, that is so sweet."

She sucked on the joint, then passed it back to her new playmate. Instant attitude adjustment. Why stress about her father? He was who he was; he was never going to change.

When the joint had burned down to a roach, her insignificant other reached for it again, but Cammie had just flicked it into a trash receptacle. "Excellent. I needed my mood altered."

There was a stoned gleam in his eye. "Yeah?" He leaned in and kissed her softly.

What the hell. It was just a kiss. Kissing wasn't cheating. She kissed him back. And while it was nice, it wasn't Adam. God. She was turning into such a good girl, she could puke. She gently pushed Rock 'n' Roll Doctor Actor away. "I don't think so."

He shrugged. "Worth a shot. Although your dad is such a son of a bitch, if I *did* seduce you, he'd probably *have* me shot."

They both found that comment hysterical, laughed until they were gasping for breath, then headed back to the bar. She gave him one soft little kiss on the lips and took off, stoned and more than a little drunk, but proud in a silly way that she hadn't done what she'd done so many times before: picked up a hot guy just to prove to herself that she could.

Maybe Adam was right. Maybe she really *was* changing.

Waiting for the Other Manolo to Drop

Cammie had already called down her order to Stephen, a new cook that her father and Patricia were trying out for a week of breakfasts before they fired Ricardo, the current cook, who did dinners four days a week and three meals on Saturdays and Sunday. Cammie had ordered two soft-boiled organic brown eggs, a butter croissant with a slice of fresh Brie melted on top, a small glass of fresh-squeezed grapefruit juice, and a sixteen-ounce mug of Sumatran coffee with two tablespoons of fresh cream and one packet of Splenda.

When she drifted into the kitchen fifteen minutes later—ready for school in a Notice green-and-white floral sarong-style skirt and a Hot Kiss white tank top—she was pleased to see that breakfast was already on the new Thomas Bell designer kitchen table with interlocking black tile and white glass squares; six gun metal chairs with plush pillow upholstery surrounded it. Stephen was at work at the restaurant-style stove with ten burners and three ovens. Her father, Patricia, and her loathed stepsister, Mia—Patricia's fourteen-year-old valley girl of a daughter who had come to live with them a few months earlier—sat around the table, eating.

Cammie's father wore his signature gray power suit and was reading the *Los Angeles Times* (you could always tell the agents from the producers in Hollywood— agents wore suits, producers wore jeans); Patricia was still in her lavender paisley silk Monique robe and was reading the *Hollywood Reporter*. Mia, meanwhile, was hunched over a science textbook, doing homework that she'd neglected the night before. Cammie was gratified to see that Mia was wearing her own clothes and not Cammie's.

"Mornin'," her father grunted, barely looking up from the newspaper. Neither Patricia nor Mia acknowledged her presence. This was not unusual—she and her stepmother were barely on speaking terms, and she and Mia hadn't been doing much better since she'd caught Mia wearing a brand new Dolce & Gabbana black gathered-chiffon corset blouse of hers just a few days earlier. In retaliation, Cammie had marched into Mia's room and used the gardener's clipping shears to shred Mia's favorite distressed leather jacket into brown confetti.

She sipped her coffee, reflecting on the night before. Okay, so she'd flirted a little with Rock 'n' Roll Doctor Actor. But she'd stayed true to Adam, and more important, she'd been true to herself. Her father's head was buried in the Living section; he was reading the review of the new Martin Scorsese film destined not to win an

Oscar no matter how good it was. So much for them "discussing" what had happened last night. He just didn't give a shit.

Cammie picked up the front section of the paper and scanned the headlines. The mayor was meeting with the governor in Sacramento. Big whoop. The Russians had sent more cosmonauts to the International Space Station. Double whoop. Gas prices had hit a new peak in California. Yawn. The Bel Air Grand Hotel had burned to the ground.

Well, there goes prom. Oh yeah. Part of her felt extremely relieved.

She thrust it at her father. "You see this?"

He glanced at the paper. "Yeah. Too bad, huh? We were there last night."

Cammie quickly scanned the story. No one had been hurt in the blaze, but the hotel was ruined. It had burned quickly because there was no sprinkler system and because the city fire hydrant system was antiquated. The fire evidently had smoldered in a second-floor bathroom waste bin before erupting in full—

Fuck me hard.

She'd been in a second-floor bathroom with her new pal. She vaguely recalled him reaching for the roach and her carelessly tossing it into the waste bin right before their kiss. Had she made sure that the roach was extinguished before she'd offed it?

Double fuck. She was a fucking *arsonist.*

"Cammie?"

She looked up from the *Times*. Mia was staring at her.

"You look kinda sick."

"Thanks, I love you, too," Cammie sneered, desperately trying to cover her horror. *Oh my God, I'm responsible for the destruction of a Los Angeles landmark!* Okay, the hotel had been toast forever, but still, she hadn't intended to turn it into toast *literally.* This was terrible!

She nibbled at her lower lip, chewing off her Tarte lip gloss. There wasn't any way the fire inspectors could find out it was her, was there? No way. Rock 'n' Roll Doctor Actor wouldn't dare say a word; he'd have to admit what he'd been doing in the bathroom.

But even if no one ever found out she had caused the fire, she'd know. What was she feeling? Something . . . strange.

Guilt.

That was it. So this was what guilt felt like. It was not a feeling with which she was well accustomed.

"Excuse me, Cammie," one of the maids announced, appearing in the archway. What was her name—Svetlana, something like that? She looked like she could break bricks with her bare hands. "A friend of yours is out front. Sam?"

Oh shit. Somehow Sam had found out. And if Sam had found out, what about the police? Was Cammie looking forward to graduation at Vacaville prison?

She opened the front door to blinding sunshine. Sam was right there, in jeans and a white fitted Cavalli T-shirt, holding the *Los Angeles Times.* She waved the morning paper in Cammie's face. "Did you see this?"

"Of course." A small flock of red finches took off

from the huge bird feeder Svetlana had erected to the right of the front door. "What brings you here? Bird-watching?"

"I wasn't in the mood for the whole family-at-breakfast thing," Sam explained. She gestured to the newspaper. "What asshole would throw a cigarette butt in a waste basket?"

A guilty heat buzzed inside Cammie's head. "Someone who hates old hotels?" She kept her face totally impassive. "Anyway, why do we care?"

"Because prom is fucked."

Cammie shielded her eyes from the sun. "I've said that all along."

"Prom is not about *you*, Cammie. I mean our *location* for prom is fucked."

"Let's do something else. Fly to Rio, how about that?"

"How about that your boyfriend wants to go?" Sam reminded Cammie, with an intense look. "Anyway, I've already been on the phone to the prom weenies. They wanted to move it to the school gym, complete with streamers hanging from the basketball hoops and a disco light. I did an immediate intervention."

Cammie lifted her hair off her neck; it was a scorcher of a morning. "That was nice of you, even if your school spirit *is* nauseating."

"It's not school spirit, it's . . . wait. I did tell you about my movie, right?"

"No. What movie?"

"A documentary I'm doing on prom, which is totally going to launch my directing career."

"I'm waiting for the other Manolo to drop."

"Picture, if you will, the Beverly Hills High School B-list preparing for prom, desperately trying to scratch their way to the A-list," Sam explained. "A commentary on the teen social structure of the rich and famous. Prom is a perfect microcosm of said social structure. I told the B's I would help them with prom and supply the A's."

"And being B's, they're clueless to the neediness oozing from their pores that will be oh-so-visible to the camera," Cammie filled in. The truth was, this was a very shrewd idea on Sam's part.

"They think they're all about to be movie stars."

Cammie smiled. "You're an evil genius worthy of my friendship."

"I'm expanding the concept. Other proms. What it says about teens and their social strata. Like that."

"Want to come in and ask Mia about proms in the valley?" Cammie offered. "Because that's like a foreign country."

Sam shook her head. "Too much to do; I can only stay a minute."

"So what new place did you find?"

"You know how my dad is doing that remake of *Ben Hur*?"

"Sure." Jackson Sharpe's *Ben Hur* remake was the talk of the town. Half the industry was aghast that

Jackson was remaking one of the great films of all time; the other half couldn't wait to see a fresh take on *Ben Hur* with decent CGI and a twenty-first-century budget.

"They built the Colosseum outside of Palmdale for the big chariot race. My dad called the producers this morning; they're not shooting there on prom night. Ta-da, it's ours. For prom."

"A toga party for prom?" Cammie scrunched up her nose. "Isn't that a little *Animal House*?"

Sam laughed. "Feel free to wear the designer duds of your choice. Can't you just picture it? Ancient Rome—which, by the by, fell due to its inhabitants' unbridled decadence, juxtaposed with the equally unbridled decadence that is our prom. The haves and the have-nots, et cetera, et cetera. It's so perfect I could kiss me."

Cammie nodded approvingly. "It *is* great, Sam. I'm impressed."

"Impressed enough to help me with the movie on prom night? I have a zillion things to do and, like, no time to do it now."

Cammie thought about that one for a moment. She *did* feel guilty about burning down a Los Angeles landmark. Helping Sam with her film would be a kind of penance. She only wished she could share the truth with Sam, who appreciated irony more than anyone else Cammie knew. But she didn't tell. Instead, she said yes.

Hey, That's My Bathrobe!

"The chariot race set from *Ben Hur*," Anna concluded. She'd just finished filling Ben in on the latest plot point in the prom saga; Sam had relayed the whole story to her at school. Ben had been training for his new job at the club and hadn't seen the news. He'd picked her up at eight to take her out for dinner. He wore baggy Lucky jeans—very low key and therefore very sexy, with a sky-blue Lacoste tennis shirt. They'd agreed to go casual, so Anna had on jeans, too, with a white T-shirt and her favorite gray flannel sweater, so well worn that it was as cool as cotton.

"A movie set for the prom," Ben marveled as he steered his black BMW from the 405 onto the exit ramp for the 101 north. "Leave it to Sam."

"Miss Resourceful," Anna agreed. The sun was just beginning to set; spectacular colors refracted in the western sky—the upside of Los Angeles smog.

"I kind of liked that old hotel," Ben mused aloud as he changed lanes. "A client of my dad's lived there whenever she was doing a movie. When I was, like, fifteen she slipped me a key to her suite and told me to visit her."

Anna made a face. "Please tell me she was under thirty."

"Not even close."

"Now tell me you didn't take her up on it."

Dimples twinkling, he steered with his left hand and put his right hand over his heart. "Do I look like a kiss-and-tell kind of guy?"

She studied him for a minute. "You have the smuggest look on your face."

"You are *so* much fun to tease. No, I didn't take her up on it. Damn." A traffic jam—it was the end of afternoon rush hour, after all—forced him to brake quickly. "I gotta hand it to Sam—she knows how to pull strings. Half the schools in L.A. have their proms on Friday night, the other half on Saturday. Every decent place was booked months ago."

"Same thing in New York. Where are we headed?" Anna queried.

"Nowhere, if the traffic doesn't thin out."

"I just didn't expect you to take me to the *valley*."

His eyes flicked to her and then back to the freeway, where the traffic had mysteriously begun to move again. "You haven't lived here long enough to be a snob about the San Fernando Valley."

"'Home of the unwashed masses?'" Anna joked. "That's what Cammie calls it. I'm not a snob, and you know it. And the answer to my question is . . . ?"

"What color is your prom dress?"

"What are you talking about?"

Ben burst out laughing. "I was artfully changing the subject so that I didn't have to answer your question."

"So you're keeping me in the dark about our destination," she surmised.

"Exactly. Let's just say that tonight you'll get the chance to try something you've never tried before. And we'll leave it at that."

A grizzled old man in rags carrying a plastic garbage bag over his shoulder was walking along the blacktop that bordered the expressway. "Poor guy," Ben murmured.

"It's funny," Anna mused. "My mother does all this charity work, but it's always for chic causes: museums, the symphony, the ballet. If she walked by that man begging on a street corner and he had his hand out, she wouldn't even see him."

Ben's eyes flicked to Anna, then back to the road. "You're nothing like her, you know."

She smiled. "This might sound awful, but that's one of the nicest things you could say to me."

Anna had loved Ben's self-assuredness right from the start, when they'd met on the plane; it was sexy. What made it even hotter was learning that it was tempered with kindness. Goodness, even. He cared about people and hated to see anyone get hurt.

She opened the console where he kept his CDs, knowing that Flogging Molly would be on top; it was Ben's current favorite band. Instead, she found something else. "Ani DiFranco, *Not a Pretty Girl*?"

"She's this alt chick singer who was big in the

nineties." Ben nodded toward the CD. "That's Maddy's. She wanted me to hear it."

He flicked on his blinker and got into the right lane, then took the Coldwater Canyon exit to Studio City. "Her prom's the night after yours."

Maddy. Lately, the girl's name seemed to come up whenever she was together with Ben lately.

"That's nice," Anna commented, hoping she sounded much more pleasant than she felt—she had a niggling little suspicion that Maddy's interest in Ben was a bit more than friendly.

"She's going with Jack," Ben continued.

Thank God.

"Great!"

She saw him knit his eyebrows.

"Not great?" Anna ventured.

Ben puffed some air out between his lips. "Look, Jack is a good bud of mine, but . . ." He hesitated. "Remember when I was fooling around and I said that all guys were dogs?"

"Who could forget such poetry?" Anna teased.

"Let's just say that when it comes to girls, Jack has had major canine moments." He turned left onto crowded Ventura Boulevard, the main drag of the valley. It was just as packed with cars as the 101 had been.

"You're worried about her," Anna filled in.

"Well, yeah," he declared, as if it were obvious. "She is the last of the innocents, Anna, I mean it. No way is she ready for Jack Walker."

Anna put the Ani DiFranco CD back in the console. "I think you should relax. Maddy has done a lot of things harder than going to her prom with Jack. She moved to a new town, went to a new school—"

"So did you."

"I didn't have my stomach stapled," Anna reminded him.

"Kids still give her shit at her high school," Ben interjected. "Amazing what assholes people can be."

"It's sweet that you feel like a big brother to her, Ben, but I think she's a strong person. Maybe she's ready for new things."

"Maybe." He didn't sound convinced.

Ben swung a right turn and pulled over to a valet stand in front of a dark wooden building. The gold-filigreed sign announced, SWINGERS.

No. It couldn't be. Anna had read somewhere that the valley was the center of the porn industry. Had Ben had brought her to a *swingers'* club? *This* was the new thing he expected her to try? How could he . . . why would he . . . ?

Anna folded her arms. "I am not going in there."

His face was the picture of innocence. "What's wrong?"

Her hand gripped the armrest even as the black uniformed valet came to open her side door. "You know exactly what's wrong, and you have the nerve to call *Jack* a dog?"

Ben shrugged, his face an odd mix of confusion and

bemusement. "Well, we can leave if you really want to. I just thought it would be fun if we had a chance to swing dance together before your prom Friday night."

Swingers. As in swing dancing.

She hauled off and punched his right bicep. "Very funny!"

Ben threw his head back, laughing so hard he was practically crying. "I wish you could see yourself right now."

"You . . . you . . . !" she sputtered.

"I'm sorry, I'm sorry." He managed to catch his breath.

She wasn't mad. Now that she knew it was just a prank, she found it quite hilarious.

"Just wait, Ben Birnbaum," she told him, with her most serene smile. "I will *definitely* get you back."

Ben stepped out of the shower and turned off the water, still laughing to himself over Anna's reaction when he'd pulled up to Swingers. There was something so self-contained and ladylike about her; it was fun to break through that façade. He knew another side of Anna, one that hardly anyone—hell, maybe no one—but him ever saw. He'd seen her in moments when she'd given herself up to passion, moments when she'd turned the tables on him and made him lose control. Afterward, she was the same proper beauty.

It was much more than that, too. There was her depth, her intellectual sophistication, her sensitivity.

Both of them found their parent of the same sex to be shallow. Both of them wanted to protect people they cared about. It was amazing, really, that on the deepest level they had so much in common. And then there was the fun of being with her. She was full of surprises, even now. As it turned out, Anna already knew how to jitterbug. She'd had dance lessons in seventh grade as part of cotillion, where old-money rich kids were sent to learn how to behave in polite society. Anna kept him entertained with stories about all the trouble she—and especially her best friend, Cyn—had gotten into there.

He reached for his white terry cloth robe on the hook behind the bathroom door. No robe. *Huh.* That was where he always put it. Whatever. He wrapped the oversized towel around his waist and padded down the hall to his bedroom. Usher was wailing from Maddy's room. Her door was open. Ben saw that she wasn't alone. She was slow dancing in there, with Jack. Their bodies were as close as two bodies could be without actually touching.

The mystery of Ben's misplaced bathrobe was solved: Maddy was wearing it.

"Hey," Ben called.

They turned to him. "Hey, man, how's it going?" Jack greeted him. "Maddy wanted to practice her dancing for prom."

Ben wasn't sure how to play this. Yes, they were dancing, but Maddy was in his bathrobe. "Uh-huh."

"See, Jack came by to talk to you, but you weren't around," Maddy explained hastily as she turned down the CD player. "Then I thought, I mean, I haven't done much dancing, you know, like when no one could get their arms around me. I wanted to practice, really. Yeah."

"Um, that's my bathrobe you're wearing."

"I'm so sorry," Maddy replied earnestly. "I was freezing after I showered and mine is in the laundry and I was sure you wouldn't mind." She reached for the sash. You want it back?"

"No, that's cool. So, you about ready to pack it in, Jack?" he added pointedly. He wanted a chance to talk to him.

"Sure." He pecked Maddy on the cheek. "I'll call you, okay?"

"Okay."

Ben walked Jack downstairs to the new foyer but stepped in front of the door before either of them could open it.

"What is up with you and her, man?"

Jack held his hands up. "Whoa, easy does it. There's nothing up."

"That didn't look like nothing."

"How about you don't get all bent out of shape over nothing?"

"Look, Maddy has the social maturity of a chick who is maybe fourteen. Don't run your game on her, Jack. I mean it."

"Is that what you think I'm doing?" His friend's eyebrows rose.

Ben shot him a jaded look. "This is me, remember? I know exactly how you are with girls."

"What, you don't think it's possible that we're just friends?"

"Seriously, man. Leave the girl alone."

"Uh-huh." He shook his head.

"What?" Ben demanded.

Jack waved a hand in the air. "Forget it. Believe what you want to believe. I'm outta here."

When he was gone, Ben stood by the door, mulling his options. He thought about stopping at Maddy's room to talk to her and set the record straight but decided it would be better if he just left things alone. Tomorrow, he'd figure out some way to explain the unfortunate facts of life to her. Or wait. Maybe it would be better coming from a girl. Maybe Anna could talk to her.

Yeah. That was a good idea.

The Prom Weenies

That Sam had never before invited Jazz or Fee, or any of their B-list friends for that matter, to her home was a given. However, she'd decided that her home was the perfect locale to begin the interviews for her documentary. She wanted her subjects to be dazzled and intimidated. They'd try too hard and look even more pathetic on screen, she figured. Yes, it would be mean, but she wanted this documentary to be a critical darling. That meant making it as snarky as possible. Critics loved snarky, audiences loved snarky, and studios loved snarky. That was why a movie like, say, *The Opposite of Sex* got the kudos and *A Walk to Remember* got dissed, even though Mandy Moore's film made a ton more money than Christina Ricci's. She did feel a little guilty about using the prom weenies in this way, but what the hell. No one ever said art was easy. Besides, acclaimed documentaries dissed their subjects all the time. Just ask Michael Moore.

Parker Pinelli had been the obvious person to help her with the project. Bearing a striking resemblance to the late, great James Dean, only taller, Parker was easily the best-looking guy at Beverly Hills High. He'd also played small film roles, most of them utterly forgettable, unless you counted an on-screen kiss he'd shared with a certain overexposed, talent-free blond heiress before she was run over by a bus. In the movie, that is.

Anyway, Parker was definitely an A-list guy. Sam was the only one who knew that, contrary to assumptions, Parker did not have A-list money. He didn't even have B-list money. In fact, he was broke. She'd learned the truth on their alternative senior trip to Vegas and pledged that she'd keep her mouth shut. Learning the truth about Parker had made Sam view him in a whole new light. Before, she'd dismissed him as just another talent-free wanna-be, albeit with money and great looks. Not hardly. He'd prove to her in Las Vegas that he had real acting ability, when he'd carried off a scam that would have made DiCaprio in *Catch Me If You Can* jealous. He was a complex, talented guy.

The Jackson Sharpe estate in Bel Air covered ten acres. Sam's father had paid seven million dollars for the property alone (his fee for doing *Blue Raider*, in which he'd played a benevolent Robin Hood–type who freed a village in Mexico from evil conquistadors, had been twenty-two mil, with action on the back end, too).

The property had once been owned by William Shatner, who had sold it post–*Star Trek* and pre-Priceline. Jackson's first act as owner had been to turn a wrecking ball on Shatner's eight-bedroom mansion and erect one twice the size, with an exterior taken directly from a Swiss château that had captured his fancy while he was filming a Swiss action thriller called *The Zurich Way*. The original château had boasted a cobblestone driveway that wended through lush stands of cedar trees, so Jackson had brought in thousands of cedar trees from Lebanon. There were hedgerows separating the château from the road; Jackson had hedgerows planted with such fast-growing shrubbery that the view of any tourist who hoped for a glimpse of "America's Most Beloved Action Hero" was hopelessly blocked.

While the front of the estate boasted massive hand-hewn granite blocks, soaring two-story windows, and a driveway that circled a fountain designed by the architect I. M. Pei, the true glory of the place could be seen from the back. The grounds were spectacular. During his "golf" phase, Jackson had installed three full par-four golf holes, each with three tee boxes, so he could play a full nine holes without leaving the premises. There were two tennis courts, one grass and one clay, plus an Olympic-size swimming pool. Recently, the pool had been drained and the bottom tiled with a giant hummingbird design in honor of the birth of Jackson's new daughter (and Sam's stepsister), Ruby Hummingbird Sharpe. There were also three guesthouses and a grove of fruit trees.

Sam prepared carefully for Fee and Jazz's arrival. They arrived in Fee's red Audi; Sam had a white-jacketed parking attendant, who doubled as Jackson's hitting partner when Jackson was in the mood for tennis, take their car in front of the estate. Then the girls were greeted by Roger, the new butler, a tall, cadaverous Englishman whose claim to fame was having worked for a certain famous British fantasy writer who'd struck platinum with a series of novels about a boy wizard. Rather than take them through the mansion, Roger had followed Sam's strict instruction to bring the girls around to the rear and then up the stone staircase to the second-floor bar, with its ultramodern steel furnishings by O'Malley and Clarkson and primo sound system. The bar was attached to the indoor pool house, which housed both a pool and an indoor waterfall; any stray whiffs of chlorine that might penetrate to the bar were eliminated by an ionic air purifier system recessed in the ceiling. The picture windows looked south over Beverly Hills.

"Hi," Sam called to the girls from the white Pampas sofa, as Roger ushered them inside. Parker, who sat next to her with his feet up on the Louis XVI antique coffee table, raised a drink in greeting. The video equipment was ready, prepointed at a pair of 1950s-era barstools about five feet away.

"Hi," Fee responded, looking extremely nervous. "Oh wow, hi, Parker, we didn't know you'd be here."

"This place is awesome," Jazz added, fidgeting nervously with the rings on her left hand.

Sam offered a cool look in response, knowing she'd succeeded in making them feel the three *I*'s: impressed, intimidated, and insecure.

"You girls look amazing," Parker told them as he idly

swirled the ice cubes around in his drink. It was the perfect thing to say. Both girls preened. In actuality, Sam could see that both had tried way too hard without any real clue as to what actually looked good on them. This was a fashion failure that Sam knew well—it was an easy pit to tumble into. Jazz wore supertight, white Earl jeans and a Chloé cotton peasant shirt that exposed an obviously faux tanned stomach the color of rust. Plus she'd doubled her usual too-much-makeup; you could have ice skated on the layers of LipFusion lip gloss she'd slathered on. Meanwhile, Fee sported an APC aqua Indian-style minishift adorned with beads and tiny mirrors that hung shapelessly on her straight-up-and-down figure and was so short that Sam desperately hoped she hadn't forgotten her sporting underwear. She'd piled on a dozen necklaces, far too much for the dress to handle.

"What can I have Roger get you to drink?" Sam asked, motioning the girls to the two bar stools. "Manhattans? Cuban rum and Coke? Or maybe a Chassagne-Montrachet '82? It's chilled to thirty-eight degrees, which should be perfect."

"Uh, champagne, I guess," Jazz chirped. "This is just *amazing*."

"Roger, two mimosas," Sam ordered, then smiled at the girls. "And a Diet Coke for me. I'm working, after all."

"Very good, Miss Sharpe," the butler intoned, and moved off to fix the drinks.

"Wow, Jazz, check out the view." Fee pointed at the vista of Los Angeles.

"You should see it at night," Sam commented. "Mind if I start the cameras?"

"No, it's fine. Right, Jazz?"

"Right!"

"Great." Sam didn't have to budge an inch. As Roger brought the girls their drinks and placed them on coasters on the table, Sam took the remote control from the same table and aimed it at the cameras. They started automatically.

"That's really cool," Jazz said, then took a sip of her drink. "This rocks."

Sam shrugged. "So, you're up to speed on our change of venue?"

Fee's eyes shone. "I was so bummed out when I read that the Bel Air Grand burned down. I started crying at the breakfast table."

"Me too," Jazz chimed in. "She called me right away. We thought we were ruined!"

"I still can't believe you got the Colosseum set from *Ben-Hur.*" Fee shook her head in disbelief.

"Yeah," Sam said modestly, "but it adds a whole level of complication. Have you talked to the caterer? They're going to have to bring in their own kitchen. Bus companies? There are going to be kids who'll want to head over there in a charter. You'll want to do an after party someplace else, too. Chateau Marmont, Breakers on the Beach would be good. *Not* the Century Plaza. Drop my name, it'll help. So?"

For the next ten minutes, Fee and Jazz—they were almost like one person, the way they finished each other's sentences—gave Sam the rundown on the adjustments they'd already made due to the new location of prom. Though Sam didn't let on, she was impressed with the girls' efficiency. What she didn't understand as well was who these two girls really were. She knew her film would suck hard unless she got inside their heads.

"So, Jazz, Fee," Sam began, looking to refocus their discussion. "All of that is great. Have you been looking forward to prom, like, forever?"

"For sure," Jazz said. "I started cutting out photos of prom dresses when I was in middle school, to tell you the truth. I keep them in a little folder."

"She cuts out wedding gowns she likes, too," Fee added helpfully.

Jazz twirled a lock of hair nervously around one finger. "I just like to be prepared for things, you know? My mom grew up on a commune. She never went to prom, and she eloped with my dad wearing torn jeans. I want something different."

Huh. That actually *was* interesting. Sam had a weakness for anything involving moms, since her own had taken a permanent leave of absence a long time ago. She and Jackson had divorced when Sam was nine.

"How did your mom feel about it?" Sam wondered.

Jazz twirled her hair again. "She kind of has mixed feelings. Like, on the one hand she still has disdain for, like, material possessions. But she loves me and she really wants me to be happy."

Sam got an unexpected lump in her throat. It must be great to have a mother like that. Or maybe she was just romanticizing it. Like so much of Beverly Hills, it was an airbrushed version of reality.

Sam nudged a shoulder toward Parker; the motion was their prearranged signal for him to join the girls on camera. He moved to Jazz, lifted her hand, and kissed it. "That's beautiful, Jazz. Really." He looked at her soulfully. "Your boyfriend must be psyched. A girl who is that romantic, that passionate . . ."

Sam knew how mesmerizing Parker could be up close and personal. Jazz stared at him, speechless, her hand still in his. "Who's the lucky guy?"

"Um . . . Jeremy Knowles. He's more like a friend, kind of. He's secretary of the student council."

Parker was clueless—Sam was certain he didn't know who was on student council, had never known who was on the student council, and couldn't have cared less who was on the student council—but he nodded solemnly, playing his role to the hilt. "I'm not sure he's good enough for you, Jazz."

"Who are you going with?"

"I had a relationship, but . . ." Parker swallowed hard, looking away as if he were about to cry.

"You can tell us," Fee urged, leaning unconsciously toward Parker.

Parker feigned reluctance to continue. "This actress . . . I know . . . I thought she really . . . cared about me. But then I saw her at Au Bar, macking with—look, I'm not a namedropper. But a certain guy on a really bad TV series."

Fee grabbed Parker's arm. "Jesse McCartney? Chad Michael—"

"It was probably someone else," he interrupted. "Anyway, I really thought this girl and I had something special, but now—"

"She broke your heart?" Jazz asked.

Sam was pretty sure there were actual tears in her eyes. Her first reaction was: *This is great.* Her second reaction was: *I am being a complete manipulative bitch.* She kept the camera rolling just the same.

Jazz still had her hand on Parker's arm. "I'm *so* sorry she hurt you, Parker."

He nodded sorrowfully. "If only you didn't already have a date . . ."

Fee gasped. "Oh my God. Are you asking Jazz to *prom*? She's going with someone!"

"Parker!" Sam cried, pretending to be annoyed.

Parker held his hands up. "That was totally out of line. I'm sorry. I need to get some air. I'll be back."

Parker left the pool house—the footage of Jazz and Parker would be priceless—and Sam continued to get the girls to open up. She was amazed at how they were willing to spill the most intimate details of their lives just because a camera was whirring.

At that moment, Sam got another brilliant idea: What better way to get the truth about the prom weenies than to have them film each other? It would double the number of people she'd have shooting, thus doubling the amount of footage she would have at her disposal. Prom prep, hair, makeup, meetings with caterers, the band . . . the possibilities would be endless. They could film their friends, too.

When she made the suggestion, Jazz and Fee were so excited, they literally ran to Sam and hugged her. They talked over each other to express their delight at not only being in the film but helping to create it.

"You'll get your names in the credits, too," Sam promised.

After that, they couldn't throw personal information at Sam fast enough. Their loves, their heartaches, their hopes and dreams. Intimate family secrets. It was fascinating, in a twisted, voyeuristic sort of way.

"My parents fight pretty much all the time," Fee confessed. "My mom always thinks my dad is flirting with the actresses he coaches and—"

Sam's cell phone rang, interrupting Fee's flow. Sam checked the number.

"Gotta take this. It's my dad. He calls me from the set all the time." This was a big fat lie, of course—a phone call from her dad was a rare thing—but it would help her dazzle the prom weenies. She put the phone to her ear.

"Hello?"

"Hey, sweetie." His warm voice boomed through the earpiece.

"Hey. How's the shoot going?"

"Really great," Jackson exulted. "I swear, we're gonna make people forget about Heston. There's been a little glitch, though. I know I told you that you and your friends could do prom here Friday night. But we're behind schedule, gotta shoot that night. I cleared you for Saturday, though."

Sam gripped the phone hard. This was awful news. Everything was arranged for Friday night, and she'd pulled every string she could to arrange it. What about the limo rentals and the caterers and the hotel suites? But showing Jazz and Fee any sign of panic would be the worst thing she could do.

"Perfect, Dad."

"Great, sweetie. Okay, gotta get to makeup. 'Bye."

Sam hung up and sparkled in the direction of her company. "I've got the best possible news. We have to postpone prom by twenty-four hours."

This was the kind of crisis that brought out the best in Sam. For any other high school senior, changing the night of prom with four days to go would have been a reason to join Dee at the Ojai Psychiatric Institute and not come out until Thanksgiving. Making the change would require the precision and detail necessary to undertake a hostage rescue mission in a dangerous rogue nation. Fortunately, Brigadier General Samantha Sharpe had the finances and the firepower to carry out the mission. She issued orders to the prom weenies, who issued orders to the sub–prom weenies:

Do it. Whatever it takes.

A detailed e-mail went to every ticket buyer. Photographers, florists, videographers, caterers, limo drivers, parking attendants, cleaning crews, hotels, and security were informed and offered whatever was necessary to change their services to Saturday night. If they were already booked for Saturday night—say, for the Reseda High School prom in the lovely Reseda High School gym—they were encouraged to subcontract that job and come to the Colosseum. Sam reminded them all that they did not want to get on the wrong side of someone as powerful as Jackson Sharpe.

There were only two things that didn't work. One was the after party; there just wasn't a cool-enough locale available. People would have to fend for themselves, except for Sam and her friends—Cammie had offered the stretch of Hermosa Beach where her father's television drama was shot.

The other problem was Eduardo. She called him as soon as she got the prom weenies out the door. Sadly, he said, there wasn't much he could do. It wasn't like his family could change the date of the anniversary party for his parents. He'd still come to Los Angeles on Thursday to spend a couple days with Sam, but he would have to leave on Saturday morning as scheduled. He was so apologetic that Sam actually felt bad for him.

When the depressing transatlantic phone call was done, she headed out to the redwood back deck to finish off the bottle of Cristal that had gone toward the major portion of Fee and Jazz's mimosas. She was surprised to find Parker there, taking in the view.

"You're still here?"

"I thought you might need a friend after that phone call."

She and Parker had talked briefly before she'd called Eduardo; there was no need to fill him in.

"What the hell," she sighed, raising the champagne bottle to her lips. "I knew it was going too well."

"He's still coming, but can't come to prom?"

Sam nodded.

"That isn't enough?"

Sam offered him the half-empty champagne bottle. He took it. "No. It's not. I want everything. And so do you." She sighed as he chugged the Cristal. "You kicked ass with the prom weenies."

"Thanks." He wiped his lips.

She regarding him carefully. "I used to think you were a sucky actor."

His lips tugged into a half-smile. "Oh, really?"

"The truth is, you're *so* good that you fooled everyone into thinking you're someone you aren't. Hard to do."

He passed the Cristal back to her. "You know, if Eduardo can't take you, you should go with me."

Go to prom with Parker? It was indecent, really, how handsome he was; those eyes, those lips . . . Sam had read somewhere that humans had a nearly impossible time separating good looks from internal goodness. Looking into Parker's eyes, she could easily understand why that was true. She had to lean back to get her bearings.

"Are you playing me, Pinelli?"

"You're about the only one I'm *not* playing, Sharpe. Come on. You just lost your date, and I don't have a date."

Sam thought for a moment. She'd heard worse ideas. She'd have to be there for her documentary anyway, and Parker was helping her. It sort of made perfect sense. Plus, she didn't mind being seen with a guy as hot as Parker. Let the prom weenies wonder.

"We go as friends. Right?" she offered cautiously.

Parker casually looped an arm around her shoulder. "Absolutely. You in?"

Sam nodded. "I'm in. Come on, we've got work to do."

Hipsters and Wanna-bes

By the time Ben came home from his shift at Trieste, his head was pounding. The work wasn't hard, but he'd had the relentless beat of techno dance music in his ear for the past eight hours. They'd put him on the door, which struck Ben as ironic, since he wasn't even old enough to get in without a fake ID himself. Ben was supposed to be a management trainee, and the manager had decided that giving Ben a taste of the many different jobs at the club was the best way for Ben to learn.

Trieste was the club of the moment. By ten o'clock there'd been a line of hipsters and wanna-bes all the way down Hollywood Boulevard, hoping for the nod from Ben that would admit them to the inner sanctum. Anyone who was anyone didn't have to wait, of course. Part of the job description was to know the difference.

This wasn't always easy. Film directors notoriously looked like shit. Even some movie and TV stars looked like shit without professional makeup. Fortunately the doorman with him, Lenny Lucci, nearly seven feet of bald Italian steel who'd been working the doors of the top Hollywood clubs for two decades, knew everyone. Lenny bounced full time and did movie stunts part-time. If Ben had a question about whether or not to admit someone, he'd subtly catch Lenny's eye. Lenny would barely nod or shake his head, and Ben would proceed accordingly. Like God, Lenny never made mistakes.

Otherwise, admittance was completely at Ben's discretion, though Lenny had laid out God's rules with great clarity. Always admit hot single women. Sometimes admit hot single guys. Couples were boring, so only let in fifty percent. Ben had to admit that the power to make or break the evenings of the cute girls— long hair, short skirts, tight tops—was a heady experience before it got a little bit disturbing, reminding him too much of Beverly Hills High's social pecking order. Take Maddy, for example. If he hadn't known her and she was in line, she wouldn't have been able to get in. The long frizzy hair, pale innocent face, zero style sense. Even after her weight loss, she'd be left on the outside looking in. He was so over that shit.

He let himself in the front door. Thinking about Maddy made him think about Jack—and his good mood was instantly ruined. Jack was running a game on Maddy, he was sure of it. If Jack hurt her, Ben would feel responsible. He hadn't even had a chance to speak to Anna today about talking to her.

When Ben padded up the stairs and down the hall to his room, he saw that Maddy's door was wide open and the lights were on. He stuck his head in to say a brief hello, but she wasn't there. There was definitely something on her computer screen, though: an image of Maddy lolling in bed, obviously naked save for a strategically deployed bathrobe. Ben's robe.

Jack had taken the photo; he felt sure of it.

"Hi."

Ben whirled to find Maddy smiling at him in the hallway. For once, she wasn't wearing his clothes, just an oversize blue-and-gold University of Michigan sweat suit.

"You're mad at me," she surmised. "Because of the pictures."

"Nah. I am teed off at Jack, though. He's being a real dick—pardon my language."

"No, he isn't!" Maddy insisted, wide-eyed. "He's really sweet to me."

Because he wants something. How can I get this across to her so she'll believe me?

Buying time, he suggested they go downstairs, get a drink, and hang out on the back deck. Five minutes later they were sitting outside on two handmade oak rockers that Ben's parents had had shipped back from a medical conference in Nashville. It was so quiet, they could hear crickets chirping.

"It's so nice here," Maddy murmured. She took a sip of her Diet Coke. "I wish I could live here forever."

Geez. He took a swig of his Corona. "Mad, I don't want to hurt your feelings. But . . . things between you and Jack might not be what you think they are."

"He's *your* friend," Maddy said earnestly. "That's why I know I can trust him."

Ben swiped a weary hand across his face. Geez, this sucked. What a cliché. The innocent girl from the Midwest getting taken advantage of in Hollywood by the older calculating guy. The only twist here was that Maddy wasn't an aspiring actress.

"Tell me the truth, Mad. How many photos did Jack take of you?"

"A few," she muttered self-consciously, staring at the redwood floor of the deck.

Maybe there was still time to stop this runaway train.

"I know you already invited him to your prom Saturday night, Mad. I don't think it's a very good idea."

"*What*? Then I wouldn't have a date!"

"That might be a better idea than going with Jack," Ben opined, a bit stiffly. "You could . . . go with some girlfriends, maybe."

"That's what I used to do when I weighed three hundred pounds. And it sucked, okay? It really, really sucked. I pretended that it was fine, you know? Like I really wanted to just hang out with my friends, but inside I was dying. I used to dream of being with a cute guy. Now the dream can come true."

If Jack took Maddy to the prom, who the hell knew what would happen afterward? Maddy would be so caught up in her dream come true that she'd probably do . . . pretty much anything.

Hold it.

Maybe there was something he could do. Anna's prom was Friday night; Maddy's was Saturday night. It could work. Anna was the most understanding girl in the world. She'd appreciate what he was doing for poor Maddy.

Why not?

"Hey, Mad? What if I got you a different date? Say . . . me?" Ben asked.

"You?" Maddy's eyes shone in the moonlight. "You'd take me to prom?"

"Sure. As friends, but . . . yeah."

"That would be . . . fantastic." Then she frowned. "Won't Jack be mad?"

"Let me worry about Jack," Ben assured her. He put down his beer. "So, this'll be a feat. Two proms in one weekend. Anna's one night, yours the next. I'd better keep my tux clean."

Maddy impulsively jumped up from her rocker and threw her arms around Ben, kissing him on the left cheek. "I can't believe how lucky I am to have you," she told him.

"It's no problem," Ben told her, extricating himself from her grasp and standing up. She stood too, her eyes luminous in the moonlight. "Let's call it a night, huh?" They started into the house together. "Hey, Mad, one last thing."

"What?"

"Whatever you thought you were doing with those pictures . . . you might want to delete them from your computer."

Maddy bit her lower lip. "You think it's a bad idea?"

"Don't you?"

She shrugged as they walked through the breezeway.

"Yeah, I think it's a bad idea," Ben told her again. "You'll sleep better. So will I."

The Big L

S am leaned into Eduardo and he kissed her temple. It was bliss to be with him again. He had indeed flown in from France on his father's jet, a new Cessna Citation ISP, a model her father had considered before opting for his Gulfstream several months back.

All afternoon she'd been so nervous, waiting for him to arrive. Visions of naked European sex kittens danced in her head, and they were all dancing for Eduardo. She had to find the absolutely perfect thing to wear so that he'd be happy to be with her, instead of with one of those girls named Françoise.

She'd tried on at least a dozen outfits, but each one had seemed wrong; she'd ended up leaving them on the floor of her huge walk-in closet. Finally, she'd settled on a filmy black-and-fuchsia Roland Mouret baby-doll top—the floaty black material fell in graceful folds from just under her bust to just below her loathed hips—and dark, boot-cut Valentino jeans.

As she was dressing, a housekeeper had brought two dozen long-stemmed red roses in an etched-glass

Tiffany vase to Sam's suite. The little card read, *Until you're in my arms. —Eduardo.*

Take that, you naked European sex kittens! Sam was infused with a mix of relief and joy—a feeling that lasted but a nanosecond. After which she felt just as nervous and insecure as she had before.

Eduardo had checked into his bungalow at the Beverly Hills Hotel before coming to the Sharpe estate to pick her up in his rented platinum Porsche 911 Carrera. He'd dressed comfortably in Randolph Duke black pants and a black T-shirt. It was a relief to know that Eduardo would be neither intimidated nor impressed by where she lived. His family was one of the richest in all of South America. He professed not to care that she was Jackson Sharpe's daughter. Sam believed him.

Then the doorbell had sounded, and a moment later she'd been in his arms, wondering how she could have been so jittery and crazy about being reunited with him. His general male gorgeousness nearly took her breath away all over again. Five foot nine or ten, with smooth copper skin stretched over powerful muscles. His hair was dark, his eyes even darker. He was easily as handsome as any famous actor in Hollywood. Yet, for some reason that was unfathomable to Sam, he wanted *her.*

Now they were sitting side by side on a Persian rug at the Mor Bar in Santa Monica; they'd been at the club for almost two hours. To her surprise, he'd made reservations before they arrived—his father, a highly respected Peruvian politician from a regal Spanish bloodline, had suggested the place because it was so romantic. She didn't want to come right out and ask, in case she'd jumped to the wrong conclusion, but it seemed to mean that Eduardo had talked about her with his dad.

The air in the dimly lit club was redolent of exotic North African spices. All the patrons doffed their shoes and sat on rugs or lolled against scarlet velvet pillows under a beet-red canopy. Giant hookah water pipes rested on each low-slung marble table. Sam and Eduardo had passed on the hookah, but they had enjoyed a Moorish feast—stuffed grape leaves, couscous, thyme-scented hot pita bread, and fresh hummus, babaganoush, and a lamb stew. It was all meant to be eaten with the fingers, washed down with the Moroccan wine Eduardo had expertly ordered, a Les Coteaux de l'Atlas Rouge Premier Cru 1999—deep ruby red with vanilla undertones.

Sam had eaten half of the grape leaves—they were delicious—and stopped there, until Eduardo fed her some lamb stew and couscous. As she snuggled close to her boyfriend and ate from his fingers, she could just make out the couple at the next table. Their lips were locked and he was half on top of her. Her skirt was up around her waist, revealing a minuscule lace thong; his hand was cupping her butt. No one in the club blinked an eye.

Eduardo followed Sam's gaze. "Too public," he commented in his lightly accented voice, and popped the pita into Sam's mouth. "That is childish. Not my style."

She chewed and swallowed. "Not mine, either."

Only the cellulite-free can afford to be exhibitionists.

Eduardo put a large, warm hand to Sam's cheek. "Did I tell you how beautiful you look tonight?"

"Must be the dim lights," Sam joked.

His eyes searched hers. "Samantha. Why is it that you cannot accept your own beauty?"

This type of conversation always made her wildly uncomfortable, and she never knew what to say. The truth? It didn't seem to be in her own interest to point out that he was the only guy who had ever found her so beautiful. If she *did* point it out, maybe he would suddenly realize that all those other guys had been right after all.

A trio of musicians on a small, raised stage began to play something bluesy in a minor key. Eduardo rose gracefully and held a hand out to Sam. "Dance?"

He eased her to her feet and held the small of her back as he led her to a small parquet dance floor near the musicians, where they joined two other couples. How easily she slipped into his arms; how perfectly they fit. For a minute or two, she swayed to the music, pressed against his chest, eyes closed.

"When I dance with you like this, it makes me sad that I will not be able to have you in my arms at your prom," he murmured.

Prom. Damn.

"You can't change your plans?"

He frowned. "My parents' anniversary party."

She smiled sadly. "I understand."

"In my family, blood is everything. Would you miss your parents' anniversary party?"

Sam was sure he meant this rhetorically, which was why she didn't answer. The bitter irony of it wasn't lost on her. She'd missed Poppy's baby shower and would have been delighted if she heard tomorrow that her dad and his new bride were divorcing.

"Maybe I should skip prom and go to Mexico with you," Sam suggested. As soon as it was out of her mouth she wished she could take it back. It sounded like she was inviting herself to meet his family, and that hadn't been her intention at all.

"To miss your prom . . . I could never ask you to do that," Eduardo insisted.

Whew. Evidently her gaffe had blown right past him. Anyway, even if she didn't give a shit about prom, she *did* care about making her prom movie. Her directing talent was what made her different, unique, special—or at least it would one day, and the sooner the better. Sam found few things more pathetic than children of stars whose only claim to fame was riding the coattails of a rich and famous parent.

"You will go to prom with your friend Anna?"

"Anna has a date," Sam explained, feeling increasingly sorry for herself. The music ended and Eduardo held Sam at arm's length so that he could look into her eyes.

"But this is terrible. I see you are sad. What can I do to help?"

He looked so stricken that Sam wanted to reassure him. "I'll be fine," she insisted. "Really."

"You will go, yes?" he prodded.

"Yes."

"With your other friends, perhaps?" Eduardo prompted. "I can't stand to think of you alone."

She felt torn. Part of her wanted to tell him about Parker. She doubted Eduardo would be mad or jealous, because there was nothing to be mad or jealous about. But she couldn't bring herself to say the words, maybe because she knew how her own mind raced with jealous fantasies whenever she wasn't within a hundred feet of Eduardo. Was it possible that he was the same way?

"I'll have lots of friends there," Sam assured him. "Don't worry about it."

They headed back to their table and ate some more, mostly with Eduardo feeding her. That she was with a boy who *wanted* her to eat never failed to amaze her. He held some wine to her lips to wash down a bite of grape leaves and followed the wine with a kiss. Then he dipped his finger in the wine and ran it over her collarbone and into the décolletage of her baby-doll top. She closed her eyes and gave herself up to the bliss.

"I have a surprise for you, Samantha," he whispered.

"What?" she asked, eyes still closed.

"I will be returning to L.A. in a month. For the rest of the summer."

She opened her eyes. "Really?"

He nodded. "I will be an intern at the Peruvian Consulate here until the end of August. My father was able to arrange it."

"That's . . . fantastic!"

He laughed and pulled her into his arms. "I was hoping for that reaction. Long-distance love is difficult."

Love? He had just used the *L* word. If it were the Big L, with him here all summer, they would both have the chance to find out. All summer? It would be just like Anna and Ben.

"You are so beautiful, Samantha. I want to make love to you," he whispered.

Whoa. Talk about saying exactly the right thing at exactly the right moment.

She glanced downward at his Randolph Dukes and couldn't help it. As he kissed her again, she wondered what was underneath.

"Is that what you want, too?" he asked huskily.

One part of Sam was ready to head back to his hotel. Another part . . . the truth was, she felt shy. It was ridiculous. She'd had sex before; usually while drunk and/or high, always with all the lights off. She'd never *made love.* That seemed so much more intimate, and scary.

"I don't know," she admitted.

His strong arms encircled her again. "We do not need to rush. You will let me know when you are ready, Samantha. A month from now, I will take you dancing and we will have our own private prom."

She felt like looking around for the girl who had inspired these feelings in Eduardo, because it was so hard to believe it was her. She knew she should bring up Parker and prom right now, but it felt so out of sync with the moment. It would come across like some over-the-top moment from *Days of Our Lives.*

Besides, they'd have the whole summer to talk about it. About everything.

MAC Matte Red

Anna gave her car to the valet and eyed the endless line that snaked down Hollywood Boulevard on the wrong side of Trieste's red-velvet rope. Just like at New York's trendiest clubs, there was nothing about the building but the line out front to indicate that this was Hollywood's club of the moment. The outside of Trieste looked like an industrial warehouse. There wasn't even a sign, just some worn numerals above the door.

She knew she could walk right in; Ben had assured her that her name would be on the guest list. She was glad she didn't have to wait, glad she didn't have to endure the humiliating process of having someone look her over to decide whether or not she was cute enough or rich enough or famous enough to be allowed inside, but the whole thing made her uncomfortable, too.

She'd been to pretty much every club in New York by the time she was fifteen; in fact, a professional-quality fake ID had been her best friend Cyn's birthday present to her that year. Her sister, Susan, was a party girl, and Anna had gone clubbing with her any number of times.

Somehow she usually ended up feeling apart from everyone else, almost as if she were outside a movie scene she was observing. Maybe it was because she was always keeping an eye on Susan. If she didn't do it, who would?

Relax. Your sister is at the Kripalu Center in Massachusetts and totally sober. Your boyfriend works here. You're fine.

"I'm a friend of Ben Birnbaum," she told the door guy, a short, skinny guy in his early twenties with a rat-like face and dirty blond hair gelled to a point atop his head. He was dressed all in black—black T-shirt, black jeans, black jacket, black wingtips sans socks. A huge bald man stood next to him.

"Now you're a friend of mine," the skinny guy told her with a deviant grin, his large front teeth bucking over his lower lip. He motioned her forward.

"Hey, you didn't even check to see that she's on the guest list!" a girl in line yelled, pointing a savage index finger at Anna. She had a pumpkin-shaped head and wore her dark hair in some variation of a mullet. Her short, thick legs were encased like sausages in skintight jeans; her enormous breasts spilled out of a cheap red-sequined T-shirt.

"Take a look at her," the doorman commanded. "She's on the list even if she isn't on the list. And you, Great Pumpkin? You might as well go down the block to Bar-Bar. There's no line there, if you catch my drift."

Anna wanted to kick the obnoxious rat-faced man in his black-clad shins. But she settled for a whispered

"You are an ass" in his ear as she slipped into the club, and felt better for having done it.

A bored-looking girl with sexy, cropped black hair and sequined, black-rimmed, cat-shaped eyeglasses stamped the back of Anna's hand with a Day-Glo green stamp, then directed Anna toward the juice bar. To put herself in the spirit of things, she'd deliberately chosen the kind of sexy outfit that the old Anna never would have worn. She'd donned a white Hermès silk crepe chiffon blouse with a loose-gathered neckline that allowed the blouse to fall off one shoulder or the other, and a fitted gold-and-white Philosophy by Alberta Ferretti cotton bias-cut skirt that ended a good two inches above her knees. She'd piled on a few beaded necklaces her father had brought back for her from a business trip to India (this would be the first time she'd ever worn them), and had finished off the outfit with aqua Balenciaga sandals that tied at the ankle with ribbons. She'd parted her hair on the side so that it fell over one eye and, on a whim, had dug out her MAC matte red lipstick and rubbed some onto her lips. When she'd assessed herself in the mirror, she'd felt satisfied that a new Anna was looking back. Ben had e-mailed her that morning to say that after a quick stint at the door, he'd be working the juice bar at the club for the rest of the night; why didn't she stop by for a while to keep him company? Though she'd e-mailed back that she really wasn't a club person, she'd decided sometime in the afternoon that her attitude was both ridiculous and knee-jerk, based on the Anna she used to be. She *would* go to his club; she'd surprise him.

She headed into the cool, dimly lit nightclub. It turned out to be an interlocked series of themed spaces. The first was about the size of two basketball courts and decorated to look like a massive hospital emergency room. Bottles of alcohol were suspended in medical supply bags over the longest bar Anna had ever seen. The sexy waitresses wore open white doctor's coats over bikinis with stethoscopes around their necks and served drinks to customers in beakers instead of cocktail glasses. Extra wide gurneys dotted various conversation areas instead of couches; some held couples in serious mack mode. Under the techno-pop music, Anna detected an echoing heartbeat throb.

She didn't spot anything resembling a juice bar, so she asked a passing white-coated doctor-cum-waitress who looked as if she were channeling Jennifer Aniston in her Rachel-haircut days.

"Juice bar?" Anna mouthed, over the pounding music.

The waitress pointed toward the far wall, where Anna saw an opening that led to another room. She mouthed, "Thank you," and started to wend her way through the packed bodies, managing to avoid stepping on any open-toed female shoes or having any beers spilled on her blouse. Guys were checking her out much more than usual—it had to be the sexier look. When a drunk club-goer with a frat guy's broad face leered at her and licked his lips, for a brief moment she felt humiliated and wished she were in her usual, more conservative clothes. Then she realized *he* was the asshole and mentally gave him the finger.

The next room, which turned out to be the main dance room, had been decorated to look like a cave, with stalactites dangling from the ceiling and stalagmites emerging from the floor amid the dancers. Giant backlit images of 3-D bats were painted on the walls. The floor was some special kind of glass, lit from below; its color changed from bloodred to sea green to snow white and back again. Not that any of the hundreds of people in the cave were paying any attention, as just about everyone was dancing. Anna had to creep along the walls to make her way through.

At the far end, she pushed through two swinging doors and found a short, wide passage filled with fresh air—a delightful change after the sweaty musk of the cavernous dance hall. This passage opened into the night, where Anna was surprised to find a large outdoor patio circa mid-twentieth-century suburbia. Life-size cardboard figures of President Eisenhower, President Kennedy, and other world leaders dotted the conversation areas as if they were invited guests. Strands of tiny white lights were strung through the branches of a dozen leafy trees. Plastic lawn furniture was arranged around individual barbecues, where chefs in old-fashioned aprons grilled burgers and hot dogs. In the center of everything was a plastic-sided aboveground backyard swimming pool common to that era, with a dozen people splashing around in it (mostly in their underwear). A voluptuous redhead was swimming in a sheer white mesh bra that had clearly been worn to be seen in that pool. At the far end of the patio was a small stage with band equipment. The band, sporting early Beatles haircuts and Nehru jackets, was sitting at a picnic table on a break.

Anna spotted Ben at the juice bar, where he was dumping a cupful of strawberries into a blender while two Hollywood writer types—both guys in their forties, both in baseball caps—waited for him to fix their drinks. When Ben saw her, his face lit up. He held up five fingers, meaning, she figured, that was when he'd get free.

She sat in a lawn chair and watched him work, as two cute girls sidled up to the juice bar. Anna tried not to think of how many times a night girls had to be hitting on Ben. A lot. Ten smoothies later, someone from the kitchen mercifully relieved him, so he was able to ease over to Anna.

"Mango-Papaya Ben Special," he pronounced as he sat down and handed her a tall, frosted glass filled with something thick and orange. "Try it. Ten bucks a pop to the general public."

She took a sip. It was fantastic. "No alcohol?"

He shook his head. "You're in the no-booze room. We get all the AA types." He took the drink from her and tasted it, then handed it back. "Damn, I'm good."

"Hey, I'll be the judge of that," she teased.

His eyes flicked over her. "You look fantastic." He reached out and touched the chunk of blond hair that flopped over Anna's face. "You should wear your hair like that for prom."

She smiled. "Saturday night. I'll try to remember."

"What are you talking about, Saturday night?"

"Sam sent an e-mail to everyone," Anna explained. "Sam's dad is shooting on Friday night, so they moved prom to Saturday. It was a last-minute thing. I was so sure you had to be on her e-mail list."

Ben rubbed his forehead wearily. "Shit."

She couldn't understand his reaction. What difference did it make, really? He'd told her that Saturday night would be his night off until the middle of June, but that he could get her prom night off, too.

"What's wrong?"

"Saturday night is Maddy's prom."

"Jack is taking her."

"He was."

"*Was*?" Anna echoed, alarmed.

Ben exhaled loudly. "I found some photos that Jack took of her, wearing . . . not much. She thinks it's some big romance, but the guy just wants to get laid."

"So *you're* going instead?"

He looked sheepish. "I didn't think it would be a problem, I was just trying to help the girl out."

It was a long moment before she could absorb what he was telling her. "You're playing knight in shining armor to Maddy's damsel in distress."

He shook his head. "Damn, I can't believe your prom got changed. The odds of that are nonexistent."

"Evidently not."

He cocked his head at her. "Wait, are you *mad*?"

Mad? Yes, she was mad. Was she overreacting? Well, too bad. She felt how she felt, and for once she was going to be up front about it. She opened her mouth to tell him off, but he spoke first.

"You don't really think I'm going to take her to her prom instead of taking you to yours, do you? I'll just explain to her what happened. She'll understand that you're my priority. Anyway, she idolizes you."

Anna shut her mouth, extremely glad that no words had actually come out, because she would have sounded like a small-minded shrew. *Of course* she was Ben's priority. *Of course* he'd still be taking her to prom. Embarrassed at her own reaction, she shifted mental gears. Maddy would be really disappointed if Ben couldn't go to prom with her now. She couldn't very well reinvite Jack after blowing him off.

Ben was right; Maddy was just a clueless kid who needed a little help. Well, Anna was willing to help her out, too.

"I've got an idea. What if you take Maddy to her prom early, for a little while, and then pick me up later on?"

The admiration on his face made her feel wonderful.

"Really? You'd do that?"

"Sure."

"You are the best, Anna." He gathered her into his arms and gave her a soft kiss. "How did I get so lucky?"

She kissed him back and then rested her head on his shoulder. Love could make a girl act in strange and

bizarre ways. So what if it was Ben-to-the-rescue with
Maddy? He did that because he was such a caring guy.
She loved that about him. A niggling voice asked her
why he felt the need to do it quite so often. She told the
voice to shut up, and kissed her boyfriend again.

For the next hour or so, Ben mechanically made
ten-dollar smoothies for an ever-growing number of
partyers at the juice bar. Anna hung out for another
thirty minutes and then went home. That wasn't necessarily a bad thing, because the young actress who played
the daughter on that WB show with the rapid-fire
dialogue about the hip mom innkeeper and her school-
bright/street-dumb daughter kept hanging around the
bar, flirting with Ben. He didn't mind. Flirting wasn't
cheating, and cheating was something he had zero interest in. The only other time he'd felt that way had been
in the very early days with Cammie, and that was only
because she was hotter than any other girl on the planet
except for maybe Anna. He'd quickly learned that a
little Cammie went a long way; he was glad that episode
of his life was way behind him.

He had three blenders going at all times, and still the
line of thirsty people didn't seem to dwindle. The only
consolation was a growing pile of cash in the tip jar—
actually, a goldfish bowl with a swimming goldfish at the
bottom separated from the money by a layer of
Plexiglas. Not that he needed the money, but it was nice
to be rewarded for a job well done. He'd taken the job

at Trieste to get some real-life experience in the club business and hoped that this summer gig might lead to a management position. If he had to make smoothies, though, as part of his training, he was more than game.

Ben expertly snapped off one of the blenders and poured a banana-coconut smoothie for the former star of a seventies TV show that, in the past few years, had been made into two movies with a new trio of babes. The former star still had the same famous, flowing blond hairdo, but her way-too-much-plastic-surgery face was a little scary. He almost recommended to her that she have a consultation with his father.

"Hey."

Ben looked up from the sliced white Jersey peaches he was dropping into another blender.

Jack was staring at him. He was alone, casually clad in jeans and a Princeton T-shirt.

"What's up?" Ben asked tersely.

"We need to talk."

Ben shrugged, then added pitted Okanagan cherries to the peaches. "I'm working, man."

Jack ignored that comment. "What is this about you taking Maddy to prom?"

"Suddenly you care about a high school prom?" Ben turned on the blender.

"Suddenly I'd say it's none of your business. What are you trying to do, run the world?"

"I'm *making* it my business." Ben snapped the blender on, then leaned close to Jack so that he could be heard over the whirring of the Blendec. "Admit it, dude. You just want to get laid and we both know it. Go play some other girl who's in your league."

Jack shook his head. "You don't know what the hell you're talking about."

"Sell that to someone who's buying." Ben turned off the blender, poured one reddish thick shake into a tall fifties Coca-Cola glass, dropped in the extralong licorice straw, and handed it to the bearded guy with thick curly dark hair—Jerry Garcia, risen from the dead, so to speak—who'd been waiting patiently.

"Screw you," Jack shot back at him. "For a smart guy, you don't know shit."

"Right back atcha, man." Ben turned to the next customer. When he looked again, Jack was gone.

Ben figured that Jack's problem was, he couldn't *not* seduce a girl, especially one who seemed so ripe for the picking. It had never disgusted Ben before, mostly because it had seemed like a joke. Now, it thoroughly did. Big-time.

TMI

Anna's father had hired a new cook, a regal-looking Ethiopian woman named Mimi who had come to the United States two decades ago and had proven herself at restaurants ranging from her own small place in Washington, D.C., to the Buffalo Club here in Los Angeles. Mimi was now the mother of toddler twins and had retired from the restaurant business, but Jonathan Percy had induced her to come to his Beverly Hills mansion for a few hours a day to prepare lunch (if he was home) and dinner, since he'd recently taken a liking to Ethiopian food. Mimi had accepted the offer, on the condition that she be allowed to remodel the kitchen to fit her needs.

Anna had endured a boring morning at school; it just seemed so pointless this late in the academic year, when she knew she'd be at Yale in the fall. Wanting a break, she invited Sam to come home with her for lunch. Mimi was a fantastic chef; they'd have a great meal. Sam had volunteered to bring over some rough footage of Fee and Jazz for her film so that Anna could see it, but Anna had demurred. Sam's movie was Sam's thing. She'd mentioned something about how she was revising the concept of her film, but Anna hadn't paid a great deal of attention. She wasn't comfortable with the whole prom-weenie thing, so she figured the less she had to do with it, the better.

The two of them stepped into the new kitchen—it now featured a restaurant-quality metal double oven, a Catamount brick oven for pizza, an eight-burner stove on an island, and a handmade solid maple table topped by white marble and surrounded by eight handcrafted Italian mahogany chairs. The cabinetry was similarly maple, and three additional south-facing windows had been cut into the wall, maximizing the amount of natural light in the room.

A multicultural feast awaited them on the table. Big plates of the famous Ethiopian flatbread called *injera* in the Ethiopian language of Amharic, smaller plates of steamed vegetables, plus an entire planked salmon seasoned with cilantro from Mimi's home spice garden.

"Yum." Sam pulled up a seat at the table. "Where's the master chef so I can thank her?"

"I think she goes home for a while, then comes back." Anna cut a segment of the salmon and put it on her floral-print Wedgwood plate, then broke off a piece of *injera* and used the bread to scoop up some of the fish.

Sam tore off some *injera* and popped it into her mouth. "Tastes kind of like sourdough bread." She chewed and washed it down with the iced spice tea Mimi had thoughtfully left for them. "So, you ready to see my killer documentary footage after this? I brought it anyway."

"Not really, if that's okay with you," Anna replied honestly. "You know how I feel about it."

Sam shrugged. "Whatever. Your loss. Oh, I got one of my dad's drivers to take us tomorrow night in the stretch, by the by. Everyone can fit. You and Ben, me and Parker, Cammie and Adam, Dee and fill-in-the-blank hot guy Cammie finds for her."

"Well, it's a little more complicated than that."

Anna quickly explained how and why she and Ben would be arriving later, so that Ben could first escort Maddy to her prom.

"Wow, so this chick used to weigh how much?" Sam asked, as she dug into the stewed chickpeas.

"Three hundred pounds, maybe," Anna replied, remembering that her friend had an unnatural fascination—no, obsession—with weight loss. "But she had to have surgery to do it. You realize that people die during that surgery? She was huge, though. Can you even imagine how cruel kids must have been to her? Ben feels protective of her. It's sweet." She couldn't decide whether to take more az*iffa*—lentil stew—or *buticha*, a side dish made of jalapenos, green onions, and garbanzo flour. Remarkably, it tasted more like perfect scrambled eggs than anything else.

"That's the Ben I know and love," Sam remarked as Anna scooped up a little of each side dish.

"Ben as white knight, you mean," Anna translated, because it was what she so often thought herself.

"That's what he does, right?"

For reasons she couldn't name, Anna felt defensive. "He didn't save *me*."

"Bull."

"Sam, I did *not* need saving."

"Didn't you guys meet on the plane when you were first moving here? Didn't he save you from the asshole music producer you were sitting next to, who kept hitting on you? He swooped in and saved you. Admit it."

Anna had never thought of it like that. It was odd, because in her own family she was usually the rescuer, not the rescued. It was also true. He had swooped in and saved her.

"Is this Maddy chick cute now?" Sam asked, tearing off another piece of the soft flatbread.

"Kind of. She's very curvy, but I don't think she makes much of an effort. You know, baggy clothes, thick eyebrows, frizzy hair—"

"Good," Sam opined. "Because you definitely wouldn't want Ben to take a hot girl to prom."

"Don't be silly," Anna scoffed. "She's like a little sister to him. A family friend."

"Uh-huh," Sam said knowingly.

"It's *true*."

"Please. If she looked like Cammie, you'd freak."

Okay. That was true, too. In fact, she was already having regrets that she'd suggested that Ben take Maddy to her prom first. Obviously Maddy had a massive crush on him. Many a guy had been swayed by that kind of intense attention from a girl.

"Does Eduardo know you're going to prom with Parker?" Anna asked, in a deft—she hoped—effort to change the subject.

Sam shook her head. "Doesn't matter. It's no big deal."

Could Sam really mean that? She scooped up some mashed chickpeas with a piece of *injera*. "He's your boyfriend. He deserves to know."

Sam waved away her friend's concern and reached for her iced tea. "It's just two friends going to a school dance together. He's helping me with the documentary. It's totally cool."

"When does Eduardo leave?"

"Tomorrow morning. Early."

The kitchen phone rang; Anna rose to answer it. "Anna Percy." She spoke automatically.

"Well, I'm glad to see that someone hasn't lost her manners." Her mother's voice was as wellbred and melodious as ever. "But shouldn't you be at school, Anna?"

Anna hadn't spoken to her mother in more than a month. This wasn't surprising, though, because Jane Percy spent as much time in Europe, visiting the various young artists whose work she collected, as she did at the family town house on the Upper East Side of Manhattan. (Anna suspected her mother also collected the artists more than occasionally, but it wasn't a conversation they were ever likely to have.)

Bone-thin with a classic short blond haircut and

vintage couture style, Jane Percy exuded class. She could, and did, trace her ancestry back to the *Mayflower*. She and Anna's father had been divorced for years.

"I came home for lunch with a friend," Anna explained. "How are you, Mother?"

"Very well, darling," Jane replied, which meant nothing. Jane Percy would have said, "Very well," if she were sliding off the deck of the *Titanic*, because that was simply what one did. "Is your father there? I need to talk to him about something in the trust for Susan. The office said he'd left for lunch and he isn't picking up his cell."

"I haven't seen him, but I'll tell him you called," Anna promised.

"Write it down, Anna," Jane instructed, as if she were a small child.

"Where are you calling from? Which number should I give him?"

"Manhattan. For a few weeks, anyway. There's some ridiculous snafu with your sister's trust fund—it's all very tedious." Her mother's voice cut out a couple of times in the middle of the last sentence; a sure sign of call waiting. "I've got to take this, Anna, it's my attorney. Call me, sweetheart."

Jane hung up. So did Anna, feeling instantly out of sorts. Talking to her mother generally did that to her. Her mother might say, "Call me, sweetheart," but both of them knew that their relationship didn't involve calling each other for no good reason. Anna couldn't remember her ever having received a phone call from her mother that didn't have a purpose other than to get caught up on one another's lives. Whenever Anna did call her just to say hello, she got the sense that Jane was busy with something else. More than that, every conversation they did have left Anna feeling as if she wasn't living up to some mythic standard of how Jane Percy's perfect daughter should act.

"Your mother?" Sam asked as Anna sat back down.

Anna nodded. She'd been enjoying her lunch with Sam. Now, despite the good food, she felt almost empty.

"Don't complain. At least she calls you. I haven't spoken to mine since 2004."

"You never talk about her," Anna noted curiously, pouring each of them more iced tea. The most Anna could recall was Sam saying that her mother's marriage to Jackson had crashed and burned about nine years ago. Other than that, Anna knew nothing.

"What's to talk about? She was a feature writer for the *Los Angeles Times* when she met my dad. I think it was either an interview or the premiere party for *Star Wars Episode VI: Return of the Jedi.* I know they were friendly with George Lucas back then. They had me, got divorced; she took a job with a paper in North Carolina and married a guy who teaches at Duke. The end."

"'The end'?"

Sam shrugged and wiped her mouth with one of the pale blue extra cloth napkins that Mimi had left at her place setting. "The end."

Anna could see that Sam was trying to hide whatever

feelings she actually had about this situation. From the *This Is How We Do Things* Big Book (East Coast WASP edition), she had learned not to pry. On the other hand, she knew what it felt like to not get along with your own mother.

"Why did she and Jackson split up?"

Sam grimaced. "Evidently they got into some weird free-love/open-marriage thing." She rolled her eyes. "I learned that in one of his heart-to-heart oversharing moments. My father operates in two gears: ignore me, or TMI—too much information. No wonder I'm fucked up."

"Aren't you curious to see her?"

"Hardly." Sam threw down the used napkin. "She doesn't even send me a goddamn birthday card."

Anna felt terrible for her friend. Sure, her own mother was pretty cold, aloof, and judgmental. At least she was around . . . occasionally.

"If we decide to have kids, we can do better," she finally suggested optimistically. "Can't we?"

"Shit," Sam responded. "We sure can't do any worse."

Adam sat at the kitchen table in basketball shorts and a faded vintage New Riders of the Purple Sage T-shirt, nursing a Dr Pepper and poring over the catalog for Pomona College—he'd been accepted at Stanford, Georgetown, and Williams, but he was pretty set on nearby Pomona, in Claremont, California. He wasn't one of those kids who couldn't wait to leave high school behind. Frankly, he'd miss his buds and his b-ball team—those guys were the best. But in another way, he was more than ready to move to the next stage of his life. He'd chosen Pomona carefully, liking its small size and low student-to-faculty ratio. He'd be able to play basketball there, which he knew would be unlikely at one of the big Division I-A schools. Best of all, it was within striking distance of Los Angeles. Adam knew it might be old-fashioned, but he didn't want to be too far from his mom and dad. He liked them, they liked him. It was a blessing.

His situation was very different from Anna's. He knew she was going back east, to Yale. Sam would be at film school at USC. Cammie had been accepted at Pepperdine, though she was making noises about deferring enrollment and going to work for some entertainment-related business, like David Brokaw's public relations firm. As for Dee, he had no idea. Parker wasn't going to college at all; he just planned to audition and support himself any way he could. Translation: Wait tables.

Adam's parents always joked that ultimately Adam would become a lawyer, too—"go into the family business." They'd met in law school at the University of Michigan and had practiced contracts law and litigation together for the past decade. Their simultaneous hiring by a law firm in Century City—the joint offer had apparently been close to seven figures—was what had brought Adam and his family to Beverly Hills from Grand Rapids, Michigan. Adam doubted that future for himself, though. Too conventional.

He heard the front door open. "Adam, you home?" his dad called out.

"In the kitchen!"

His parents stepped though the kitchen door, both of them wearing their lawyer costumes—dark, perfectly cut suits. It amused him, because his folks did not have suit-type personalities. They were actually easygoing, casual people and had always been very hands-on parents. Each of them cared about the world, and they had raised Adam to care, too. They took on quite a few liberal pro bono cases—meaning they got paid nothing— and were very involved in Democratic Party politics. His father even made noises from time to time about running for elected office.

For a pair in their forties, they were cute. His dad was better than six feet, long and lanky, with short dark hair and round John Lennon–style glasses that he needed all the time but wore only for reading. His mom, on the other hand, was petite, with a pixie-style Audrey Hepburn haircut that worked with her fine-boned feminine features.

In the parental sweepstakes of life, Adam figured that—on balance, of course—he had come up a winner.

"It's after eight, sweetie, did you eat dinner?" his mom asked with smile as she slung her briefcase up on the white kitchen counter. It was the same counter that had been in the house when they'd bought it a year or so before; the Floods were the only people in their zip code who didn't redecorate within a month of buying a new home.

Adam nodded. "Your lasagna from last night. Better the second day."

Mr. Flood had already opened the refrigerator door and cracked the top off a can of Guinness. It was his one indulgence—he drank one a night after work, and always from a Guinness glass he'd brought back from a business trip to Dublin where he'd had a chance to tour the brewery.

"Ah," he said, as he poured the dark liquid. "Nectar of the gods."

"How's the case going?" Adam asked, clearing off some room at the table for his parents by stacking the Pomona catalog and that morning's *Los Angeles Times* and putting them on the fourth chair at the table. His parents were trying a breach-of-contract suit on behalf of one of the movie studios, where a star was claiming that his unplanned trip to drug rehab was a satisfactory excuse for having to miss two weeks of shooting.

"Okay." His mom sighed loudly and stepped out of her heels. "Except one of the jurors passed the defendant a love note today. She had to be replaced with an alternate."

"Which is what we hope doesn't happen with your prom date," Mr. Flood cracked. He took his beer glass and pulled up a seat at the round, 1950s-style Formica kitchen table that had also come from their house in Michigan. "You have to remember to let a Guiness settle in the glass, son. Let the head form. Don't rush things."

Adam grinned. "Thanks for the tip. Since when are you a fan of Cammie, Dad?"

His father sat and hoisted his Guinness in a toast to Adam. "As long as you're happy, kid. Now it's ready."

He took a sip. "Ah. That almost makes the love note in court worthwhile. You got everything planned? Limo? Tux? Shoes? Corsage?"

Adam nodded. Earlier in the day, he'd stopped into Mr. Williams' Formals, the tuxedo shop in Westwood, to rent a tux. It had turned out that the store was basically a one-stop-shopping for prom night. He didn't have to bother with a limo—Sam was providing one for all her friends—but he had rented a nice-looking Ted Lapidus suit and dress shoes, and arranged for a corsage that the seemingly gay salesman advised would work best against Cammie's strawberry blond hair. "Never," he'd sniffed, "go by the color of the gown; much too matchy-matchy."

"I didn't go to my prom," Mrs. Flood recalled as she went to the fridge for a Vernor's vanilla soda, a Detroit-based drink to which she'd been partial ever since Adam could remember. When they'd moved to California, Adam remembered how overjoyed she'd been that she could buy it at the local Ralph's supermarket. "It was the seventies—too politically incorrect."

"I went." Mr. Flood grinned widely.

"I don't like that smile, so don't tell me about it," Adam's mom noted with a smirk as she popped the top of her soda and took a sip. "Oh! Adam, I almost forgot. We got something for you in the office today. I think it's in your briefcase, Alan."

Adam's dad put down his glass and opened his shiny black briefcase, extracting a thin manila ten-by-twelve envelope from beneath a messy pile of court documents and yellow legal pads.

"What is it?"

"Remember when you asked Mom and me to do a little background check on that case involving Cammie's mother? It's done."

Mr. Flood tossed him the envelope. Adam caught it, his heart thudding as he contemplated what might be inside.

"Our firm's investigator put it together for us, actually," Mrs. Flood explained, slipping into one of the kitchen chairs. "I guess there was a lot of stuff under seal until recently."

Adam held the package gingerly. "You haven't read it?"

"No," she replied after another long sip of her Vernor's. "And if you want my professional opinion, now that you've got it in your hands, neither should you. Let Cammie decide what she wants to do with it."

"Thanks for doing this," he told them automatically, his brain going a mile a minute. After Cammie had gotten so upset on the beach, he knew he should have called his parents off. He could tell himself that he'd forgotten all about it, but was that true? Or did he want to show Cammie he could defy her instead of always acquiescing to her wishes and whims? Or was he just so curious about the events of that night long ago that he was going to find out what he could, come what may?

He fingered the envelope. Hell if he knew.

"I have no idea what's in there, champ," his father declared. "But you're dealing with a dead mother. It could be really upsetting for Cammie, whatever it is."

Adam frowned.

"Be sensitive to that," his mother advised. "Don't be surprised if she doesn't say anything at all to you. Or even if she just throws the whole thing away."

"We once did this pro bono case for a woman who was adopted. She was looking for her birth mother," his dad said, tracing a circle in the condensation on the side of his glass with his forefinger. "That's what she thought . . . until we found who she was looking for."

"She tore up a file just like this one," Mrs. Flood recalled. "Just couldn't handle the idea of opening it when the time came. I'm going to shower off the Los Angeles grunge; then we have to write that damn brief for tomorrow on that hearsay objection you made. You were correct, the judge is just being picky. You coming, sweetie?"

"Sure." Mr. Flood drained his Guinness, put the empty glass in the dishwasher, and pointed at the envelope. "Use good judgment, okay?"

Like *that* was helpful. His parents always advised him to use good judgment when they knew that Adam had a difficult decision to make.

Ten seconds later, he was once again alone in the kitchen, staring at the envelope that his parents had brought home. His mom and dad were right. The best thing to do would be to call Cammie, tell her about what they'd found, and just deal with whatever her reaction was. He knew that, but he still couldn't quite bring himself to pick up the phone. Instead, he tossed the package atop of his Pomona catalog on the chair, where it silently called to him like a siren to Odysseus.

Maybe there was another way. What if he looked at the contents? Checked it out himself? If it turned out it was nothing, he could just put the whole damn package through his parents' home paper shredder and it would be like it had never happened. Yeah, that made sense. Of course, if there was something unexpected inside, something he was sure that Cammie would want to know, he'd call her right way. He'd figure out what to say to her, too. Or seal the envelope back up. Or . . . something.

What the hell. He tried to open the envelope seal carefully, but the glue was too secure—he ended up tearing the top of the package. Finally, though, he had it open, and extracted a thin sheaf of papers that were held together by a single paper clip. The first few pages were absolutely routine; he sighed audibly as he flipped through them. Police reports, photos of the Strikers' yacht, toxicology reports on the people who'd been on board that—

Holy shit.

Adam forced his eyes back to the top of the page and reread it slowly and carefully. Then he reread it again, feeling sick to his stomach.

How could he ever tell Cammie about *this*?

Cheesy Romantic Chick Flick

Eduardo's bungalow at the Beverly Hills Hotel was aglow with lightly scented vanilla candles, dozens of them, set on every surface—the pearl marble counters of the kitchen and the bath, the clear Lucite Philippe Starck table and chairs and butcher-block countertops in the small kitchen, the white glass coffee table between the taupe Minotti leather sofas. Same thing in the bedroom. The antique nightstands on either side of the four-poster bed held more than a dozen small tapers between them. The aroma of the rose petals he had sprinkled across the hand-embroidered Belgian lace quilt lingered in the air.

Sam lay on the bed in Eduardo's arms; the lovely quilt had fallen to the Persian rug sometime during the previous torrid hour. He was naked. *She* was naked. The truly amazing part of the equation was how okay she was about it.

They had finally done it. Made love, in a torrent of passion that had lived up to every fantasy she had ever had about the experience.

Well, not *every* fantasy. If it were going to live up to *every* fantasy, her body would be better than Cammie's.

"You are so beautiful, Samantha," Eduardo murmured into her hair.

Damn, the boy meant it.

Sam had always wondered if making love would really be all that different from drunken sex. Maybe all that carried-away shit was just what perfect-looking actresses feigned with perfect looking actors who usually weren't so perfect-looking in real life. The director of photography and the editor would stretch the images so the actors got longer and leaner. Lighting made them look ten years younger. A soft-focus lens eliminated pimples, bumps, and bruises.

Sam was a Hollywood kid who knew every Hollywood trick in the book. And now she knew something else: the truth about making love and for the first time feeling beautiful in the eyes of a boy who adored you. Compared to this, drunken sex sucked ass.

"Are you happy?" Eduardo whispered.

"What do you think?"

She could feel his smile though her eyes were closed. "You *sounded* happy."

"Don't let it go to your head."

To think that she'd been nearly petrified with nerves when they'd stepped into the bungalow. After dinner in the Polo Lounge, they'd strolled through the lush gardens of the hotel back to his place. Eduardo had gotten some assistance from the hotel staff; the candles were already lit, the rose petals strewn. What touched her most, though, were the dozen tulips in a vase by the bedside. She had once mentioned in passing that tulips were her favorite flower.

Once inside the door, he'd gotten a decanter of 1935 Taylor's vintage port from the bar and poured them each a small glassful. They'd sipped it by the roaring fire. There'd been no pressure. He had meant what he said, he told her. As much as he wanted to make love to her, he would wait until she was ready. He'd kissed her. Kissed her again. And . . .

She was ready.

In a perfect world, she'd have been light as a feather and he'd have carried her to the bedroom; he looked strong enough to do it, too. She was thankful he didn't try. She was also thankful that he didn't do any of the following: Sit on the bed and ask her to undress for him. Begin to undress her himself. Begin to undress *himself*. Instead, when they were in the bedroom, he kissed her some more, so much that she wanted to be in his arms forever. It was amazing how her self-consciousness fell away with her clothing. The look in his eyes had told her everything: she was beautiful to him.

"How about if we spend the rest of our lives in this bed?" she suggested, snuggling against him. "We would only get up for the occasional shower."

"Our friends and family might come looking for us," Eduardo teased.

"We could plant a rumor that we ran away. Tibet sounds good."

He kissed her hair. "I've been to Tibet. The food is not so good. Someplace more romantic. How about Saint-Tropez?"

"Been there. Too many Americans."

"True," he mused. "Same thing with the Scottish moors . . . I've got it. Corsica. By yacht from Italy. They have the best cheese in the world."

She craned around and gave him an arch look. "You want to go to Corsica for the *cheese*?"

"I would go just about anywhere with you, Samantha." He kissed her softly again.

"Except my prom."

Eduardo smiled. "I've already promised my family. Take photos for me. Then I can see how beautiful you looked in your dress."

"How about if I just wear the gown for you sometime?" Sam asked. She knew that there hadn't been much chance of Eduardo changing his mind and staying, but it had been worth asking him. If he'd said yes, she would just have worked it out with Parker, who wouldn't have argued. He didn't want to make an enemy out of Sam. Now, she had to tell Eduardo about Parker, which she still hadn't done.

"I know you, Samantha. You would never wear a formal gown twice."

She laughed. Right on the first try. He understood her *and* thought her thighs were hot. What a guy. She just wouldn't think about tomorrow night, she decided. Sam curled into him and kissed him lightly. It was just like a cheesy romantic chick flick—the hyper talented woman with the thunder thighs who gets the hottest guy to fall not just for her brains but for her body too.

But Sam didn't give a damn—she was too busy starring in it.

Pink Velvet Prada Pumps

B en loaded another blenderful of blueberries, peeled kiwi, and sliced peaches, surveying the crush of club goers that had closed in around his smoothie stand.

He shook his head ruefully. An article in *L.A. Weekly* had come out the day before, reviewing the hottest new clubs in town. Trieste had been at the top of the list. The article guaranteed that the club would stay hot for months, but for the real trendsetters it was the beginning of the end. They never went to a club that had been written about in the newspaper, even if it was the city's alternative weekly. Slowly but surely the place would become post hip, full of valley and South Bay kids, European tourists, and various wanna-bes. They'd flock to Trieste like low-rent travelers to the cheapest all-you-can-eat buffet in Las Vegas.

The orders came fast and furious and Ben found himself playing a game as they did, trying to guess the size of the tip that would come from the particular customer. This one for the burly bodyguard of a twenty-something singer who'd gone from triple-platinum superstar to laughingstock after starring in one of the worst movies ever made, then resurrected her career with her first decent CD since the twentieth century. Tip? Five bucks. He'd guessed three. A banana-and-guava special for one of the *Big Brother* winners. Tip? Two bucks. He'd guessed four. Coconut, passion fruit, and cherries for a former guitar player for the Dead Kennedys. He thought he'd get a fiver. Tip? A twenty.

Finally, the boss showed up—a clean-cut Wall Street type who'd made a fortune by getting out of Internet stocks right before the bubble burst and then selling AOL and Amazon short through their precipitous declines.

"Thanks for your hard work," he told Ben. "Now go take a break. Next week I'll get you in the back office, or else your father will mess up my wife's next surgery on purpose."

Ben's relief—a tall, thin young woman in a red tank top and tight black trousers, with two lip piercings and spiky black hair, stepped in for him.

"I'll be back in twenty minutes," he told her.

"Got it covered." She was already taking orders.

He drifted away from the juice bar toward one of the backyard chaise longues and realized he was hungry. A Trieste burger would be tasty—they made them with buffalo instead of beef—so he put in an order with one of the barbecue chefs, then sprawled in a lawn chair, realizing he was famished.

Shit. Not him.

Jack Walker was back at Trieste. He wore skinny

black jeans and a black T-shirt with a skull on it, very punk. The moment he spotted Ben, he waved and dodged through the crowd, then pulled up a wicker chair of his own next to Ben's. "Hey, man, can we talk?"

He knew Jack; the guy wasn't likely to go away until Ben let him say his piece.

"I've got twenty minutes and a burger to chow down. So you might want to cut to the chase."

Jack nodded. "I'll leave you about eighteen minutes to yourself. I just wanted to apologize."

Ben was taken aback. "That's unexpected."

"Look, you're right. I can see how you might think Maddy is easy pickings."

"Thanks."

Jack raised an eyebrow. "Hey. I've seen you dawg with the best of 'em."

"In the fall, yeah. I'll grant you. But they those were college girls. Maddy's junior-high material."

Jack looked amused. "I hear you got me uninvited as her prom date."

"Good news travels fast."

"I just wanted you to know that I'm cool with it."

"Ben! Buffalo burger's up!" the chef with the body art on his neck called.

"Thanks, Willie." Ben got up and retrieved the paper plate with his oversize buffalo burger. It was served on a fresh-baked hard roll with sides of cabbage salad and baby red potato salad.

"I can't quite figure out your game," he admitted to

Jack, as he bit into the potato salad and then sat down. "Is this some kind of lead-me-not-into-temptation thing?"

"You think you have it all figured out, my man." Jack chuckled, then stood. "Anyway, we good?" He held a hand out to Ben.

He and Jack were practically best buds at Princeton; he didn't want to see the end of that just because of Jack's penchant for women. He understood where that came from; it all had to do with growing up poor in New Jersey and wanting to show the world and his own soul that he was a guy with power. Maybe his friend would get over it. Maybe he wouldn't. If he didn't, he wouldn't be the first Princeton graduate to be a first-class womanizer.

Maybe Jack was more mature than he'd thought. He sure hadn't expected him to be man enough to apologize.

He bumped his buddy's fist with his own. "Yeah man, we're good."

Sweet.

From the far side of the outdoor patio, Cammie eyed Ben and Mystery Punk sharing a manly bonding moment, doing one of those primitive anthropological gestures that had long ago replaced the handshake. Ben looked hot as ever, damn him—as much as she loved Adam, part of her would always smolder for Ben. Whether that was because he had dropped her and she had something to prove because she still had feelings for him, or because he'd had the balls to call her on her considerable bullshit, she wasn't sure.

Cammie wasn't at Trieste for Ben, though. She'd come for Dee, vowing to make good on her promise to secure her a hot prom date. The weird thing was, until that very afternoon, she'd had one. His name was Zack Bronson; he was the tall, skinny, but undeniably smoking drummer for the neo–New Wave band Fluffer, which had just been signed by her father's agency. Everything had been fine until Zack had called before dinnertime to say that Warner Brothers wanted him to play a showcase in Miami on Saturday night, which meant the prom fix-up with her friend was definitely off, so have a nice life and peace out.

Asshole.

That left Cammie a girl on a mission to find a young, reasonably sane, definitely smoking-hot guy who was free the next night and would like to go to a high school prom. She could have hit any number of clubs in search of such a guy, and told herself that she'd picked Trieste because it was the flavor of the month and not because Ben was working there.

She watched Punk Boy throw back his head and laugh at something Ben was saying. *Hmm.* He was kind of cute in a skinny Johnny Rotten/Sid Vicious kind of way. He might have possibilities.

She snaked through the crowd to where they were sitting on a couple of lawn chairs under a big tree. "We can't go on meeting like this," her voice purred.

"Cammie!" Ben sounded genuinely pleased to see her

as he rose and gave her a great big bear hug. She felt the contours of his hard body and had the fleeting thought that it would be nice if the hug didn't end, though of course it did.

"Welcome home." She smiled nonchalantly, pulling over another of the wicker chairs and turning a sexy smile on Punk Boy. "Hi. I'm Cammie Sheppard."

"Jack Walker. How's it going?"

She could see his immediate attraction to her in his eyes. Cammie loved when that happened, much as she *expected* it to happen.

"So, you're a friend of Ben's," he gathered, his admiring gaze fixed on her. "Lucky Ben."

"You have no idea." She crossed her legs smoothly, because she knew that in her pink-and-white floral Kenzie baby-doll minidress and her pink velvet Prada pumps, it was all about her legs. She was gratified to see Punk Boy's gaze head south . . . and stay there.

"He let you *go*?" Jack's eyes didn't budge from Cammie's bare thighs.

"Yo, let's change the subject," Ben suggested, then took the last bite of his burger.

"Sure," Cammie agreed easily, leaning toward Punk Boy. "And who are you?"

Punk Boy gave her the coverage, coverage being a film studio's two-page version of any story when no one wanted to take the time to read the actual book. Friend of Ben's from Princeton. In town for summer. Internship with Fox. Living in guesthouse. Hot car on loan.

Got it. It was getting better and better.

When Ben announced that he had to return to the juice bar because his break was over, Cammie made it clear that she was perfectly happy to hang with his friend. With his friend, Jack launched into an epic about the new reality show he was helping to develop—*The Pickup Artist*. The gimmick was that hidden cameras would follow various guys and girls to clubs and through malls in a competition to see who had the best pickup batting average.

Cammie pretended to find this concept fascinating, though in actuality she felt certain she could puke a better idea. Meanwhile, Ben had a tiny blond waitress with a gymnast's muscular build bring over two orange sherbet smoothies, which gave Jack an opportunity to expound for fifteen more minutes on the various personalities at Fox, a third of whom were or had been clients of Cammie's father.

Finally, Jack got to the question she had been waiting for.

"I was thinking, Cammie. Tomorrow night, maybe you could show me a few of those clubs."

Deft. Not.

"Wow, I'd love to," she lied, then shifted to the truth. "But tomorrow night is my high school prom."

Jack nodded. "Yeah? And you're not too cool to go?"

Cammie laughed genuinely for the first time. "I am, actually, but my *boyfriend* had his heart set, so . . ."

She'd calculatedly thrown in the *B* word, knowing that Punk Boy would be disappointed.

Sure enough, he sighed.

God. Guys were so goddamn predictable.

"Boyfriend, huh?" Punk Boy sighed again. "Should have known."

"Yes, you should," she agreed, giggling on purpose and touching his arm. Physical connection was always good. "You know, I just thought of something."

"Yeah?"

"I've got a close friend who wants to go to the Beverly Hills High School prom tomorrow, but her date fell through at the last minute. If you're not busy, maybe you'd want to take her."

"Not a chance." He shook his head. "I have a policy against blind dates."

Cammie was momentarily stuck. Then she got an idea.

"Come with me."

She marched over to Ben's juice bar, where he was in the midst of preparing yet another three smoothies simultaneously. As she'd suspected, Punk Boy followed.

"Ben?"

"Yeah?"

"Dee needs a prom date for tomorrow," Cammie explained enthusiastically. "Your friend isn't sure. Tell him how cute she is."

Ben turned off one of the blenders. "Real cute. But—"

She cut him off. "See? You just got a guy's opinion. Besides . . ." She moved close enough to Jack that her breasts pressed lightly against him. "We'll get a chance to dance too."

Cammie had Punk Boy put his digits into her BlackBerry and told him she'd call him in the A.M. about the logistics. Mission accomplished. Now if only she could remember Punk Boy's name.

Mystery Punk Boy

"I can't believe Eduardo's gone," Sam told Anna wistfully, as they pushed through the front door of Boss Sushi on South La Cienega Boulevard. "It was amazing. I already miss him."

"He'll be back soon, for the whole summer," Anna reminded her. "Lucky you."

Sam nodded.

Early in the week, they'd agreed to get together on Friday after school for prom prep. When the prom had been rescheduled, the prep date had been rescheduled too. But frankly, Anna was surprised that Sam wasn't already up in Palmdale, running preprom like a five-star general. She had assured Anna that with Monty already at the facility, plus Fee and Jazz with their handheld cameras, there would be more than enough footage to sort through.

Once inside Boss Sushi, Sam waved to some people she knew. The restaurant was dimly lit, with well-spaced wooden tables and Sinatra on the sound system. Boss Sushi was one of the city's hottest eateries, and her father was friends with master chef Tom "the Boss" Sagara and had even secured him a small role in *Ben Hur*. Once the Boss spotted Sam, he rushed out to kiss her on both cheeks and promised that he'd provide the freshest and best sushi and sashimi, no need to bother with a menu. He sat them in a booth and recommended the minced yellowtail with avocado and shiso, wrapped in Japanese radish. A black-clad young waitress with red hair cropped close enough to render her scalp visible brought them a carafe of the house wine—a gift from the Boss—a chardonnay so light and crisp that it tingled on the tongue.

"So, you're free for the whole afternoon, right?" Sam asked. She poured some chardonnay into her crystal goblet.

"Why?"

"I've got a stylist coming over with prom dresses for you, Dee, Cammie, and me. And yes, I told them to bring you size twos and fours—for which I hate you."

Anna was a bit taken aback. She'd already planned to wear a pale blue chiffon Chloe gown. She'd worn it once before to a state dinner at the White House. (Jane and Jonathan Percy each regularly made predictably sizable donations to both political parties. No matter who won, they'd still have access.) The White House banquet had been no great shakes—chatting with one of the president's daughters had been surprisingly uninteresting. But the wife of the Belgian ambassador had asked where Anna had found the grown, which was flattering.

"Uh-oh, you're pissed," Sam decreed. "I see it on your face."

"No, I'm not," Anna insisted. And she really wasn't. With Sam, she'd learned to expect this kind of surprise.

"Oh, great, then!" Sam grinned. "Whatever you were going to wear—forget it. This stylist does all the chicks on the best-dressed list every year. And . . ."

She peered at Anna more intently. "There's still something going on. Spill."

"It's not the dresses." Anna struggled with how to say what she wanted to say. "It's . . . your film. I know you want to be a director, and I know how talented you are, and—"

"And *what*?"

"I just . . . I wonder if you want to jump-start your career—to make yourself look good by making some other people look bad."

Sam leaned back, put her hands behind her head, and laughed. "Anna. You don't have to pull your punches with me. Just say it: You think I'm going to do a hatchet job on the prom weenies. Is that it?"

Anna took a meager sip of her wine. "Yes. And I don't see what's so funny."

"*You* are funny. You're so lucky you didn't grow up here in Hollywood, Anna. You would have been eaten alive before you graduated from nursery school."

"Don't change the subject," Anna warned. "It took a lot of courage for me to bring this up with you."

Sam laughed again. "I know. And I want you to know

you don't have anything to worry about, even though I don't let my friends dictate my art, especially when they have no idea what the finished product is going to look like and didn't want to see any of the edited footage and decided to jump to conclusions without even knowing the facts."

Anna blinked slowly. "I am totally confused."

"Okay, maybe in the beginning I was thinking about a prom-weenie hatchet job. But since then, I changed my concept for the film."

"To what?"

Sam fiddled with a straw wrapper. "The bizarre thing is, once I started to get to know the weenies, I actually kind of sort of . . . like them."

Anna's face lit up. "That's so sweet."

"Don't let it get around. As soon as you start seeing people who are different from you as actually three-dimensional, it's a lot harder to dis them. So my new concept is a lot more . . . affirmative."

The Sinatra CD ended and was replaced by Billie Holliday singing "Strange Fruit"—a song Anna adored. She leaned forward. "I am so glad that you changed your mind."

"Look," Sam continued. "You knew a lot of writers and painters in New York. You know that art is an evolving thing. Your first concept isn't always going to be your best concept. Last night with Eduardo . . . it was just so . . . real. Honest. Open. Authentic. When I woke up this morning, I realized that as much as Jazz and Fee want to be part of something they're not, everything they're doing for prom they're doing with their hearts. They really, truly, deeply care about this. That's what I want my movie to be about. How here in Beverly Hills, where party-giving is an art form, two high school girls can put their hearts into putting on a great party. Heart in a heartless town. That's what I'm going for."

Anna couldn't help but grin. "Sam Sharpe, you're a genius."

"True. Now, moving on," Sam replied briskly. "I have a surprise. At any—"

She was interrupted by the waitress, who carried an enormous tray with plates of sushi and sashimi, and identified each as she set it down: salmon, tuna, shrimp, and eel.

"Sam!"

The voice had come from the doorway. Anna turned and was surprised to see Dee trotting toward them. With her was a gangly guy, all arms and legs, with the faraway squint of the nearsighted. He had red curly hair, nervous eyes, and a prominent Adam's apple that bobbed up and down like it was attached to a yo-yo string. His ears stuck out a little, and he wore ironed jeans with a crease.

"Here comes my surprise," Sam explained to Anna happily. "On her day pass. With . . . you know, I have *no* clue who that guy is. I hope not her new boyfriend."

She rose to hug Dee. "I'm so glad you're here!"

"Oh wow, this is so fantastic!" Dee gushed.

Anna rose and embraced, Dee too, pleased to see her

up and around—maybe even getting back to a normal life. "It's good to see you. You've got to be feeling a lot better."

Dee's face was absolutely devoid of makeup. She wore Bebe khakis, a little faded olive-green T-shirt, and red Vans sneakers. Anna didn't think she'd ever seen her so dressed down before. The look worked, though . . . maybe even better than ever.

"Sit, sit," Sam told Dee and the gangly guy, ushering everyone into the booth.

"This is Marshall Gruber," Dee said, introducing Gangly Guy. "He's my warden for prom."

"Chaperone," he corrected, in a reedy voice. "I'm a clinical intern at Ojai."

Sam gave Anna a dubious look. It was great that Dee could get a pass for prom, but for her escort to bear such a striking resemblance to the guy from *Napoleon Dynamite*? This was definitely not the stuff that prom dreams were made of. What about the date that Cammie was supposed to procure? Meanwhile, the waitress hurried over with more plates and another large platter of sushi.

"Dig in," Sam instructed Dee and Marshall. "The yellowtail is amazing."

"Oh no." Marshall looked horrified. "I'm vegan. Just rice. Unbleached, if they've got it."

Dee nabbed a piece of yellowtail—evidently, her own former vegetarianism had vanished along with her bipolar symptoms—and bit into it. "Freedom," she declared, after she'd happily savored the fresh fish. "It's awesome. A whole afternoon with my friends, plus prom."

Friends plus chaperone, Anna thought. She tried not to stare at Marshall, who was using his chopsticks to pick apart the white rice on his plate, seemingly grain by grain.

"There's no nutrition in white rice," he scowled. "A person might as well down cyanide."

"Marshall? Maybe you'd like to sit at the sake bar?" Sam suggested cheerfully. "Far from the evil ivory rice?"

Marshall shook his head. "No. I have to be with Dee."

Dee rolled her eyes. "Sam? Did you hear anything about my *actual prom date*?"

Sam shrugged. "Nothing from Cammie, but she's supposed to meet us at my house in about an—

"Hey, Dee!"

With movie-perfect timing, Cammie swung into the restaurant unannounced, clad in a flouncy tiered Crazy Chic orange gauze skirt and a pink-and-orange bandeau top. "I've got news. Too good to hold until later."

Dee jumped up and hugged her, then introduced Marshall. Since there were no free chairs, Cammie slid onto Marshall's lap. He stiffened up; she glanced down.

"Is that a chopstick in your pocket, or are you glad to see me?" she teased.

Sam and Dee laughed; Anna tried not to show too much bemusement at Cammie's crack. As for Marshall, he blushed beet red and scooched out from under Cammie.

"My date?" Dee prompted. "Or else—"

"Done deal," Cammie announced, plucking a seaweed wrapped Pacific albacore roll from the platter. "His name is Jack Walker. Friend of Ben's from Princeton. Very punk-bad-boy hot."

Anna stopped with her chopsticks dangling in mid-air.

Jack Walker? The same Jack Walker who had hit on Maddy? Had to be. She couldn't imagine Dee going out with such a player; she had to still be emotionally fragile.

On the other hand, Dee looked *so* hopeful.

"I know him, Dee. He's cute," Anna assured her, hoping she was doing the right thing.

Marshall cleared his throat, which made his Adam's apple bob like a bobble-head doll in his throat. "Um, excuse me. Dee's pass specifically says that I'm escorting her. I've got it in the glove box in the car. I'll go get it to show you."

Cammie draped an arm casually around Gangly Guy's shoulder. "There's no need for that. You are escorting her, Marshall. So is Jack. Consider it . . . a variation on a double date."

The intern nodded solemnly. "I suppose that's all right, but I can't allow any alone time that could be an opportunity for illegal drug or alcohol activity or sexual relations that would not be conducive to the therapeutic process."

Cammie stroked Marshall's hair. "Marsh, honey, can you excuse us? We've got some girl talk to do."

"Sure," he agreed, apparently satisfied now that he knew he'd be with Dee at prom. "I'll go to the sushi bar and watch the fish swim around before they're murdered."

As Anna watched him depart, she didn't notice the teen girl with long, thick dark hair who was approaching their table from the opposite direction.

"Hi, Anna. Wow. Am I interrupting?"

To Anna's surprise, there stood Maddy. She wore oversize khaki pants and a navy T-shirt large enough to house a small island nation. Her hair was roped in a long, frizzy braid; she carried what looked like an overnight bag.

"No, of course not," Anna told her. "What are you doing here?"

Maddy looked embarrassed. "Can I talk to you for a second? In private?"

Anna nodded, excused herself, and led Maddy to a short corridor by the rear restrooms.

"Are you, like, pissed?" Maddy asked as they found a quiet spot. "I would have called your cell but I forgot to ask Ben for your number and he wasn't home but I remember he said that you were having lunch here. I could have called the restaurant and asked them to page you, but I didn't think of it until I got here."

"It's okay. You did the best you could. So what can I do for you?" Anna asked. She still couldn't figure out what was such a big emergency.

"The thing is . . ." Maddy hesitated. "Okay. I should just say it. Okay, I'll say it. My mom sent me a prom dress. I don't have a lot of money to go buy a new dress at the Beverly Center or anything like that. None of my old clothes fit. I wanted to show you the dress so you could maybe tell me if it's okay."

Anna was touched and a little ashamed that she'd ever been jealous of this girl. She was so . . . young. Innocent.

"I'd be happy to look at your dress," she declared.

"Gosh! Thanks!"

Maddy opened her overnight bag and extracted the dress. It was hot pink polyester, with rows of ruffles from the neckline to just under the bust, and little cap ruffled sleeves. Plain and tentlike, it fell straight to the floor.

All in all, it was perhaps the most hideous garment Anna had ever seen.

"What do you think?"

"I think you should put it back in the bag," Anna told her, in as neutral a voice as she could manage.

"You don't like it," Maddy declared. "I knew it sucked."

"You can do better." Anna was formulating an idea as she spoke. "Listen . . . would you like to come sit for a while with me and my friends?"

Maddy's face lit up. "Really? If it's not an imposition . . . that would be great!"

Anna linked her arm through Maddy's and led her through the crowded restaurant and back to the table, signaling the hostess—an Eva Longoria look-alike (which had to piss her off, because that meant she wouldn't get any roles unless someone was casting look-alikes)—to add another chair to the end of the booth.

As Maddy sat down, Cammie gave the girl the once-over. "Who are you?"

"A friend of Anna's. Madeleine McGee. You can call me Maddy. Everyone does."

Cammie eyed Maddy's oversize T-shirt. "Whoever you are, were you wearing that T-shirt before you gave birth?"

Anna cringed. She should have expected Cammie to make such an obnoxious and rude remark, but it was such a mean thing to say.

Maddy's reaction, though, was completely disarming. Instead of getting mad, she grinned broadly. "I used to be really fat and I haven't bought new clothes yet because I'm going to lose even more weight. Plus I don't have all that much money, to tell you the truth." Without further prompting, she launched into the story of her stomach stapling, leaving no stitch untouched, even digging into her pocketbook for her well-worn "before" picture to illustrate.

As the photograph was making the rounds, Sam snapped her fingers. "I know who you are. You're the chick living at Ben's house."

"That's right!" Maddy exclaimed, almost jumping out of her chair that the great Sam Sharpe had heard of her. Thus prompted, the story of how she'd come to move into the Birnbaums' house tumbled out, followed by a rhapsody about Ben himself and how it was so wonderful of Ben to take her to the Pacific Palisades junior prom that same evening.

With this last disclosure, every eye at the table swung to Anna.

Oops.

"Well, that's true," Anna allowed, doing rapid damage control. "I *suggested* that Ben be her escort, then come over to our senior prom. I mean, you only have one junior prom, right?"

"Cool!" Cammie cried gleefully. "That is so Esalen Institute—my aunt did Esalen years ago before she became a Scientologist. You two are *sharing* Ben."

"Well, why not? You don't have him anymore." Dee touched Maddy's forearm. "Cammie and Ben used to be an item."

"Wow! Before he fell madly in love with Anna?"

"What do you think?" Cammie jibed.

"Maddy, are you at all hungry?" Anna jumped in, wanting to change the subject so Maddy wouldn't become the object of Cammie's pique. She'd been in that position herself; it wasn't much fun. "Why don't we order another—?"

Maddy shook her head. "I can't eat much because my stomach is smaller, remember? I'm always hungry but I can never eat; that's just the way it is. It's worth it, though, 'cause I look at you guys and you're all so, like, thin and perfect. It makes me feel like I'm still a moose."

Cammie eyed the garment bag. "What's in there?"

Lie. Anna wished that telepathy were not just a figment of science-fiction imagination.

Maddy told the truth. "Umm, it's my prom dress. My mom sent it."

"Show it to me," Cammie ordered, in a voice that brooked no opposition.

Slowly, Maddy took the horrid garment from its carrying case, mumbling again how she hadn't picked it out, how her mother had sent it to her from Michigan. As the dress came out of its bag, the table fell deathly silent. Even Cammie couldn't seem to grasp that someone's own *mother* had suggested that her daughter wear such a frock.

"Does your mother *hate* you?" Cammie ventured, in a voice that sounded more shocked than mean.

"I know. It's ugly." Maddy looked crushed as she wadded the dress up and stuffed it back into the bag.

"Please. It's beyond ugly," Cammie snorted. "It's like, post ugly. It should be shredded and burned before it breeds and multiplies."

"You need a different dress," Dee agreed, squinting at Maddy. "If you don't mind my asking, what size are you now? It's hard to tell because your clothes are so baggy."

"Twelve, maybe? Fourteen? I haven't really shopped much."

This is the moment, Anna thought.

"Sam? You know, that stylist is coming over later. . . . Maybe we can call and see if she could bring Maddy a different dress."

Maddy smiled wanly. "I'd love that, Anna, but I can only afford about maybe . . . fifty dollars?"

Cammie was aghast. "For what, a lipstick?"

Anna looked pointedly at Sam; Sam picked up on the glance immediately. "Know what, everyone? I have an idea: definitive makeover for this girl. Makeup, hair, nails. And for God's sake, a new gown. On us. What do you say?"

Dee nodded. "Great idea. I'm feeling it."

Anna took in Maddy's uncertain face. "You deserve it, Maddy. You've *earned* it. Let us do this for you."

She meant every word. For a while there, insecurity about Ben had stupidly gotten in the way of her usual belief in the power of kindness. She was not going to let that happen again. Every once in a while, a situation came along where she could use the advantages life had given her to make someone else's life a bit better. This was definitely one of those situations.

Maddy gulped hard. "Wow. You must be the four nicest girls on the whole planet."

"Not exactly," Dee observed. "One of us is *too* nice, two of us are rarely nice, and one of us—that would be me—has neuropsychological issues."

This truth went over Maddy's head completely. "But what about appointments for hair and stuff?" she asked. "My prom is *tonight*."

Sam dug her BlackBerry cell phone out of her limited-edition gold Fendi spy bag and pressed Kiki's speed dial. "If you're rich enough and famous enough, you don't need an appointment. Maddy McGee, welcome to the City of Angels."

Perfect Little Waist

"It's good to be the queen," Sam remarked with exaggerated hauteur, as she watched Suki, an expert in the patented Japanese thermal reconditioning hair process called the Yuko System, go to town on Maddy. The Yuko System would transform her long frizzy mess into glossy, pin-straight, perfect hair. That is, until the new frizz began to grow in; then the process would have to be redone. The Yuko System was five hundred dollars a pop, exclusive of washing, styling, and blow dry.

No one ever said beauty came cheap.

It was an hour and a half since they'd left the sushi restaurant, and the girls were gathered in Sam's twelve-hundred-square-foot bedroom suite; Maddy sat before a dresser mirror on a hard-back chair that Roger, the butler, had brought up from the den and positioned on top of an artist's dropcloth. Suki had cheerfully explained during the early part of Maddy's process that she'd been born at Encino-Tarzana Medical Center and been christened Krissy Atkinson. Once she'd embraced Japanese thermal reconditioning as her professional calling—eschewing a gig at the Supercuts in Sherman Oaks—Krissy/Suki had given herself an appropriate Japanese-sounding name. She claimed it had increased her business by a factor of five.

While Maddy was being reconditioned, Sam lolled on her California king bed with the clean, silver-poled, roofless canopy. Her notion had been, since time was of the essence, to bring the mountain to Maddy—hair, makeup artist, etc. In a matter of a couple of hours, the makeover project had turned her room into prom central for all of them.

Across the room from Maddy, Cammie was sitting at a nail tech's portable table. Meanwhile, Dee was in the bathroom, getting a seaweed wrap from Katarina from Spa 310. Her escort, Marshall, had been content to wait downstairs in Jackson's library, though Sam had graciously offered him a thermal reconditioning process too.

All this activity meant that Sam and Anna would start with the personal attention of Gillian Garrett, a professional shopper and stylist on retainer for two of the major movie studios. It would be Gillian's job to help them peruse the various prom dresses she'd brought over in a panel truck—they currently hung on the costume rack in Sam's five-hundred-square-foot closet.

Tall, thin, heavily tattooed, and multiply pierced, raven-haired Gillian was known for her own quirky couture, such as creating dresses from shower curtains, glitter, and a glue gun. Where she really shone, though, was shopping for others. Based on a quick description of the client and his or her tastes, she had a sixth sense for the styles and designers that would be a perfect match.

"Remember when we got dressed her for your dad's wedding, Sam?" Dee called through the open stained-mahogany bathroom door. "I found that great gown for you but you didn't want to wear it because it was size . . ." Her voice trailed off. "Never mind. Your dress size is not important. Real beauty comes from within."

"Quoth the size nothing," Sam quipped, drawing her legs up and crossing them. "Okay, Gillian, show us what you got. Start with her." She hitched her thumb toward Anna, who sat on a pale pink leather desk chair.

Gillian checked her notes. "You're the . . . five-foot-eight size four who likes clean lines and classics. Right?"

"Yes, exactly."

Sam could see Anna was impressed. Good. She was about to prove that she knew Anna better than Anna knew herself. She'd been very careful with Gillian, very specific, in describing what kind of gown should be brought for each of her friends and Maddy. She was a director, dammit, and a director had to have an eye for that kind of thing.

There were six possibilities for each of them. Anna eyeballed the dresses and narrowed the choice down to two: a sleeveless black silk Oscar de la Renta that fell in a chic narrow column almost to the floor and a strapless Chanel haute couture gown of the palest silver, pleated over the bust and very fitted, which dipped in the back to the waist.

"Try the Chanel," Gillian instructed. She stood off to the side with her arms crossed, as if she could divine the proper dress for Anna just by observing her.

Anna did, and then stepped in front of Sam's 270-degree full-length mirror.

"That dress looks as if it were made for you." The stylist was pleased. "Have you ever considered modeling?"

"I'm only five-eight," Anna demurred. She turned her back to the gold-gilded mirror that had been imported from Germany and looked over her shoulder.

"I know you're not worried about the butt view," Sam opined. "You look perfect coming and going, for which you should die a slow and painful death."

Maddy, whose head was now bathed in chemicals and covered in a robin's-egg blue Gore-Tex wrap, admired Anna from across the room. "Wow. I would *kill* to be as skinny as you are."

Gillian took a small pad of paper from her back pocket, scribbled the gown's price on the top sheet, and passed it to Anna, who nodded at the four-figure price tag. Like her mother always said, you got what you paid for.

"Lovely. I'll take it."

"Excellent." Gillian pocketed the paper. "Well, *you* were easy. Who's next?"

"Let's get it over with," Sam muttered as she stood up and started to pull off her clothes. What the hell. All her friends knew what she looked like in her pink silk La Perla underwear—a prizewinning pear that not even stomach stapling could improve.

Sam had insisted on black. Gillian had followed her

instructions . . . partly. Four of the dresses were indeed
black. Another was midnight blue, and the sixth was forest green. The green Monique Lhuillier was out on principle—in sixth grade Sam had worn a green skirt and her
so-called friend Blu had chortled that her ass looked like
the Jolly Green Giant on steroids. It had taken a full
year of psychotherapy with Dr. Fred to get past that
one. She worked her way through the hip-hiding black
dresses: an off-the-shoulder drop-waisted Lanvin and a
John Galliano bias-cut chiffon number with pleats that
began at various places between her waist and her thighs.
Neither of them was right. Nor were the Bill Blass and
the Stella McCartney that followed.

Shit.

"You're not happy," Gillian surmised. "Try the midnight blue one for me."

Sam dubiously fingered the soft, blue textured silk
gown.

Gillian nodded. "I know what you're thinking. It'll
make your hips show. Trust my instincts, Sam. It's why
you hired me. That's the very first one that I pulled for
you. The cut is amazing, designed to show off your
manubrium."

"The upper part of your sternum," Anna translated.

"From which your clavicle and your first two ribs
articulate," Sam added. "I didn't sleep through biology,
thank you very much. Fine. I'll try it. Although I don't
know what's so fucking hot about exposing your
manubrium."

Gillian helped her slip the blue Emanuel Ungaro over her head. A layer of braided chiffon encircled her neck and continued down the center of her chest to the tops of her breasts. The three inches of chiffon across the bust were skintight, but then the dress fell into floaty folds of material, disguising Sam's lower body and emphasizing her upper body.

"Get it made for you in every color," Cammie decreed, as Gillian zipped Sam up.

Sam admired her reflection.

Damn. She looked good. Possibly even . . . really good.

"That is an amazing dress," Anna agreed warmly.

Huh. Sam checked out the always-dangerous rear view. Her butt and hips were hidden. Her crappy-ass fat legs were hidden. If only Eduardo could see her in it tonight.

"Sold," Sam declared. "You're a genius, Gillian."

"The price." Gillian scribbled on another piece of paper.

"Screw the prices Gillian," Sam declared. "Since when do we care about price?"

"How nice." Gillian smiled. "And Sam, that dress is a size—"

"Don't tell me!" Sam interrupted, clapping her hands over her ears. "Don't ruin the moment! I don't want to know."

Gillian held up eight fingers.

Sam lowered her hands. "You're shitting me."

The stylist shook her head. "The only place the dress is fitted is where you're small."

"I *should* get this made in every color," Sam chortled. "We so need champagne to celebrate."

Gillian unzipped her; Sam stepped out of her dress and picked up the portable phone on her 1930s antique French Art Deco nightstand. A moment later, she'd called the kitchen and arranged for refreshments. Meanwhile, Maddy returned from the shower in Sam's floral cashmere robe, having just washed the Yuko chemicals out of her hair.

"I wish I was you," she sighed.

Huh. What a strange comment. Sam considered all the times she'd looked at other girls who were prettier or thinner or who had hotter boyfriends and had thought exactly the same thing. Then she realized what Maddy had meant—to live in a place like this, with stylists and manicurists who came to your house, where money was no object and anything you wanted was at your beck and call.

She shrugged inwardly. Life was weird. Sometimes you were the windshield of the Jensen Interceptor, sometime you were the bug. This was her world. She hadn't asked for it, hadn't done anything to merit it. It was just the way it was. That she could welcome Maddy into it for an afternoon made her genuinely happy.

When Anna went into the bathroom for her facial from Katarina, Sam took the manicure seat to watch Cammie choose her prom dress. Cammie's selection was instantaneous—a draped white satin Versace so tight that it would be impossible to wear underwear, not even a thong. Casually, she stripped down to the buff, careful not to smudge her fresh manicure, and then let Gillian do the dozens of tiny hooks hidden by a row of pearls that fastened the dress.

One glance in the mirror was all Cammie needed to approve.

Christ. Cammie looked like every guy's fantasy: luminous, pouty-lipped face; strawberry blond Boticelli curls down her back; high, full breasts; tiny waist; curvy hips; and no underwear. Sam was tempted to call the kitchen and cancel the food order, vowing never to eat again.

As Cammie took another moment to admire herself, Suki flat-ironed Maddy's hair—the second-to-last step in the process before the chemical neutralizer. Meanwhile, Dee stepped forward to choose her gown. Gillian had intuited that tiny Dee would be easily over-whelmed by too much fabric, so she suggested a simple but fitted strapless pastel pink Roland Mouret gown with a white overlay.

Sam's BlackBerry rang. "Yeah?" she answered, eyes on Cammie prancing around in that damn gorgeous dress. If it was the kitchen, she would cancel the food order.

It wasn't. Instead, it was Monty, out in Palmdale, giv-ing her an update on the filming. Everything was going according to schedule. He'd interviewed the caterer, the band's manager, the florists, the parking attendants, and the security people, just as Sam had directed.

"You asked them all the questions I gave you?" Sam queried, now all business.

"Check," Monty replied. "Do I get an AD credit?"

"We'll see. How about Fee and Jazz?"

"I just talked to them," Monty reported. "They're having a blast with their handhelds."

Sam smiled. Everything was covered. She was so busy that she wasn't even obsessing about Eduardo. She had a dress that fit her. It didn't get any better than this. Well, it did. She could be going to prom with Eduardo. But this was a very, very nice second best.

The food—caviar and hand-cracked sesame wafers, melted Brie with slivered almonds, a fruit platter of sliced kiwi, passion fruit, tangerines, and peaches *and* Taittinger compte de champagne rosé—had been delivered and consumed, and Maddy's hair was finally done. Sam had the stylists and her friends remove or cover all the mirrors, decreeing that Maddy could not see herself until the makeover was complete. Sam knew that what they were doing was goddamn archetypal.

"I can't fucking believe that we're doing *Clueless*," she told her friends.

"*Ten Things I Hate About You,*" Cammie chimed in.

"*She's All That,*" Dee commented.

"*Drive Me Crazy,*" Cammie added.

"*Never Been Kissed.*"

"*Pretty in Pink*."

Anna spoke up. "I get it. Like *Pygmalion*."

Cammie shot her a withering look. "*Pygmalion*? No, Anna. *Pygmalion* is not the topper to that list. The topper to that list is *Not Another Teen Movie*."

"How does my hair look?" Maddy asked nervously.

"Sensational," Dee assured her, nodding her head vigorously. "When my hair grows out I'm going to do it too. I swear."

"Remember, you must keep it absolutely dry for the next forty-eight hours," Suki reminded her, as she pumped her own vanity-brand glossing spray over Maddy's new-look straight 'do. "Don't even sweat around your hairline. I'm serious."

"I promise." Maddy gave Sam an uncertain look. "I'm sure this costs a fortune."

Sam waved her off. "I told you. Money is no object today. It feels good to do something nice for a change."

"Don't worry," Cammie immediately chimed in. "Her inner shrew is still alive and well. And for what it's worth . . . I'm glad we did this for you, too."

Sam laughed. "Geez, I hope someone recorded that comment for posterity."

Gillian moved to the clothes rack. "Maddy, Sam described your style as Anna Nicole Smith with taste."

"I wish." Maddy gazed anxiously at the selection of prom dresses. "They all look too small."

"You think you're bigger than you are, probably," Anna assured her. She poured a small glass of champagne and offered it to the girl, thinking it might calm her a bit. "Why don't you just pick your favorite?"

Maddy waved off the champagne and surveyed the dresses. "I just . . . I have no idea."

"Mind?" Cammie stepped in front of Maddy and held up a jewel-toned floral print silk gown by Tashia. "Out—it will make you look like fat walking wallpaper." She tossed the dress onto Sam's bed and moved on to the next, an Asian-inspired aqua-and-black cashmere gown with a wide satin sash just below the bust. "Also out. You'll look pregnant. Let's see . . . the red Ya-Ya is *definitely* out." She shot Gillian a disdainful look. "No one over a size six should wear red, for God's sake. The purple Emanuel Ungaro just all around sucks, which leaves us with . . ."

Cammie lifted a two-piece lavender silk top-and-ballgown combination by Marc Jacobs. "Ah. This."

"I like it," Anna declared.

Maddy hesitated. "Lavender? Won't I look bigger in lavender?"

Cammie thrust the padded, scented hanger toward Maddy. "Rarely do I say anything remotely supportive, but if this doesn't look hot on you, I'll go to prom naked."

"Cammie, you're an exhibitionist. You'd *like* to go to prom naked."

Sam stifled a snort and grinned at Dee, who was sitting on the floor by the food, nibbling on a piece of passion fruit. Since when was Dee Young funny on purpose?

Maddy shyly took the hanger. "Can I change in the bathroom?"

"Be my guest," Sam told her.

While Maddy was changing, Gillian opened a large steamer trunk that contained dozens of pairs of shoes in various sizes. With her excellent taste, she'd brought Manolos, Jimmy Choos, Gravatis, and Baldinis that perfectly complimented all of their gowns, in sizes from five to ten. "When you're done with everything else, knock yourselves out."

"Here goes nothing!" Maddy called from the bathroom.

"Hold on!" Sam instructed. She quickly double-checked the mirrors. They were still all covered. "Okay, come out."

Maddy stepped into a room rendered speechless.

The lavender bustier top showed off her impressive cleavage and creamy shoulders. It ended an inch above where the full-cut floor-length skirt began. The combination was a miracle. There was skin, but no adipose tissue.

"Well?" Maddy asked anxiously, as she stood just outside the bathroom door.

"Wait until you see." Anna grinned, motioning Maddy toward the mirrors. "You look like a princess."

"A big, fat princess?" Maddy worried. "When can I see?"

"Soon," Sam assured her. "After Valerie is done with you."

"Who's Valerie?"

Sam clicked open her BlackBerry and pressed speed dial. "Roger? Send Valerie up, please."

Two minutes later, the renowned eyebrow queen of Los Angeles stepped into Sam's room. Slim, blond, and in better shape than most women ten years younger, Valerie had done the brows of anyone who was anyone in Hollywood. And she was about to do Maddy's.

"I don't do house calls; this is a favor to your father," Valerie told Sam disinterestedly, gazing around at the group. Her eyes landed on Maddy. "You, with the unibrow. You're the one, right?"

Maddy, who still stood by the bathroom door in her prom dress, nodded and rubbed the faint pelt between her brows self-consciously. "I tried waxing. It hurt."

"Suffer for beauty," Valerie insisted. "Go change. Love the outfit, by the way, and your hair is to die for. Let's make your face match."

A half hour and a several yelps of pain later, Maddy had elegant, perfectly arched eyebrows two shades lighter than her new straight hair.

"That makes an amazing difference," Anna announced. Sam had told her many times about the powers of Valerie. Now she was a believer. "You're going to love it."

"I want to see." Maddy was practically pleading from her seat at the manicure station, which the eyebrow queen of Los Angeles had transformed into a brow-and-makeup center.

"Nope. Makeup first," Valerie declared, brushing nonexistent eyebrow pluckings from her black cashmere turtleneck/black Anne Klein trousers combination. She then opened the levels of her traveling makeup box as the other girls gathered around to watch.

Valerie was a consummate artist. She used Cle de Peau ivory concealer under Maddy's eyes to soften the dark circles, then sponged a translucent creamy base all over Maddy's face. "The trick is to make sure your natural skin shines through." Valerie explained her work as if she were teaching a class. "Your freckles are cute, so we'll leave them."

Colorless loose powder came next, to set the base. Then Valerie focused once more on Maddy's eyes, blending shades of soft matte beige, taupe, and pink eye shadow, and following that with a deftly wielded eyebrow pencil. Three coats of Blinc Kiss Me black mascara onto curled eyelashes, then it was back to the cheeks with cream blush, plus a touch of Valerie's signature fairy dust sparkling powder above it on the cheekbones.

Finally Valerie went to the lips: Burt's Bees lip plumper, followed by a rose lip pencil, followed by a high-shine clear lip gloss. The makeup artist stepped back and squinted at her subject. "I'm good, if I do say so myself. Okay, gotta go, have a class at Yoga Booty in forty-five." She turned to Sam, who was standing with everyone else in a cluster around the makeup table. "Sam, I'll send the bill."

"Thanks, Valerie. You're a lifesaver."

"I know." Valerie gathered up her weaponry and departed.

"You guys *have* to let me see," Maddy pleaded. She stood up as if to go to the big mirror, but Sam blocked her path.

"Nope," Sam told her. "Go put on your prom dress first. In the bathroom."

"I'll help," Anna volunteered.

"I'll do it," Sam responded quickly. "I want to make sure she keeps that dress clean."

She couldn't help it. Sam simply had to compare Maddy's body with her own, which turned out to be a bad idea. No matter how shy Maddy was in her Wal-Mart white cotton underwear—very shy, indeed—the truth was right there for Sam to see. Maddy might tip the scales at a higher number, but her body still put Sam's to shame. Her waist was easily ten inches smaller then her bust, and her hips were maybe an inch smaller than her bust. Hourglass, all the way. It might not be the Hollywood look of the moment, and there were plenty of surgery scars, but hot was hot and Sam knew it.

Shit. An image of Eduardo entwined with a dangerously curvy French girl—Veronique? Danielle? Martine? —whose body was just like Maddy's flew uninvited into her head. The image morphed into a feature that Sam was helpless to turn off.

Stop. This is not about you.

Okay. She could rise above this.

She helped Maddy into her lavender prom dress and

Jimmy Choos, instructed her to close her eyes, and led her back into the bedroom. Anna, Cammie, Dee, and Gillian had unveiled the 270-degree mirror; Sam positioned Maddy right in front of it. "Open up," she instructed.

Maddy did. Her jaw fell; her eyes grew enormous.

"Is that me?" she whispered faintly.

"This is just like *The Swan*!" Dee cried happily.

Maddy's eyes pooled with tears. "I just can't . . . I can't believe . . ."

"Don't cry, for God's sake!" Cammie commanded. "You'll ruin the makeup."

"You look beautiful, Maddy." Anna hugged her warmly.

Maddy looked around at them, overwhelmed. "You guys just met me, and then you go and do something unbelievable like this. I don't know what to say, except thank you."

"You're welcome," Sam replied.

So. Maddy had a better body than she did. She was also, with newly arched brows and decent makeup, considerably prettier. Still, Sam's heart momentarily went out to the girl who previously had been hidden under a mountain of fat. Which was remarkable, because Sam's heart rarely went out to anyone. For the second time in twenty-four hours—the third, if you counted her change of heart with the prom weenies—it felt good.

Cinderella Likes Older Men

Ben straightened his bow tie and went to the refrigerator for the first of the two corsages he'd be bestowing that evening. Anna had asked for something simple and white, so hers was freesia blossoms from Floral Originals by Gregory on Wilshire Boulevard. Maddy hadn't specified what color she'd be wearing, so the gay salesman had recommended a white orchid surrounded by white baby roses, which wouldn't clash with whatever color gown she'd be wearing. While he'd been getting dressed—a Hugo Boss three-button tuxedo with a classic white shirt without ruffles and a black bow tie, Maddy had slipped a scrawled note under his door, suggesting that he wait for her in the kitchen. That was fine. It wouldn't matter what she looked like. He was going to help make a wonderful night for her and treat her like a princess, albeit of the little sister varie—

Maddy stepped into the kitchen. "Hi, Ben." She was so nervous she could barely get the words out.

Whoa. Ben could not believe what he was seeing. She wore a lavender gown. No, wait. It was a low-cut top and a long skirt, the combination skimming gracefully over her curves. Her hair was glossy and straight, her brows . . . her eyes . . . her lips . . .

Ben was a guy, which meant he couldn't decipher everything she'd done. There was no doubt, however, that the Maddy he was looking at bore little resemblance to the Maddy he knew. No way could she be mistaken for anyone's little sister.

"Maddy. You look beautiful."

"Really?" She gazed across the room at him from under sooty, smoldering lashes.

"Really. Wow."

"That's what I was hoping you would say."

Ben held out the white corsage. "For you."

She came to him, took the box, but fumbled opening it—now, this was the Maddy he knew—so he unwrapped the corsage for her and slipped it on her left wrist. "I never had one of these before," she breathed, turning her wrist this way and that. "I feel like I'm in a movie."

"You *look* like you're in a movie," he remarked. "So, Shall we?"

Ben held out his elbow for her to take his arm and escorted her through the house and out the front door . . . where he had arranged a surprise.

"A limo! A stretch limo!" she exclaimed, grasping his arm tightly. "Oh my gosh, I've never been in a limo. Holy cow, we have to get pictures!"

Ben laughed as she dug a disposable Kodak camera

out of her evening bag and took some shots of the black limo. Then she asked the driver—a middle-aged Russian man with close-cropped dark hair in a black suit and tie—to photograph the two of them with his vehicle as a backdrop.

Ben checked his classic Steinhausen wristwatch, trying not to make it too obvious. He'd promised to meet Anna in Palmdale at ten-thirty. No way was he going to be late.

Pacific Palisades High School's junior prom was being held at the Getty Center, the huge new art museum perched on a hillside at the south end of the Sepulveda Pass between Westwood and Sherman Oaks. Traffic on Sunset and Sepulveda boulevards was actually moving, so the limousine pulled into the Getty Center roundabout within twenty minutes of having left the Birnbaums' front door. There, the Golden Boys Valets were stationed—the company's conceit was that all the handsome young out-of-work actors who moonlighted for the agency had to bleach their hair blond. A Golden Boy built like a linebacker helped Maddy from the limo, since one couldn't drive up to the Getty Center itself. Instead, a silver monorail train ran from the roundabout up the hillside to the museum proper.

As the limo headed for the three-story parking structure, Ben and Maddy joined a small group already waiting for the monorail. Though the girls were in gorgeous gowns and the boys in crisply pressed tuxedos,

Ben marveled at how young they looked. Was it really such a big jump from high school junior to college freshman? Maddy shyly greeted one girl in a strapless red velour gown, but other than that, she didn't seem to know these kids. Moments later, the four-car white monorail pulled up. Ben and Maddy stepped inside for the quick trip to the museum itself. There was only one other couple in their monorail car—a muscular Latino guy with a blond girl who had extremely long, extremely straight hair.

"The architect who designed this place is Richard Meier. Did you know that?" Maddy asked nervously, sounding like a guidebook audio CD. "There's a mix of buildings, beautiful gardens, and open spaces, with a view of the whole Los Angeles basin."

Ben nodded politely as the monorail rounded a soft curve. It was a hazy night in Southern California—the lights of the city swirled like the stars in a Van Gogh painting.

"They used sixteen thousand tons of travertine from Bagni de Tivoli. There are fossilized leaves and feathers and branches still in the stone."

Ben smiled gently. "I know, Maddy."

She looked surprised. "You do? This docent from the museum gave a speech at an assembly last week."

"I got the same speech when I was in high school."

"Oh." Maddy started to bite at a hangnail, then remembered she had a fresh manicure and stopped herself. "Were Sam and Cammie there, too?"

He raised his eyebrows. "How do you know Sam and Cammie?"

"We all did prom prep this afternoon. Anna and Cammie and Sam and Dee. At Sam's house."

Ben smiled, very pleased. "Anna really came through for you, huh?"

"Actually . . . I think it was all of their idea. But Sam was the one who set up the hair and makeup and had this cool stylist bring over dresses. The worst part was my eyebrows. Ouch! But now I know you have to suffer for beauty."

They reached the top of the hill and stepped out of their monorail car, then followed several other couples into the complex. Ben had been here before but always marveled at the Getty Center's astonishing architecture. There were seven gleaming white, geometrically intricate buildings, each containing art from a different era. A dazzling riot of plants and flowers stood sentry to the walkways while a natural stream led to a cascading waterfall that poured into a sparkling blue pool with a floating maze of azaleas. Some couples were wandering around the gardens; a few were already making out. In one of the arbors a small stage had been set up, where a harpist played a sedate version of the REO Speedwagon classic "Keep on Loving You." As Ben and Maddy watched the harpist, an angelic-looking girl in a pink tutu and fairy wings slithered over and sprinkled fairy dust on their shoulders.

"What was that for?" Ben asked, brushing the pink glitter from the lapels of his tux.

Maddy giggled. "This year's prom theme is fairyland. I voted for the eighties, but lost. Come on. Let's go inside, where the real party is."

They walked to the south end of the plaza, boarded the long escalator, turned right at the top, and entered what was normally the Getty Center's main restaurant. Glass-walled, it offered a panoramic view of the low-slung Santa Monica mountains to the west and north, their dark shapes visible against the deepening blue of the evening sky. For the event, the staff had arranged circular tables with fairy-tale-themed centerpieces around the room, while a dance floor and stage had been erected at the west end of the restaurant. Enormous blown-up cells from animated fairy-tale movie adaptations adorned the walls, and the servers were dressed as characters ranging from Snow White and the Seven Dwarfs to Rapunzel. The band hadn't yet started its first set, but a DJ already had the place rocking; kids jammed on the dance floor to Kanye West's "Golddigger."

"Maddy!" An angular-faced skinny girl with braces, her unnaturally burgundy hair adorned with pink baby's breath that matched her pink-and-white strapless gown, ran over to them and hugged Maddy as if they were sisters who had lost each other in wartime. "Oh my gosh, shut *up*! You look fantastic!" she squealed.

"So do you!" Maddy squealed back.

"No lie, you look amazing. I hardly even recognized you!"

"Really?" Maddy's face lit up as she grabbed Ben's arm, practically dislocating it from his shoulder in the process. "Theresa Kushner, this is Ben Birnbaum. Ben, this is my friend, Theresa. She was on the prom committee."

"You did a great job," Ben affirmed politely.

Theresa beamed as the deejay brought "Golddigger" to a close. "Thanks. The little garden fairies throwing fairy dust on people? That was my idea. And my mom does PR for the Roasters; that's how we got them to play. We almost lost them to Beverly Hills High!"

"Lucky you," Ben grinned.

God, had he been this young two years ago? It didn't seem possible.

Maddy's eyes strayed intently around the room, as if she were looking for someone. Theresa tapped her on the shoulder. "Hey, Earth to Maddy!"

"Have you seen Mr. T?"

The skinny girl nodded toward the crowded dance floor. "He was dancing with Miss Brewster last time I saw him. But that was like twenty minutes ago."

"Miss Brewster?" Maddy echoed. "But she's so mean to us!"

"Yeah. But she's got big boobs and her dress is to die for. Anyway, I gotta go. My boyfriend drank so much in the limo that he's already hurling behind the Renaissance Pavilion. See ya."

By the time Theresa departed, the five members of the Roasters—four grungy white guys with a Rastafarian black lead singer—had taken the stage to an enormous cheer from the gathered crowd. They launched into a rocking ska-tinged tune at earsplitting volume.

"Dance, Maddy?" Ben shouted, over the lead singer's soaring wail.

She was in his arms the moment they hit the dance floor. To Ben, it felt . . . not odd, but different, to be holding such a voluptuous girl. Maddy was as different from Anna as different could be.

Not only that, she was definitely looking over his shoulder.

"Watching for someone?"

"Oh, you know, just want to see who shows up," she replied, making a point of gazing up into his eyes. "You're a good dancer, Ben. Am I doing it right?"

Ben was bemused. "You're doing great, Maddy," he assured her.

"Hi, Maddy."

Maddy stopped dancing as a tall blond man with rimless glasses danced by with a well-tanned, bleached-blond young woman in his arms. *Ah.* Ben remembered—this was Maddy's math teacher, the infamous Mr. T. He'd met him at Joe's Clams. He looked great in an Armani tuxedo. Meanwhile, Ben thought that Theresa had described his dance partner—this had to be Miss Brewster—correctly. She did indeed have huge boobs, cantilevered atop a black-and-white polka-dot spaghetti-strap chiffon dress, with a full, flirty skirt. For the life of him, Ben couldn't imagine what kind of bra was holding up her basketballs.

"Oh. Hi, Mr. T." Maddy smiled radiantly and called back as the two teachers danced off into the crowd.

"Your teacher seems like a good guy."

Maddy's smile turned into a frown. "You think?"

They kept dancing. Was it Ben's imagination or had Maddy just deliberately pressed up against him? *Damn.* Much as he tried, he couldn't exert control over certain anatomical reactions. Maybe this was what she thought she was supposed to do? Maybe her amazing makeover had filled her with confidence and she was trying stuff out on him?

"Do you think people looking at us think you're my boyfriend?" Maddy asked, as they continued to dance.

"Maybe." He'd have to remind her—diplomatically, of course—that he was involved in an exclusive thing with Anna, which made him the wrong target. He realized that it couldn't be easy for her for it to be prom night and for her not to have a boyfriend.

She rested her chin in the nape of his neck. *Double damn.* Ben could feel beads of sweat pop out on his forehead. This was not what he'd had in mind *at all.*

Fortunately, the song ended; when Ben suggested they go outside for a while, Maddy happily acceded. They stopped for some "fairy punch"—Ben wished it had been spiked with Stoli—and joined a few of Maddy's friends at a round table on the restaurant patio that overlooked the city. Ben barely caught their names—Barry and Amy, Twilla and Joel, Heatherly and River. They weren't the geekiest kids at prom . . . but they were close to it. The guys seemed like clones of each other. Not only had they obviously rented their tuxes at the same store, but each sported a thin wisp of a moustache; their hair ranged in length from very short and spiky to medium short and spiky; and each had had a piercing somewhere on his face.

As for Amy, Twilla, and Heatherly, they were a triumvirate of blond, redhead, and brunette, but each with at least one facial feature that would knock them off the pretty list. Ben hated to admit this, but it was true. Twilla's eyes were too close-set; Amy's lips were almost painfully thin; and Heatherly's nose resembled a snowball that had been thrown at her face and smushed on impact. Ben was, of course, polite and friendly, complimenting their dresses, etc. They giggled giddily in response.

That they were not A-list was confirmed by the obvious A-list kids who fired glances of disdain in their direction as they entered or left the restaurant.

Ben checked his watch. Good. Time was passing mercifully quickly. Another half hour and he could make a graceful exit for Anna's prom in Palmdale. The limo would take him home, he'd get his car, and then the driver could return to the Getty Center to wait for Maddy.

"Want to take a walk in the garden?" Maddy asked.

"Sure."

Anything to kill some more minutes.

They said good-bye to Maddy's friends; she took his arm as they headed back past the restaurant for the escalator that led down to the central gardens. With the sun fully down, the gardens were spectacular, lit by tens of thousands of tiny pink lights strung through the trees, plus a rotating series of theatrical gobos atop several of the pavilions that projected tableaus from famous Grimm's and Hans Christian Andersen fairy tales on the terrace floor.

Maddy held tight to Ben's arm as they strolled. "I wish this night could last forever and ever."

"You're like Cinderella at the ball, huh?" Ben asked kindly.

"I am?" She stopped, took his hands, and gazed into his eyes. She looked ethereal, beautiful, bewitching.

Uncomfortable, Ben shoved his hands into the pockets of his tux pants. "Sure."

"I always wanted to be beautiful, you know? Like all the time I was so fat and everything, I used to dream that one day some kind of magic would happen and— *poof!*—I'd be pretty."

"It wasn't magic, Maddy. It was your accomplishment."

They stopped by the central fountain and people-watched for a while; more couples had come downstairs to enjoy the fragrant night air and the transformed surroundings. Ben thought to himself about how much longer he'd have to hang around. An hour, maximum, he decided. Hopefully less than that.

"Do you think I need to work out more?" she asked suddenly, raising the hem of her top to expose a couple of inches of creamy flesh.

Ben gulped hard.

"Lookin' good, Mad," he assured her, though her attention was entirely on one strolling couple—Mr. T and the teacher with body of death.

"How good?" Maddy demanded.

The next thing Ben knew, she had snaked her arms around his neck and pressed her lips to his in a sizzling kiss. At least, it would have been sizzling if he'd wanted it to happen. It was painfully clear now. Sweet, clueless Maddy had a crush on him. He'd suspected it for a long time, but now he knew for certain.

Poor kid.

He put his hands on her hips and gently eased her away from him. "Maddy—"

"You're mad."

God. He didn't want to ruin her evening, but she had to understand the truth.

"Come with me for a sec. I want to talk to you." He put a hand on her elbow and led her to a carved stone bench at the far edge of the terrace, but where they could still see the central fountain. She sat next to him on the bench after he brushed away any nonexistent dust.

"Maddy," he told her, "I'm so flattered you can't imagine. But I'm in love with Anna."

"That's okay," Maddy replied amiably.

"No, it isn't. You know how much I care about you, but . . . not like *that*."

Maddy nodded. "Yeah, I get it. I don't care about you like *that*, either."

Okay. Now he was baffled.

"But you just—"

"Didn't you see Mr. T?" When Ben didn't jump in, she continued. "Wait, you mean . . . you really don't get it?"

Ben scratched his chin. "No, Mad, I really don't."

"Oh, wow! I was so sure that it's, like, written all over my face! And Jack is your best friend so I figured you guys talked and. . . ." She puffed air out as if it were all just so complicated to explain. "Okay, well, the thing is, I have this huuuge crush on Mr. T, my teacher? Don't you think he's like, the hottest guy you ever saw in your life?"

"Uh, I never really thought about—you've got a crush on your math teacher?"

Maddy looked at him cockeyed. "Why do you think that Jack and I got to be such good friends? And why he said he'd come to prom with me? I told him about Mr. T. and he said he would help me. Mr. T. would think of me as, like, a *girl* and not just his *student* if he saw me on, like, a *date* with an older guy."

Ben felt completely off-kilter. "Jack did that?"

Maddy nodded. "He said he knew what it felt like to really want something and that it was hard to get what you wanted if you didn't have help. Isn't that so sweet?"

Ben reeled. All his assumptions had been—

"When you said you'd take me to prom instead of Jack, I thought you were in on it! Because you're even cuter than Jack is, so that would make Mr. T. really, *really* jealous!"

"Why didn't you tell me back then?" Ben wondered aloud. He felt like such a presumptuous dick. "That night I got so mad at Jack—hey, what about those pictures on your computer?"

Maddy flushed. "Those were going to be for Mr. T, sometime. I don't know if I would have had the nerve to actually give them to him or anything. Probably not. Even Jack said it wasn't really a great idea, but when I told him I was going to do it anyway, he relented and said he'd help me." She ducked her head. "This is kind of embarrassing to talk about. Do you think I'm, like, pathetic?"

No, Ben thought. I think *I'm*, like, pathetic.

"It's fine to have a crush, Mad. But Mr. T is a lot older than you are and—"

"Hey you two. Hope I'm not interrupting . . ."

There stood Maddy's crush, Mr. T. Alone. Big Boobs was nowhere in sight. Now that Ben really looked at him, good ol' Mr. T wasn't all that old; early twenties.

"No, no, you're not interrupting *anything*!" Maddy insisted. "Ben is just a *friend.*"

"Yeah?" Mr. T asked.

"Oh yeah," Ben confirmed.

Mr. T's gaze went back to Maddy. "You look . . . great tonight, Maddy."

"I do?" Maddy seemed to float off the stone bench.

"I thought you might like to dance. If that's okay with your friend, that is."

"My friend doesn't make my decisions," Maddy declared, even before Ben could give permission. "Anyway, he has to go meet his *girlfriend.* Right, Ben?"

"Right," Ben agreed, nodding his head slowly. "But could I speak to you, Maddy? Before I go? Alone?"

"I'll wait for you at the top of the escalator," Mr. T assured her.

"Two seconds," Maddy promised. When Mr. T was safely out of view, she threw her arms around Ben. "It worked! Oh my gosh, he asked me to dance. He likes me!"

Ben cleared his throat. "At the risk of sounding parental, he's a teacher and you're a student."

"So?"

"So . . . I want you to promise me that you won't . . ." He wasn't quite sure how to put it. "You know how people think you have to have sex on prom night. . . ."

Maddy nodded eagerly.

"*No. Very* bad idea."

Maddy gave him a sly look. "What about you and Anna?"

"That's different. We're a couple, we're nearly the same age, and—" He stopped himself. "I want you to promise me that all you'll do with Mr. T is *dance*."

She nodded. He kissed her cheek and watched as she ran to the escalator. When she was on her way up, Ben headed back to the monorail. He didn't know what to laugh about more—how he'd totally assumed the wrong thing, or about how his own ego was as least as big and fat as Maddy, presurgery. Or both.

Win-Win

Where the hell was Adam?

Adam, the guy who was never late, was now holding everyone up. Cammie tapped the foot of her taupe stiletto-heeled sandal impatiently (taupe because even though her gown was white, it was mall-level tacky to also wear white heels) and checked her new Jacob & Co. pearl-faced, diamond-studded watch that had been a lame can't-we-all-just-get-along gift from her father after their spat at the late, great Bel Air Grand Hotel. If the truth be known, she felt badly that she'd had a big role in that hotel being late and great. On the other hand, who doesn't put a good sprinkler system in a public bathroom?

She stood by the fountain in the center of the circular driveway in front of the Sharpe estate along with the rest of her friends who were limoing over to the *Ben Hur* set in Palmdale. There were Sam and Parker and Anna, Dee and Jack and Marshall—Jack looked very cute in an Oleg

Cassini tux; Marshall was more *Napoleon Dynamite* than ever in his severe black formalwear.

A good chunk of the rest of the informal Beverly Hills High School high court was there, as well. Damian Williams, he of the unfortunate name—same as a villain from the Rodney King riots of 1992—but the fortunate bank account, whose father owned a string of exotic car dealerships from San Diego all the way up to San Francisco. Dark of hair, indolent of face, and fond of drink, with a thumbnail-size diamond stud in his left ear, he wore an Ecko six-button notch tuxedo with a silver cummerbund and a matching silver bow tie. He stood chatting with his ex-girlfriend, Skye Morrison, a crazy boho trustfunder with a pedigree almost as long as Anna's.

Unlike Anna, Skye was a free spirit with dreadlocks who had given up alcohol a month or so ago after an inebriated Damian had deposited his semidigested Buffalo Club roast venison in blackberry balsamic reduction on her lap. Her latest penchant was for one-of-a-kind bejeweled designer cowboy boots that easily ran ten thousands dollars a pair. She could afford them; her great-grandparents had invested heavily in the nascent West Coast oil business. Every barrel that came out of the wells by LAX helped to line her family's pockets. This was a good thing, since Skye had the academic interest of an amoeba. What she cared about was snowboarding, skiing, and staying in shape—that shape was displayed to great advantage in her custom-made, fitted Antoniette Catenacci silver gown that shimmered in the twilight, slit up both legs to reveal hand-tooled silver cowboy boots adorned with hand-painted diamond-and-ruby cowgirls.

Near Skye and Damian, standing in a little knot, were Krishna Gottesman, Jordan Jacobson, and Ashleigh Amber Anders (nicknamed "Triple A" as middle schooler for her lack of upfront assets. She'd been the first of the A-listers to pay a professional visit to Ben's father. Now, Triple A was Double D.) All three were from showbiz families. Krishna looked eerily like Tiffany-Amber Thiessen circa *Beverly Hills 90210* and was the daughter of self-help guru Howard Gottesman, whose late-night infomercials raked in a million dollars a week and were giving Tony Robbins a run for his considerable money. She was currently dating Jordan, son of a famous movie producer whose decades-long feud with Sam's father was Los Angeles legend. Jordan's father had been an early producer of Jackson's movies but then had had the temerity to beat him 6-0, 6-0 in the quarterfinals of the Beverly Hills Country Club fall club tennis championships. Jackson hadn't spoken to Mr. Jacobson since, and that had been in 1988. Jordan was a guitar player—tall, handsome, and in superb shape—and wore a Carlo Palazzi tux that looked great with Krishna's Hanae Mori Japanese-inspired jet black formal gown.

Ashleigh, like Sam, was the daughter of an actor. Her father, Charles Anders, was the same age as Jackson Sharpe. Many thought that Charles was the superior performer, particularly after he proved himself by playing Macbeth in a recent Broadway revival opposite Susan Sarandon. His current quote, however, was several million dollars below Jackson's, which Ashleigh found maddening. Ashleigh's Swedish mom, Britta, was a fashion designer. Ashleigh planned to follow in Britta's footsteps after college. She and her mother had codesigned a gown that would set off her flaming red hair—black Chinese silk brocade with a massive hot pink rose on the bodice; its leafy tendrils were green silk ribbons that curled down the front of the dress.

No one seemed to mind that Adam was late, not even Sam, who should have been more nervous because of her movie. Cammie figured it was because Sam had sent Parker's younger brother, Monty, over to Palmdale to film the B-list as they went through their prom prep. Even though time was ticking away, Sam insouciantly toted around a video camera, getting her friends' impressions of prom night. Meanwhile, one of the maids had brought out a magnum of vintage Clos du Mesnil champagne from Jackson's twenty-thousand-bottle wine cellar and had already come back once already for refills. At the far end of the driveway, so the fumes from the idling engine wouldn't bother anyone, Jackson's platinum superstretch-limo was idling in preparation for the forty-five minute trip to Palmdale.

Cammie continued to tap an impatient foot. This was getting ridiculous. Where the fuck was Adam?

"Umm, your boyfriend is AWOL," Sam intoned as she approached and focused her handheld Sony HDR-FX1 digital camcorder on Cammie.

"No problem," Cammie cooed smoothly, giving the camera her patented, sloe-eyed I'm-always-in-control look.

"Adam is always on time," Sam mused. "Didn't you guys go to dinner?"

Cammie gave the camera an above-it-all look. "Who would go to a restaurant on prom night? They're all jammed with kids from the valley. The chefs are so rushed you can't even order off the menu."

Anna stepped over to Cammie. "You should call Adam; this isn't like him."

Cammie raised her eyebrows and smiled, feigning a cool she didn't actually feel at the moment.

"I'll call his parents, then." Anna got out her cell and punched in the numbers. It irritated Cammie, but she didn't let that show on her face. It was just so Anna to jump into the fray, reminding Cammie that she'd been with Adam first. Anna probably had a decent relationship with Adam's parents, too. They probably loved *her*.

Stop, Cammie told herself. She exhaled and tried to calm down, knowing full well that she was mentally taking her pique out on Anna because she felt a bit anxious about tonight. She loved Adam as much as ever, but she knew they'd been out of sync for the last few weeks. Some of it was probably her own fault—it was like the happiness gene wasn't working for her, and she needed to replace it with the rush of chaos or the thrill of the chase.

"He's on his way," she reported. "I'm on with his father and—"

At that moment, a silver Prius rolled in through the

Sharpe estate front gate. It was Adam, and his entrance merited spontaneous applause as he stopped the car by the fountain. Damian even added a two-finger whistle as Adam hopped out of the driver's seat and hurried to Cammie.

"Man, I'm so sorry."

"Where were you?" Cammie asked, allowing him a careful kiss on her perfect lip gloss.

"I was driving my mom's Saturn and it died in the middle of Pico Boulevard," Adam explained, fumbling with his bow tie. "I wanted to call Triple A but my cell phone wasn't charged and . . ." He waved a hand. "Long, boring story. Anyway, I managed to get the car off the road, take a cab home, and get the Prius. I'm good to go."

"Good." Cammie kissed him again, for three reasons. First, she wanted to. Second, Anna was watching. Third, Sam had the camera on her again.

"Okay, we're outta here. Let's go, guys," Jordan instructed. He snapped his fingers and motioned for the limo. Two minutes later they'd all piled inside. The stocky driver shut the doors and they started to pull away, but instead of heading toward the security gate, the driver circled the fountain and turned left onto a gravel service road that led to the rear of the estate.

"'Scuse me, wrong direction!" Dee chirped.

"No it's not," Sam countered. "You didn't really think we were going to *drive*, did you? Do you know what the traffic could be like between here and Palmdale? The exhaust fumes alone could undo every oxygen facial you ever had."

The limo rounded the house, motored past the pool, tennis courts, and golf area, and stopped at the edge of Jackson's private helipad. On that helipad, a converted VH-3D twin-engine military helicopter, painted white, started its blades whirring the moment the pilot saw the limousine.

"Shut *up!*" Krishna cried happily. "We're taking a chopper!"

"How do you think my dad gets back and forth to the set?" Sam asked, smoothing her dress as the air blast from the chopper blades hit them all. "We can get there this way, but we have to limo back."

"Whatever," Ashleigh commented. "This is definitely the way to travel."

The helicopter pilot was there to greet them. With silver hair swept back from a high forehead that offset his craggy features, he looked like someone right out of central casting. "Careful of your heads, ladies and gentlemen," he called over the sound of the engines, and offered a hand to help them into the copter, a commercial version of Marine One, the official helicopter of the president of the United States.

There was plenty of room inside. The chopper had been outfitted to carry sixteen passengers plus crew. The regular seats had been taken out in favor of leather couches to which seat belts and safety harnesses had been attached. There were a big-screen TV and a small video console, along with wireless headsets for all the passengers. The interior had been dampened against noise, but there was no way to completely silence the roar of the engines or the *whup-whup* of the main blade overhead—hence the wireless headsets.

Cammie took a seat between Adam and Jack and strapped herself in; Dee was across from her, between Jack and Marshall (who did not look thrilled about their mode of transportation). To her left were Parker, Anna, and Sam. Her other friends were in a separate forward cabin. As the helicopter engines roared and Cammie felt the craft go airborne, Parker lifted the handheld camera to film them all.

"Next stop, *Ben Hur*," Sam announced happily, as they headed straight up over her father's estate. The chopper rose until Beverly Hills spread out below them like a high-priced Monopoly board, then roared forward so quickly that Cammie felt herself pushed back into the sumptuous leather seat.

Punk Boy—what was his name again? Jack!—caught Cammie's eye and jerked a thumb toward Dee. "Cute," he mouthed, since it was too loud for conversation.

"I know," Cammie mouthed back with a smile. "Hurt her and I kill you." She pointed to her own eyes with two fingers, and then to Jack. The message was clear: I'm watching you.

The flight north over the Santa Monica Mountains and through the pass to the outskirts of Palmdale took only ten minutes—far faster than a limo ride would have been, though Cammie could see that the 405 and the other freeways were clear and traffic was moving rapidly. Once they were through the mountains and into the high desert, they buzzed the Magic Mountain theme park—a kaleidoscope of color against the starkness of the landscape—and circled west, with a great nighttime view of the space shuttle's secondary landing strip at Edwards Air Force base to the north.

Five minutes later, they hovered directly over a movie set replica of the Colosseum of Rome, as if that storied edifice were still a fully functional sports arena. The parking lot was full of cars, vans, and limos; Cammie watched dozens of gawking classmates as they dropped down toward an illuminated concrete helipad a few hundred yards from the Colosseum. To the left of the helipad were the four black limousines that would squire each of the couples—in Dee's case, a peculiar trio—to Hermosa Beach for the after party and then home.

The helipad had been roped off with a red-velvet barrier; security guards from the movie studio were stationed every ten feet. As the pilot gently touched down, Cammie saw the early prom arrivals gather to see who was making such a spectacular entrance.

Like there'd ever been any question.

Jackson Sharpe's remake of *Ben-Hur* was already the buzz of Hollywood, mostly because of accounting figures leaked from the production office—the budget had already escalated from a hundred and twenty million to a hundred and forty million dollars, and that was before publicity and advertising were taken into account. Word was that dialogue was disappearing from the script in favor of more and more action, on the theory that overseas territories cared little for the nuances of English language. They mostly wanted to see shit blow up. Since serious pyrotechnics had been an impossibility in the first century, in their place was a grossly inflated, very bloody body count.

Jackson was playing the title role of Ben-Hur, which in the famous 1959 version (the story had already been filmed twice in the very early days of Tinseltown) had been brought to life by Charlton Heston. The story was an epic tale of a boyhood friendship between Ben-Hur and his former friend Messala. The action culminated in a chariot race between them in the Colosseum.

Once the helicopter blades stopped, the pilot opened the passenger doors and helped everyone down. Sam had specified that a red carpet lead from the helipad to the entrance to the Colosseum, and the prom weenies had done their job well. Monty Pinelli—Parker's younger brother who was nowhere as cute as Parker, with his stocky build, big nose, and somewhat unkempt appearance despite a Ralph Lauren tuxedo that Sam had rented for him—was stationed at the far end of the red carpet to film their arrival. Krishna gave him a kiss as they passed; Monty blushed happily.

The producers of *Ben-Hur* had spared no expense in building a Colosseum for the seminal chariot-race scene, except to construct the structure of wood with false fronts instead of the original marble used two thousand years ago. The exterior wasn't much to look at, since it wouldn't be seen in the film—any exterior shots would be done with a miniature model in the studio. The interior, though, was dazzling from the moment Cammie stepped inside, and that was without considering any of the prom decorations.

The floor of the Colosseum was some sort of brown synthetic substance mixed with tiny silicon balls (the better to reflect movie lights and to absorb any stray moisture—chariot racing in mud was not what Jackson had in mind). It covered the length of two football fields. One half of the building was given over to camera towers, a production office, and all the various and sundry spaces that were necessary to produce an action epic: makeup trailers, a commissary that was doubling for the evening as the caterers' headquarters, costume headquarters, even a stable in which the teams of horses used in the race could be kept.

The opposite side of the building, though, was a meticulously crafted vision of a first-century Roman stadium. There was tiered seating that could hold thirty thousand extras, columns by the hundreds, and arches by the dozens, with a marble royal reviewing stand that covered a quarter of the bottom tier of seats. At the far end of the structure were two matching sets of columned arches through which the chariot race would start, while the center of the racetrack was dominated by a long and narrow formal garden containing enormous statues of Roman leaders, generals, and caesars. The gardens served the same purpose as the infield at the thoroughbred track Hollywood Park.

The entire arena was lit by an array of steel football-stadium lighting towers. There was also a concert-quality sound system that had been erected for the band. After having nixed any number of possibilities, Sam had suggested that they bring in Slick Willy, a new British band that was reviving Beatles haircuts along with a good-time party sound; their first CD, *Manchester Disunited,* was number one in Britain but just beginning to cross over into America. Cammie had called Dee's father, the record producer. He was so happy that his daughter was mentally healthy enough to attend prom that he twisted arms, pulled strings, arranged for a private jet to fly the band over, and it was a done deal. The band was playing its heart out on a stage erected at the opposite end of the track from where the chariot racers would enter.

"You rock, girl!" Cammie heard Jack tell Sam, as the group—trailed by Monty—got past the last phalanx of security and joined the throng already inside the arena. At the front gate, ordinary promgoers parted like the Red Sea to let the A-listers pass.

"This is totally off the hook," Adam chuckled, surveying the Colosseum. All the parts that weren't being used had been draped in blue and white fabric, the BHHS school colors. "Back in Michigan, they had prom in the gym with a disco ball."

"I thought that kind of thing was only urban legend," Cammie teased.

He grinned at her. "For a girl who wasn't into prom, you sure look happy."

For some reason, Cammie now felt determined to be on her best behavior and mend things. It was prom night, for God's sake. She slid her arms around his neck. "Because I'm with you."

Such a simple, declarative statement and yet so hard for her to say. Why did it all get so complicated? Why couldn't a girl just love a boy and have the boy love her back? She so wanted to believe that she wasn't too fucked up to have that, for the first time in her life—to have it with Adam. Before she could summon up her nerve to tackle the pile of unspoken shit that still stood between her and Adam, Jack found her.

"Listen, I'm feeling your girl, Dee," he confided, thumping his chest with his fist.

"Excellent."

"But what's up with Napoleon D over there?" Jack cocked his head toward Marshall, who stood with Dee on the parameter of the parquet dance floor near the band.

"Her mental-health bodyguard," Cammie quipped.

"No, really. The girl's in an institution?"

"Something like that. Temporarily."

"Well, I like a woman with a past. How do we ditch him?"

"I'll leave that in your capable hands," Cammie replied. "Let's see how motivated you are. And how well you treat her."

"Very to both," Jack replied easily.

"Dee's been through some tough stuff," Adam put in. "Go easy, huh?"

"Hey, easy is my middle name." Jack winked and headed back toward Dee.

"Yeah, I bet." Adam frowned as Jack walked away. "You trust that guy?"

Cammie took his arm. "No need to worry. Jack will make Dee feel desirable and hot, and Marshall won't let Dee out of his sight. It's a win-win." She took a deep breath. "Want to go up to the bleachers for a minute? I think we need to talk."

A-List-worthy

"Sam, wow. This is the most killer prom ever!"

"You rock, Sam. Thank you so much for making this prom so special!"

"Sam, you built a Roman bath! That was so smart!"

"One for the guys and one for the girls. And one that's coed!"

"And chariot rides outside for everyone! Way cool."

"I always thought you didn't even have any school spirit, Sam, but I was totally wrong. This rocks!"

Sam Sharpe had nothing if not a great appreciation of irony, and that appreciation was certainly kicking in. Classmates with whom she'd never had a conversation, whom she'd never normally deign to speak to, and who knew better than to start a conversation with her were rushing up to her to gush no more than two sentences of praise—all they probably thought they could get away with—to thank her for saving the prom. No, not just saving it—making it into a true A-list-worthy extravaganza.

To the south of the arena, Sam had had a full-fledged Roman bathhouse constructed by the movie's production designers, complete with showers, hot tubs, and portable swimming pools, along with individual terry cloth robes personalized with each prom attendee's name and *BHHS Prom* in Roman-style calligraphy. Promgoers could indeed choose the guys', girls', or coed facilities. Outside of the arena, horse-drawn chariots piloted by Italian models (some male, some female) in skimpy togas were squiring couples and quartets on a mile-long path through the hills. Meanwhile, all the food was being cooked on enormous open pits, in keeping with the *Ben-Hur* theme.

"Big smile, Sam Sharpe!" crowed one of the event photographers, a tuxedoed older woman with a shaved head. Sam smiled as Old Baldy popped off a few shots before Fee and Jazz edged their way into the viewfinder. They each still carried their videocams, identical Sony models to Sam's.

"How'd the filming go?" Sam asked them.

"Fantastic!" Jazz gushed. "We had a bunch of friends come over to do our prom prep—we even had a makeup artist! We got the whole thing on film."

"I'm sorry I ever thought you were a snob," Fee told Sam earnestly.

"Me too," Jazz added. "I hate judgmental people and then I totally judged you. I'd just like to apologize."

"Ditto," Fee agreed.

"What can I tell you, girls, I was just overcome with

school spirit," Sam responded, managing to sound suitably sincere. A pang of something close to shame hit her. Jazz and Fee were actually very sweet—not so different from Sam and her friends, except economically. She was glad all over again that she'd changed the thrust of her documentary. It would have been unfair to bash Fee and Jazz.

Twenty feet away, Monty had the camera trained on the three of them. Sam's instructions had been clear: Focus on other people, not herself. She didn't want any more footage of herself at the actual event and detested documentarians like Michael Moore and Morgan Spurlock who insisted on making themselves the center of their work. Who did they think they were, Jonas Salk? That was why she'd asked Monty to troll around with the other camera for a while, to try to record some candid moments of the crowd.

"Students, students!" The acerbic voice of Mr. Vorhees, their vice principal, boomed out over the public address system, getting their attention. "Students, be sure to drop your vote for prom queen into the ballot box within the next half hour!"

Behind Mr. Vorhees, the band smirked. Vorhees was a tall man who looked about eight months pregnant; the belt to his tux pants lost somewhere underneath his stomach. "We'll count the ballots and announce your prom court at eleven o'clock. Good luck to one and all!"

Fee and Jazz both looked thrilled at the mention of the prom court; it actually meant something to them. Sam scrutinized the two girls. Fee wore an off-the-rack

Armani strapless royal-blue matte jersey gown—there was also a blue flower Sam couldn't name in the center of her wrist corsage. Evidently some serious color-coordination planning had taken place. Her hair was done in curls; Sam supposed that she'd been looking for sexy and messy. She'd almost gotten there.

As for Jazz, she'd chosen a diagonal pastel rainbow-striped Chloé knockoff; Sam had seen the cocktail-length designer version on Kate Hudson at Koi the week before. The dress did nothing for Jazz, though, other than emphasize her lack of bust. Though Jazz's hair was freshly streaked and flatironed, new bangs only drew attention to the fact that her nose was a little too long for her face. She needed Raymond of Beverly Hills for a consultation and a style, and Gillian to shop for her.

"Do you think you have a shot at prom queen?" Sam asked Fee.

"Oh, I'd *never* get voted to the court," Fee insisted. "Jazz, maybe."

"That's *totally* not true," Jazz countered. "Everyone is *totally* going to vote for you for court!"

"You!"

"No, *you!*"

Sam sighed. It was B-list de rigueur for girls to insist that they couldn't *possibly* get voted to prom court, because they shared some kind of unwritten rule that they weren't supposed to appear to have egos. Sam's own friends, though, would be the first to say that while they deserved to be prom queen—after all, they were the cutest, hottest, and coolest girls in the school—they would never actually *be* prom queen because they were above such drivel and everyone knew it.

After a few more questions, Fee's and Jazz's dates drifted over to try to join the conversation. Fee had ended up coming with Miles Goldstein, who had pitched a hissy fit in the principal's office when he found out that he was on track merely to be salutatorian instead of valedictorian, while Jazz's date was Roman Hoopes, an aspiring white rap promoter whose original name was Richard but who'd changed it to Roman because he thought that sounded more dope.

The arrival of the two guys was Sam and Parker's signal to depart—they drifted over to the production side of the arena without even thinking about voting. Sam settled into the Barcalounger reserved for her father and happily put her feet up. Meanwhile, Parker sat in the director's chair, pulled out his flask of Chivas, and passed it to Sam. She threw back a long swallow; it burned going down, but in a good way.

"Your film is going to rock," he told her, then took the flask and swallowed lustily. "Chivas. Better than mead."

"Let me be the judge of that," she teased, taking the flask back and drinking some more.

Parker gave Sam a serious look. "You know, Sam, you look really hot tonight."

Sam would never admit it, but hearing Parker say that

gave her a little thrill. From a purely physical point of view, he was easily the best-looking guy at prom. If only he could magically morph into Eduardo.

"Too bad your guy crapped out on you," Parker went on, as if reading her mind.

How irritating. It wasn't like she wasn't already thinking about just that.

"Eduardo didn't 'crap out on me.' He had a family engagement."

Parker shrugged and reached for the vodka. "He's missing something great. Look out there, Sam. Look."

She looked. The party was in full swing, with hundreds of her classmates dancing to the band. Most were in formalwear, some were in bathrobes from the Roman baths. They were laughing, smoking, eating, having the time of their lives. Though Monty and the prom weenies were out there shooting, she got her handheld and took some more footage. The more she looked through the lens, the more she felt that she had the makings of a great documentary on her hands. Still, she felt the loss of Eduardo so much that she belted down another huge shot.

"You did this, Sam. If you were my girlfriend, I'd figure out a way to do whatever I needed to do to be here for you."

Please. She knew how good Parker was at acting— witness the fact that he'd passed himself off as a rich kid for so long without anyone figuring it out but her.

"Don't bother sucking up, Parker."

Parker shook his head. "Man, you always think everyone is using you."

"Because they usually are."

Out near the gardens at the center of the track, Sam spotted Anna wandering around, alone. Strange. Why hadn't Ben shown up yet?

"You're right," Parker acknowledged. "They are. Look, I'm gonna go get something to eat and find Damian. Then I'll do some more filming. Okay?"

"Okay," she told him, reminding herself to keep her eye on the prize. Her cell rang as Parker loped away.

"Yeah?" she answered.

"How's prom?" The voice was lightly accented, deep, and sexy.

Eduardo.

"Not as good as if you were here," Sam responded, thrilled that he had called her. "You can't imagine what that voice does to me."

"Alas, I'm stuck in Mexico with the family. Miss me?"

Sam nodded, even though Eduardo couldn't see her. "Yup. Definitely."

"Is it fun anyway?"

"Sure." Sam watched Parker talk for a moment with his brother. "There's the afterparty on the beach; it's the set of *Hermosa Beach*."

"Ah yes, I know where Hermosa Beach is," Eduardo said.

"Someone will probably have sex with someone and regret it afterward, some longtime couple will break up badly, and a lot of someones will have way too much to drink," Sam quipped. "Prom with all its trimmings is an American institution, after all. How's your party?"

"Very large," Eduardo replied. "Maybe three hundred people. I am related to half of them—I have a very large family—and every lady over the age of sixty wants to pinch my cheek and tell me what a handsome young man I've grown into."

Sam laughed. "Sounds deadly."

"It's all right. Anyway, I just wanted to tell you I was thinking of you and I'll see you when I get back to Los Angeles for work. I'm really looking forward to the summer."

His words were perfect; they brought myriad images to her mind: being in bed with him at the hotel. Making love. Making love again. No image was as strong, though, as the dozen tulips in the vase. That he'd remembered her favorite flower when she'd only mentioned it once seemed to encapsulate everything that she adored about him.

Which was why she responded, "Me too."

Anna had been drifting around the Colosseum for the past hour, watching prom unfold but not really feeling a part of it. The guy she loved was at a different party with a different girl. She told herself it didn't matter, that having Ben put in an appearance with Maddy had been her own idea, but she wondered now whether she had been more stupid than selfless. Ben was a guy, after all. She'd seen how Maddy had looked after her prom makeover. *God.* She'd been partly responsible for that, too.

Mr. Vorhees had just made what he'd claimed to be

his last announcement for prom court voting. Anna figured she might as well cast her ballot. The voting area was below the twin arches at the north end of the Colosseum; she wended her way through the crowd, found a ballot and looked it over.

Who to vote for? On a whim, she scrawled in Dee's name and stuffed the paper in a ballot box watched over by Fee and Jazz. The new and improved Dee was someone Anna actually liked—at least, could possibly like, if she had a chance to get to know her better.

After that she didn't know what to do, so she found a quiet spot away from the band and watched people she barely knew dance, laugh, fight—all the things couples did on prom night. Her high school back in New York had been as cliquey as anyplace, yes, but she'd known almost everyone, having gone to school with many of her classmates for years. Here, she'd come in as the new girl and would go out as the new girl, notable only because she'd been taken in by Sam Sharpe and had hooked up with Ben Birnbaum. Would anybody even remember her for who she was? It seemed doubtful.

She drifted toward the dance floor. Dee and Jack were together, diminutive Dee snuggled up against Jack. Marshall stood near the stage, moving to and fro in an effort to keep Dee in his sightline. Damian and Ashleigh were dancing; Jordan and Skye were macking, even though they were no longer a couple. Even Parker and Sam were out there. The only ones not around were Skye, Cammie, and Adam. To think she'd had qualms about how Cammie might flirt with Ben. He wasn't even around to participate in that possibility.

Anna couldn't help it; her mind went back to her first date with Ben, when he'd abandoned her on his father's boat at two o'clock in the morning. A tiny part of her would always wonder if he'd do such a thing again; if, in fact, he was doing such a thing right this very moment. She wouldn't put it past him. With the new Maddy and his history—

No. There he was. Striding toward the dance floor, looking more perfect in his Armani tux than any boy she'd ever seen before. A lock of his brown hair flopped onto his forehead; his eyes searched everywhere.

For me, Anna thought, and her heart swelled and her face broke into a giant smile. *He's looking for me.*

She rose to meet him, ashamed of her feelings of the moment before and so glad that she had shared them with no one. Then he was there, and it felt as if there was no one there but the two of them; the rest of the world slipped away.

"This is a very Cinderella moment," she teased.

"The *Caligula* version," he joked back. But the look in his eyes told her how important the moment was to him, too. "You look amazing."

"How many other prom dates have you said that to this evening?"

He slipped his arms around her waist. "Wait till you hear about Maddy and her crush."

Anna arched a brow. "On you?"

"Oh, no, not me. I was merely a pawn in her chess game of love. Or lust. I can't figure out which one." He tugged her toward the dance floor. "Come on. I want to dance with the most beautiful princess in the empire."

The Vicinity of Her Heart

I t took quite a while for Cammie and Adam to wend their way through the crowd. Rather than a buffet table—*so* Club Med—Sam had directed that waitstaff dressed as gladiators and wenches circulate among the guests, offering a variety of grilled Italian hors d'oeuvres—tiny *bruschetta al forno* (native plum tomatoes marinated in fresh basil, chopped garlic, and extravirgin olive oil on focaccia squares topped with Belesca-grated mozzarella cheese), crab cakes served with a fennel-and-pepper topping, scallops wrapped in Italian bacon and mesclun greens, jumbo shrimp marinated in horseradish with lemons and Grey Goose vodka, and mushrooms stuffed with smoked Gouda and a salmon demiglace.

"Scallop?" A curvaceous, raven-haired gladiator/waitress stepped in front of Cammie, holding out the tray. "They're prepared in—"

"Already know, no thank you, but thanks for the offer," Adam told her with a grin.

"How about a drink?" the waitress offered.

Cammie shook her head. "Maybe later."

They continued making their way through the crowd, passing the granite tables that supported the goodie bags each prom guest would take home. In a rough muslin bag (that had been Sam's idea, too, as she reasoned that velvet had not yet been invented in the first century) each guest whether male or female—the bags were unisex by design—would find two coveted tickets to the *Ben-Hur* premiere slated for next summer at the Kodak Theatre, a set of twenty-four-karat hammered-gold earrings and cuff links handmade in Milan, a minivial of Jackson Sharpe's new signature cologne, a new iPod with fifty Slick Willy songs already loaded, and an official limited-edition *Ben-Hur* satin baseball jacket with the Beverly Hills High School coat of arms embroidered on the chest.

Finally, they reached the base of the north-end bleachers, where they found an assortment of faux-marble roundtop tables and gold lamé–covered chairs. Each table had a custom centerpiece—a collector's edition of the 1959 *Ben-Hur* script signed by its director, William Wyler, plus replicas of props from that film.

"So, what's up?" Adam asked, as he pulled out a chair for Cammie, and then sat next to her.

Cammie couldn't believe she was actually nervous enough to clear her throat. "We haven't really talked about that stupid fight on the beach the other day."

"It's okay. It's over. We're good, right?" He scratched the little star tattoo behind his ear—the way he always did when he was nervous.

Well, fine. At least she wasn't the only one. "I overre-acted," Cammie admitted. "I guess . . ." This was harder than she'd thought it would be.

She started again. "I think about my mother," she murmured. "A lot, actually. I'm . . . so used to doing it in private, inside my head. I guess . . . with what you said . . . I felt kind of invaded. Or something."

Adam reached for her hand. "I shouldn't have sprung it on you like that, Cam."

He scratched the tattoo again. Cammie wondered why.

"Cam, there's something I need to . . . shit."

An alarm went off somewhere in the vicinity of her heart. "What's wrong?"

"Nothing."

"Bullshit. What?" she demanded.

Adam let go of her hand and got to his feet. "Let's go dance. We've only got one senior prom. It's not that important. We can talk later."

"Adam, you're a terrible actor. Is this about what you were talking about on the beach? My mom?"

He nodded, looking miserable. "Kind of."

"Something bad?"

"I don't know. Maybe." He shook his head and ran a hand through his spiky hair. "Damn, I fucked this up. I just wanted us to have the greatest prom night. I blew it. Let's just go dance. I *promise* we'll talk later."

For a brief moment, Cammie was tempted to go with him, because she sensed that whatever it was, once she heard it, her night—and maybe even her life—would not be the same. But she couldn't help herself.

"Whatever this is . . . how did you find out?"

"My parents."

Eight years of fear, anguish, and uncertainty over her mother's death welled up inside her. "You got information from your *parents*? And you didn't tell me?"

Adam edged the tip of his tux shoes into the earthen floor of the Colosseum. "I pretty much hate me right now, if that makes you feel any better."

Cammie pushed him. "Fuck that. I don't *care*. Just tell me."

"Not here. Later. Tomorrow—"

"Now."

"Cam, please. You have to see it for yourself."

Cammie stiffened. There was something for her to see?

"What is it? And *where* is it?"

"My house." Adam hesitated. "My room. Geez, Cam—"

"Shut up." She raised a trembling palm to him. "I'm going to your house, Adam. You can come along or not."

Lean and Hungry and Hot

"So that's how I ended up in Ojai," Dee concluded. She and Jack were walking together on the wood-chip–strewn path that away led from the Colosseum set toward the temporary Roman bath-house. Every so often they had to move to one side of the path to let a horse-drawn chariot pass. Inside each chariot was a bucket of rose petals—they'd already been showered twice by laughing students coming back from the bathhouse, either in their prom clothes or in their new custom-made robes.

The night was calm and clear, with so many more stars than in the light-polluted skies of Beverly Hills that Jack could point out the Milky Way. The only dis-cordant thing was how Marshall trailed them like an overzealous bodyguard with a rock star client.

"You've really been through it," Jack commented.

"Yeah," Dee agreed, "but it was worth it. I feel lucky and grateful now. Lots of people helped me, and my true friends stayed my friends all the time I was weird. Like, when you're different, usually people will just turn away."

Damn. What Dee was saying really hit home with Jack. People turned away from his sister, Margie— practically shunned her—all the time.

"I think I know what you're going through," he murmured.

"Really?" Dee asked. "How?"

There was something about Dee's forthrightness that made Jack want to be up front. He started telling a story he rarely told—the story of his sister—and didn't finish until fifteen minutes later, when they'd found seats on a bench by the entrance to the bathhouse. All the while, Dee listened intently. Meanwhile, Marshall had the discretion to stay out of earshot, if not sightline. When Jack finished, Dee's gaze was steady.

"She's so lucky to have you for a brother," Dee declared.

It was so clear that she meant it. *Oh no.* This was not how it was supposed to be. Blind dates sucked. When it turned out that Cammie had been telling the truth, that Dee was quite the cute little package, he'd been pleasantly surprised and had immediately considered the possibility of bagging a richie-rich Beverly Hills girl. Dee was older than Maddy, after all. More worldly, he figured. Why not give it a go?

The problem was, the more time Jack spent with Dee, the more he found himself *liking* her. She was nice, sweet, certainly smart enough, and had a childlike enthusiasm for life. Her honesty was both disconcerting and damned attractive. As the evening had progressed, he found himself genuinely caring about Dee. Worse than that, he felt *protective*. Protective had not been in the game plan at all.

The moon reflected in her azure eyes; he gently raised her chin with his forefinger. He was just about to kiss her when the crunch-crunch of feet on the path was followed by a pale hand karate-chopping the air between them. Dee was so startled she screamed. Jack's instant reaction was to jump the guy to protect Dee . . . until he saw it was Marshall.

"What the hell was that for?" Jack barked.

"You could be passing illegal substances from your mouth to hers," Marshall shot back so intently that the next thing Jack expected was for his Miranda rights to be read to him.

Only Marshall was no cop, which let Jack fire back. "Only if my *tongue* is illegal, dickhead."

The chaperone was undeterred. "Rules are rules."

"Come on, Marshall," Dee pleaded. "Have a heart. Couldn't you maybe bend them a little? Like, check our mouths for contraband?"

Marshall shook his head. "It's my job."

"Job this." Jack gave Marshall a one-finger salute, thoroughly irritated. Then he took Dee's hand. "Let's go back to the Colosseum. At least the Thought Police will let us dance."

They walked around to the front of the bathhouse and climbed up into one of the waiting chariots. Their chariot driver announced his name, Antonio—six feet, two inches of curly-haired, chiseled Italian muscle in an undersize toga that revealed how much time he'd spent in the gym. Dee's eyes, though, were on Jack all the way, which made him feel great.

The ride back to the Colosseum took only a couple of minutes. Just outside the entrance was an incongruous row of green Porta Pottis used by the film-production crew. As Antonio helped them down from the chariot, Dee announced that she had to use the facilities. She excused herself and stepped into one of the portable bathrooms; Marshall took the opportunity to visit another. Jack was surprised the guy didn't ask Dee to collect her fallout for urinalysis.

"'Zup?"

Jack turned; it was the dude who was Sam Sharpe's date. What was his name again?

"Parker Pinelli," the guy filled in.

"Yeah, right. Not much, man. Where's your lady?"

"Sam? Chicks on the prom committee dragged her off somewhere." Parker glanced around, saw no prom chaperones were in sight, and took out his flask. "Me and Sam pretty much killed it, but there's some left. Chivas." He held it out to Jack.

Jack shook his head. He had the sense that Dee would prefer it if he stayed sober. Marshall too.

"Mind?" Parker unscrewed the top.

"Go for it," Jack said. "But watch the door to that one." He cocked his chin toward the green door behind which Marshall was otherwise engaged. "Dee's jailer is in there. He'll probably call out the National Guard if he sees you."

"Thanks for the heads up." Parker tilted his head and drank. "So, Cammie hooked you up with Dee, huh? What do you think?"

Jack nodded. "Great chick. Except for that asshole Marshall, this would be sweet."

"Maybe we can find a way to lose him before the after party. We're going to Hermosa Be–"

The door to Marshall's Porta Potti opened; Parker smoothly pocketed his flask before Dee's chaperone could get a foot back on the ground. Nonetheless, Marshall approached them warily, sniffing the air like a rookie bloodhound. "Is that *liquor* on the wind?"

"I think so," Parker reported earnestly. "Some girls just walked by with a bottle of contraband tequila. They went back toward the bathhouse. If I were you, I'd give chase."

"I have to do my duty," Marshall murmured, looking around. "Speaking of . . . where's Dee?"

"You just missed her," Parker fabricated, hitching a thumb at the entrance to the Colosseum. "She went inside to find Sam. You oughta head in there. Who knows what trouble she could get into? I mean, dude, it's a *zoo*."

"She didn't wait for me? She *knows* she's supposed to wait for me!" Marshall's nostrils quivered. "Excuse me."

As he strode off with razor-sharp precision toward the entrance to the Colosseum, Jack cracked up. "Thanks, man. You're a hell of an actor."

Parker folded his arms. "So, I hear you're working on some reality thing at Fox."

"I'm just interning for the summer." Jack's voice dropped lower. "But I pitched a big idea to my boss and she loved it. I call it *The Pickup Artist.* Guys see how many hot girls they can pick up; people at home vote on who got the hottest girl; that kind of thing. She's giving me a lot of time to work on it."

"Yeah?" Parker looked impressed, as Dee stepped out of her Porta Potti, the squeaky door echoing in the night. "Tell me more."

"Sorry that took so long." Dee looked around for her chaperone. "Where's Marshall?"

"Your genius friend here ditched him for us," Jack explained.

He was getting an idea. This guy Parker was perfect— really killer looking and clearly a terrific actor. He had a lean and hungry look in his eyes that Jack recognized from his own bathroom mirror. They were the eyes of burning ambition: someone on the outside, looking in.

"I need to talk to Parker for a few minutes," Jack squeezed her fingers lightly. "Can we hook up by the refreshments in, like, five?"

Dee hesitated, then flashed Jack a radiant smile. "Definitely."

"Five minutes, no more." Jack pointed to his watch, a utilitarian Coleman brand that he'd bought at Target because it had been highly rated for longevity. When you grew up like he did, you didn't waste money on stupid things like trying to impress people with your freaking watch.

"Excellent." Dee gave a shy little wave and walked away.

"She's different," Parker noted. "From how she was before, I mean. Good different. Maybe you bring out the best in her, huh?"

Jack studied Parker carefully. "You're a professional actor, right?"

"Yeah."

"I'm thinking about shooting a quick pilot for my idea; so I can show my boss what I've got in mind. Those suits are lazy; they don't read. They like to see it on the screen. Maybe I'll call you about it. Interested?"

Parker's "definitely" came so fast that Jack upped the blond boy's ambition quotient to the top quintile.

Jack checked his watch again. One minute to when he said he'd meet Dee. *Gotta hustle.* He clapped his potential employee on the back. "Glad I met you, man."

"Same here." Parker plucked a cheap business card with his name and phone number on it out of his pocket; Jack realized that Parker must carry these cards everywhere, always prepared for his big break.

Huh. Jack studied the card for a moment. It's perfect, he thought. Parker thinks he's using me, and I think I'm using him. In fact, we're using each other.

How Hollywood.

Long Blond Hair Down to Her Butt

The girl stood by the massive oak door all the way across the crowded living room—beyond his aunts and uncles and cousins, beyond his grandmother and his mother, even beyond his father, who was passing out Partagas Serie D cigars made in Havana, Cuba, to all the men at the fiesta.

She was the most beautiful girl Eduardo had ever seen.

Her long white-blond hair fell in a waterfall to the small of her back. Her cheekbones were two baby apples, her lips two silken pillows, her sooty-lashed eyes surprisingly dark against pale skin. A swanlike neck led to graceful shoulders, which curved into full, luscious breasts. Her waist was minuscule, really; it swelled to smallish hips and then to long, coltish legs that went on forever. Her dress was shimmering gold, tight around her hips.

She was ravishing. A Catalonian goddess.

As if pulled by some unseen force, Eduardo made his way to her. "Who are you?" he whispered.

"Pilar."

She was a cousin's friend, something like that. The details didn't matter. Pilar. My God, she was perfect; everything Eduardo had ever dreamed of.

He asked her to dance. She put her hand in his; he led her to the ballroom, where the twelve-piece orchestra his father had engaged was playing "Some Enchanted Evening." Her body pressed against his. Words were unnecessary. She was Pilar. Pilar the Perfect. There was no other girl but her in the universe.

After three or four songs, they drifted outside to the gazebo to sip champagne. Another cousin asked Eduardo blithely about his American girlfriend. Samantha, was that her name?

Pilar waited to see what Eduardo would say.

"Samantha *who*?" he breathed.

"Students and faculty, ladies and gentlemen, gather round!" Vice principal Vorhees's voice boomed out from the public address system. "Gather round, gather round! It's time to announce your fiftieth-anniversary prom court!"

The amplified voice shook Sam out of her fantasy. No, nightmare. Something about Eduardo and some perfect bitch named Pilar. What a horror. The last thing she remembered, she'd been thinking about Eduardo at his party. Then she'd seen the dark-haired waitress in the golden toga with the impossibly long legs. Then her mind had started to race, worry, invent.

Pilar. Where the hell had Sam even come up with that

name? Did she trust Eduardo so little that she'd picture him with someone like *Pilar*?

Vorhees went back to the mike, as few of the thousand prom guests seemed to be paying attention to his summons. "Gather round, gather round! It's time for your fiftieth-anniversary prom court!" He motioned to the band, which struck up a ragged version of the Beverly Hills High School fight song.

Focus, Sam told herself. This was the coronation of the prom queen, the culmination of the night. She'd planned on her documentary storyboard to intercut moments from this coronation through the film—she was toying with the idea of starting with it, in fact. She wanted close-ups of various queen hopefuls as they tried to hide just how badly they wanted that stupid crown on their heads. Sam scanned the crowd, which was clustering by the stage. Where was Parker? Where was Monty? She wanted to get as much film of this moment as possible; multiple camera angles of the moment when hopefully either Fee or Jazz would be named queen of the prom.

Ah. There was Monty, exactly in the position she'd assigned him—behind one of the huge black subwoofer speakers on the stage, with a telephoto lens so he could come in tight on the triumphant winner. Where the hell was Parker?

As Sam watched, two of Fee and Jazz's prom-weenie friends practically danced across the stage to the vice principal. They held a gargantuan envelope in the school colors that presumably held the names of this year's prom queen and king. When the vice principal took the envelope, Hollywood premiere–style spotlights pre-positioned on the Colosseum floor burst forth, their beams splitting the sky. Meanwhile, two more spotlights came together on Vorhees, who puffed out his chest a little. The bemused Slick Willy drummer let forth a thirty-second drumroll that ended with the loudest cymbal crash in history.

"It's a pleasure to announce your prom court," Vorhees intoned, trying to build the tension by slowly tearing the envelope open and feigning having difficulty reading the names on it. "Our first two prom princesses are Stephanie Epstein and Katelynn Thistle-Phelps!"

Two prom committee girls—friends of Fee and Jazz in variations on black de la Renta and Armani, respectively—bounded up to the stage to polite applause. Each received a bouquet of long-stemmed roses from Slick Willy's mop-headed lead singer. Sam caught Monty's eye and pointed toward the singer to make sure Monty got the moment on film.

Vorhees quieted the rowdy crowd. "Our last princess is . . . Ophelia Berman, escorted by Miles Goldstein!"

There was louder applause this time, as Fee took Miles's arm and ascended the stage. Sam found that she was glad for Fee but aggravated that Monty couldn't cover Fee and shoot Jazz's reaction at the same time. Why wasn't Parker where he was supposed to be? At least Jazz was still carrying her handheld camera and filming her friend's moment of glory.

The new prom court assembled behind the vice principal. "And now, students and honored guests, the moment you've all been waiting for."

Sam took one last look around. No Parker. *Damn* him.

Vorhees dug into the oversized envelope for one last sheet of paper. "For your fiftieth-anniversary prom queen and king . . . it's an honor to present to you Samantha Sharpe and Parker Pinelli!"

What?

Amid deafening applause, Sam stood frozen to the spot. She couldn't possibly have heard what she thought she had heard.

Suddenly, she felt Jazz's arms surround her. "We all voted for you, Sammy!" she cried.

"There wouldn't have been prom without you!" someone else yelled, and then the accolades came fast and furious as Jazz used her handheld to film Sam's stunned reaction.

"You rock! You saved our prom! Go, Sam! Go on up there, prom queen!"

No, no, this was impossible. *Me?*

Somehow, Sam's legs took her toward the stage. Parker materialized from the opposite direction, taking the stairs two at a time before meeting Sam with an Academy Award–winning grin and dipping her backward in an Old Hollywood–style kiss. Then the vice principal and Ophelia draped him in a prom king sash.

The applause and whistles grew even louder when

Slick Willy segued into a punk version of the old Miss America theme song. "Oh, great. *Now* you show up," Sam managed to hiss at Parker, away from the microphone.

"Come on, Sam," Parker cajoled. "You're the queen. Enjoy it."

When he righted her, last year's prom queen—Ivory Maxwell, the beautiful blond daughter of a horror flick director—placed the tiara with BHH in blue encrusted rhinestones on Sam's head.

"Congratulations," Ivory, who was an aspiring actress, told Sam. "Let's do lunch sometime."

"Speech, speech!" The cry went up from the crowd that pressed forward against the stage, but before Sam could make a decision about whether to say a few words—she wasn't sure she could even put together a sentence with both a subject and a predicate—Fee stepped up to the microphone.

"I think we all know that Sam Sharpe single-handedly saved our prom," Fee recounted into the mike, the words echoing around the Colosseum, every head in the place nodding fervently. "I mean, how great is this? Here we are on the set of Jackson Sharpe's next unbelievable movie. Sam, we all just want to thank you for taking lemons and making lemonade!"

The crowd roared. Sam saw Anna and Ben—they were beaming and applauding. Damian, Jordan, Skye—everyone was cheering.

The strangest thing happened. The omnipresent

voice in her head that always said that she wasn't cute enough to be the queen of anything fell silent.

Here she was, with the crown to prove it and the hottest boy at Beverly Hills High with an arm around her waist. For a brief, singular moment in time, Sam Sharpe didn't just feel happy—she felt beautiful.

The feeling was gone in an instant—when Monty stepped out from behind the big speaker. The red light of his camera reminded Sam that the magic minute was being recorded for posterity.

Oh shit on a shingle. The film.

Sam knew she couldn't be prom queen in her own movie. The judges would die laughing. Nor could she do the movie without including this section—you couldn't have a prom without a prom queen. What kind of a documentary would that be?

Damn, damn, damn. All that work, all that planning, all those storyboards. Right down the goddamn drain.

A few moments later, Parker helped Sam down the wooden ramp to the golden chariot drawn by four snow-white horses, conducted by a quartet of Roman gladiators in golden helmets. There would be a royal victory lap around the racetrack.

"Where did you disappear to before?" She asked Parker as he helped her into the carriage. Not that it mattered anymore. But she needed to focus on something besides her now-dead-in-the water documentary.

"I was with Jazz and Fee, trying to stop this *disaster*," he explained. "They came to me all atwitter and said that everyone was voting for you. I told them you didn't want to be queen, but they wouldn't listen. I tried, though."

Her anger at Parker dissipated like helium through a four-day-old balloon, and she mustered the energy to wave mechanically to her classmates as they whistled and applauded the passing carriage. The fireworks she'd arranged for went off, exploding in confetti rainbows in the sky. Sam appreciated irony more than most, and the ironies of the situation were overwhelming. Fate had conspired against her. Her documentary was finished. She could have accepted that. What was impossible to accept was that for one brief moment in time, Sam Sharpe had been chosen the fairest of them all, and the one person she really wished had been there to experience it with her—Eduardo—was two thousand miles away.

Thread by Thread

The forty-five-minute limo ride back from Palmdale had been a grim and silent affair. Cammie had made sure there was space between them on the white leather seat. The chill in the air had nothing to do with air-conditioning.

Now they were inside Adam's house, on the green leather sectional couch in the family room. The room was so cozy—stone fireplace, a big-screen TV, and a pool table—that it felt like it should be used only for convivial gatherings like Super Bowl parties or Halloween bashes for little kids dressed in scary costumes that didn't really scare anybody.

Unlike the manila envelope in Adam's hands at that very moment.

"Where are your parents?" Cammie asked. It was bad enough that Adam had the envelope—she didn't want Mr. and Mrs. Flood joining the festivities.

"Upstairs, asleep."

Adam turned the envelope over. Cammie saw the open seal.

"You opened it." Her voice was hollow.

"Yeah," Adam admitted. "I shouldn't have, but . . . I guess I thought maybe I could protect you if it was something bad."

"Bullshit. It *is* something bad, and you *didn't* protect me."

She took the envelope from him. He didn't resist. She didn't open it.

"I can chuck it, Cam. Burn it, even," Adam offered.

She cut her eyes to him. "You know me better than that."

"Yeah." He sighed. "I do."

What would be better? Slowly or quickly? Reading slowly could be like pulling a stitched wound apart thread by thread. Reading fast could be like having a heart attack.

Fast was better. You either died from a heart attack or got better.

She took out the papers. Adam had left the most relevant one right on top.

SANTA BARBARA POLICE DEPARTMENT WITNESS STATEMENT SUMMARY: DINA RACHEL SHARPE

Mrs. Dina Rachel Sharpe is the wife of movie actor Jackson Sharpe. Her statement, attached, indicates the following:

Mrs. Sharpe was on board the vessel the night that Jeanne Sheppard went overboard.

Mrs. Sharpe had been picked up by the owners of the vessel, the Strikers, at the marina in Carpinteria at 6 P.M., after the Strikers and the Sheppards had departed from Santa Barbara Harbor at 5 P.M.

Mrs. Sharpe admits to having sexual relations with Mr. Sheppard during the course of the evening. She did not or could not specify the time.

Mrs. Sharpe claims to have been returned to the marina in Carpinteria just before midnight and denies being on the vessel either when Mrs. Sheppard disappeared or when the death of Mrs. Sheppard was reported to the Coast Guard the next morning.

Numb. Nothing. Cammie felt nothing as the sheaf of papers slid to the celery-green area rug. Adam retrieved them and stuck them back into the envelope.

"You okay?"

"My father was screwing Sam's mother," Cammie muttered. The truth didn't feel real until she said it aloud. "My *father* was screwing Sam's *mother*. She was on the boat that night. Nobody told me about that."

"That doesn't necessarily mean that anyone committed a crime," Adam pointed out. He scratched at the tattoo behind his ear and started to put an arm around her, then stopped and just stared straight ahead. This was awful.

"Thanks a lot," she told Adam, her voice bitter. "You've made my prom a night to remember."

He held his palms up. "If I could do it over, I would. I'd—" He stopped himself. "Who am I kidding? I'd do the same damn thing again. I'd open the envelope, read what was in there, and then show it to you. I'm sorry."

"I *told* you to leave it alone—"

"I know—"

"But you didn't listen to me." She felt her voice rise; the louder it got, the madder she felt. That was good. It felt so much better than that cold, dead place where her heart was supposed to be. "Do you know the position you've put me in? I fucking hate you right now, you know that? I *hate* you."

"It's okay, Cam." He spoke softly and held his arms out to her.

"Leave me alone, you asshole! I mean it!"

His arms wrapped around her.

She willed herself not to lose control, not to push him away or pummel him or—worst of all—cry. Instead, she went as stiff and unyielding as a mannequin, and didn't speak until he let go of her body.

"I was right," she whispered. "All these years. I knew I didn't know everything."

He stroked her hair. His touch didn't alarm her now, didn't revolt her. In fact, it somehow gave her the courage to go on.

"Ask my dad about that night and he always changes the subject. He says I'm only making things harder for me, for him. For *him*!" She leaned her forehead against his shoulder. "My mother hardly drank. I remember how my dad would tease her—it was a big deal if she had a glass of wine at a restaurant. She was on the swim team at UCLA." She lifted her face so that she could look into his eyes. "Does that sound like a woman who fell off a boat?"

"I don't know, Cam—"

"Goddamn. My best friend's mother slept with my father, my father never says a word about it all these years, and I find out on prom night. I shit you not: John Hughes wouldn't make this movie. Freddie Prinze Jr. wouldn't be in it. Shit. Keira Knightly wouldn't be in it!"

Cammie got to her feet and started pacing in front of the fireplace. Meanwhile, Adam sat back on the couch looking visibly relieved, as if he'd emerged unscathed from a horrible storm. "Maybe . . . your dad didn't want you to know he was having an affair."

Cammie's laugh sounded dark and bitter to her own ears. Her father always had affairs. He wouldn't have given a shit if the whole world had known he was doing Sam's mom. It wasn't like the man had a conscience. Nope. There could be only one reason he'd covered it up all these years. It was time to say it aloud.

"I think they killed my mom. My dad and Sam's mom."

Adam paled. "Geez, Cammie, you don't know that—"

"Like hell I don't." She strode over to him, grabbed the envelope, and headed back the way they'd come in.

Adam bounded after her. "Where are you going this time?"

"To do what needs to be done."

Cerebral Annaland

The unofficial prom after party was at Shutters on the Beach in Santa Monica, but Anna and her friends were having their own private afterparty on the set of the new hit television show *Hermosa Beach*.

Clark Sheppard's talent agency had packaged the show, meaning that the writers, stars, and directors were all Apex clients—it meant the Apex agency got an even heftier chunk of the revenues than usual. Anna had briefly been an intern for Clark, but even her friendship with the show's wunderkind writer, Danny Bluestone, hadn't prevented her from walking away from the gig. She'd found Clark to be a venal man. Yet by permitting his daughter and her friends to have their after-prom party here, he'd proved that even the worst people in Hollywood occasionally came through for their children.

When the convoy of limousines had arrived at two-thirty in the morning, there was a bonfire already lit on the beach and a sound system set up on the patio of the hotel that was the main set for *Hermosa Beach*. The best restaurant in Hermosa Beach, the Blue Pacific, had set out a sumptuous buffet for twenty: cold cracked lobster; a marinated salad of octopus and baby shrimp; a fruit salad of fresh pineapple, coconut, apples, grapes, and almonds; a dozen different pâtés and cheeses, plus hot bread baked in a portable oven right on the beach. Two older bartenders served lemonade mojitos—mint leaves with sugar syrup, club soda, lemon juice, and vodka. For those not in a lethal-lemonade mood or who preferred to make an atempt to sober up, there was espresso that could be laced with Kahlua.

Fifteen minutes after they'd arrived, Anna and Ben were walking hand-in-hand in the moonlight along the ragged surf line where the surf washed up and then went back out to sea. They were both barefoot, having left their shoes up by the patio. Ben casually two-fingered his tuxedo jacket over his shoulder. Suddenly, Anna giggled.

"What's so funny?" Ben wondered.

"I'm still thinking about Maddy and Jack," Anna admitted. "What you told me."

"That it was all a plot for her to get Mr. T?" Ben stepped out of the gentle splash of an approaching wave. "That's not the worst of it. That teacher was into her. I made her promise that she wouldn't hook up with him."

"I hope not." The sea breeze ruffled some hair onto her cheek and she pushed it back. "But you can't control what she does."

"Yeah, I guess. . . ." He didn't sound convinced.

"You could climb down from the horse, Ben," she

ventured. "Not everyone needs you to be a white knight."

"I don't do that."

She bumped into him playfully with her hip. "Yes, you do. You've done it ever since the day I met you, when you saved me from that jerk on the airplane."

"Well, he was messed up."

"So are a lot of people in this world. You come through for everyone. But sometimes . . ."

She hesitated, unsure if she had any right to continue. Who was she to tell him what he should or shouldn't do?

"Go ahead," he urged ruefully. "Hit me with your best shot."

Right. Honesty.

She stopped and took his arm. "Not everyone needs to be rescued, Ben. I don't."

"Only when you're stuck in the window seat on a long flight next to an asshole, huh?" There was a subtle but noticeable edge to his voice.

She turned toward the dark ocean. "The reason I understand is because that was always my role with my sister, Susan." She thought about all the times she'd held Susan's head over the toilet while her sister puked up whatever illegal substance she'd ingested, all the times she'd been at parties and spent the whole evening as Susan's watchdog. "Maybe taking care of everyone else is just a kind of protection."

"You're going to Cerebral Annaland on me."

"Yeah," she laughed. "I guess I am. I just want you to know, Ben, that you don't need to save me. I can save myself."

The words made her feel stronger; and hearing herself say them, she knew they were true. She loved Ben. But she didn't need him to make her life okay.

Ben stroked her hair. "Don't you get it? One of the reasons I love you is because I know you *don't* need saving."

She raised her lips to his and they shared a kiss. Ben had jumped to the wrong conclusions about Maddy and Jack, and she'd jumped to the wrong conclusions about Ben.

Just as they were about to kiss again, a tall, skinny figure hollered for them to wait up. It was Marshall, Dee's escort from Ojai. His tux jacket and tie were gone, his shirt rumpled and half untucked from his pants. He had a tall lemonade mojito in hand—from the way he was walking, it clearly was not his first.

"Please tell me you've seen Dee-ee." He made the name Dee into two syllables.

"The answer's the same as it was the last two times you asked me, buddy," Ben replied. "No."

Marshall had lost track of Dee at prom. Anna wasn't worried, because Dee had called Sam to say she was fine and with Jack—they'd be at Hermosa Beach by 3 A.M. Anna glanced at the luminous hands of her watch. Two forty-five. Anna suspected that Dee was learning how to save herself too.

"Marshall, may I make a suggestion?" she queried.

"What?"

"Relax. Have some fun. Dee won't let you down."

"I'm fucked," Marshall moaned, then sucked a quarter of his mojito noisily through his straw. "How did this happen? How? I should call the hospital, but I'll lose my job." He wandered away up the beach—Anna saw him stop to question Skye, whose silver mesh dress seemed to dance in the reflected bonfire. His elongated silhouette looked forlorn in the night.

They were getting some espresso minus the Kahlua a few minutes later back up at the patio when Ben and Anna spotted Sam and Parker on a blanket not far from the bonfire. Parker motioned that they should join them, so they strode through the sand and plopped down on their blanket.

"How's it going, Miss Prom Queen?" Ben teased. He picked up a handful of sand and let it run through his fingers.

"Oh, bite me," Sam grumbled as she cradled a lemonade mojito. "I did all this work to make a great documentary, and it turns out it's all for nothing."

"How do you figure?" Ben asked.

Sam raised her eyebrows. "If the prom queen makes a movie about prom, it's not called a documentary. It's called a fucking *home movie*."

"I don't think royalty is allowed to say 'fuck,' your highness," Parker offered. "Not even when she's had three power mojitos. Speaking of which, I'm due for another."

"Whatever," Sam sighed. "What's done is done. And my documentary is really, really done. My father always says that no good deed goes unpunished. I think he's right."

Anna stretched out and dug her toes into the cool sand. "Actually, you gave people an amazing prom that they'll remember forever."

Sam propped herself up on her elbows and took a sip of her drink. "Good. Nominate me for sainthood."

"No, seriously, Sam. You're turned a near disaster into something really amazing."

"Coffee, this time. More Kahlua, less caffeine." Sam slurped the last of her mojito and handed Parker the glass.

"Your wish is my command, your prom queen royal highness." He rose, bowed to her, and padded off across the sand toward the bar table.

Sam's gaze followed him. "You're right, Anna, I'm a total magician." She closed her left eye, made a fist with her right hand, then spread her fingers. "Poof! Did you see that? I just magically turned Parker into Eduardo."

Anna smiled. "It's too bad that Eduardo couldn't have seen—"

"Hi, you guys!" It was Dee, skittering across the sand toward them. "I'm so happy!"

"Better be careful. Marshall's on the prowl for you," Ben warned. "Of course, last time I saw him he was down there getting loaded." He pointed toward the surf.

"Thanks for the heads up," Dee said. She wrapped her arms around herself. "I will remember this night *forever*. Prom night. The night Jack and I met."

"Where is he?" Anna asked.

"In front of the hotel," Dee replied. "I just didn't want you guys to worry."

"Well, I'm worried anyway," Ben said. "Jack's a player."

"Not with me," Dee insisted, eyes shining.

Dee really did look happy. And sane. Anna smiled at her.

"Do you think there is such a thing as soul mates?" Dee asked.

Anna was touched. "It's definitely possible, Dee."

Ben kept his eyes on Anna. "Even a player can decide to quit the game when the right girl comes along."

"I love you guys so much," Dee breathed. She hugged them each in turn. "Where are Cammie and Adam?"

"They left prom early," Sam told her with a wink "They'll either show up or not."

Dee grinned. "I'm going to Jack's guesthouse with him. I'll call Marshall so he won't worry anymore."

"What about the Ojai Institute?" Anna asked.

"I don't know. Whatever happens, it's worth it. I love you guys!"

"That's the most sane I've ever seen her," Ben remarked as Dee trotted away.

"No kidding," Sam agreed. "It's kind of scary."

Parker arrived with Sam's drink. "I saw Dee. Where's she going?"

"Off with Jack. They're soul mates," Sam filled in. She sipped her laced coffee. "Much better."

Ben nuzzled Anna and whispered in her ear. "Dee and Jack are inspiring me. How about we find a more private spot?"

He was reading her mind.

Your Promness

"**L**ast one to make a ring shot has to go skinny-dipping," Sam told Parker as they stood on the patio about twenty feet from an upended buffet table. She'd tucked the bottom of her gown into the waist of her boy-cut black lace La Perla panties. Her prom crown was in one hand, yet another mojito—she'd switched back again—was in the other. As the night had gone on, she'd found herself more and more depressed, both over her ruined documentary and at being with Parker instead of Eduardo. Her boyfriend would have found a way to make everything okay. But he was in Mexico, probably with that hot Pilar bitch—

Stop, she ordered herself. Just stop.

She bent her wrist and curled the rhinestone tiara toward her, then flung it like a Frisbee, trying to ring it on one the table legs. No dice. She overshot by five feet, losing her balance in the process.

"Steady there, your promness," Parker advised, then went to retrieve the now-battered crown.

Sam stared into the night. She and Parker were alone.

Ben and Anna had taken off down the beach. Cammie and Adam hadn't shown up—she knew exactly what they had to be doing. Krishna and Damian had come back for drinks about fifteen minutes ago and then had decided to take a walk into town with Ashleigh so that they could buy a razor and give Damian an impromptu Mohawk. For some ungodly reason, Skye had joined up with Marshall in the search for Dee—a search that Sam knew would be completely futile. Maybe Dee had called Marshall by now. Maybe not. As for Pilar—

Geez. She really *was* wrecked. The imaginary Spanish chick didn't really exist, except in Sam's paranoid imagination.

That doesn't mean Eduardo isn't with some other, equally bodacious babe, the demon voice in her head whispered. Some version of Parker's earlier words to her came roaring back.

Not enough to skip some stupid party in Mexico. "If I really wanted to be with you . . ."

"Does your worshipfulness wish to take another shot?" Parker knelt in the sand and handed her back her crown, plus a drink he'd made.

"Since we're such good buds, you may call me simply 'your royalness,'" Sam decreed. "Because *I* am prom queen. *Me.*" She took a sip of what Parker had poured for her. "Jameson. Good choice."

Parker patted the crown on her head. "Enjoy it."

"Screw it." Sam tossed her tiara away. "I'm abdicating. What good is a queen if her king doesn't attend the coronation?" She pointed at the night sky. "I hereby command you to make Eduardo appear!"

No shocker. Nothing happened.

"His loss," Parker declared.

"Whose?"

"God or Eduardo, your heavenliness. Take your pick."

Sam giggled. Had Parker always been this funny? Or did she just think he was funny because she was so fucked up?

She put her face two inches from his. "When I do this, it looks like you have one giant eye in the middle of your forehead."

"I *do* have one giant eye in the middle of my forehead. Excuse me." Parker strode out onto the beach, retrieved Sam's crown, and then deposited it around one of the upturned table legs. "Tada! I win! You pick who skinny-dips."

Skinny-dipping. She'd felt so free in Mexico that she'd swum bareass in the Pacific with Anna. It wasn't until the next day that she found out Eduardo had seen her from a boat, and that he he'd loved what he's seen. She looked around. No Eduardo. So she boomed at Parker: "I command you to partake of the sacred waters of the Pacific!"

"Absolutely, your wastedness." Parker started to fumble with the buttons on his tux shirt.

"Stop," Sam ordered.

"How come?"

"First, the ceremonial kiss from the queen."

"Yes, your highness."

Sam giggled again, then stepped drunkenly toward Parker, who had closed his eyes. She kissed him. Then she kissed him again. It was friendly, that's all. Well, maybe a little more than friendly, but not much. . . .

"Samantha?"

Oh God. She knew that sexy, slightly accented voice. It belonged to Eduardo. But it couldn't be real, because Eduardo was in—

"*Samantha!*"

Sam pushed Parker to one side so she could prove to herself that she was having auditory hallucinations.

Nothing phantasmagorical was involved. Eduardo stood not five feet from them, in jeans, a white T-shirt, and an open light blue shirt.

"I left the party in Mexico to surprise you." His voice was hard and cold. "But I am the one who is surprised."

Parker tried to go to Sam's defense. "Hey, man, this isn't what it looked like. It's prom night, Sam was missing you—"

"Shut up before I feed you your teeth," Eduardo seethed.

"But—it isn't fair. You should have told me you were coming." She knew that was a weak effort, but she was too mortified by her own behavior to think of anything else to say. Mortified and drunk.

Eduardo's eyes narrowed. "Why? So you could pretend to be the girl I thought you were?"

Fear clutched Sam's stomach. "I *am* that girl! This was stupid, I know. I was just lonely and missing you and we were goofing around and—"

"Save it, Samantha," Eduardo spat, "for someone who gives a damn."

He turned and headed back toward the hotel parking lot. Sam stumbled after him. "Eduardo, wait, please. *Please!*"

He didn't turn stop; Sam was too wasted to catch up with him. All she could do was watch him disappear around the corner of the hotel. She felt bereft, lost, alone. How had this have happened? *How?*

Parker came up next to her and put a supportive arm around her shoulders. "What's with that guy? He just loves to show up unannounced."

"Go to hell, Parker."

"Relax, Sam. Talk to him tomorrow. It'll be okay."

Funny, five minutes ago he'd been as wasted as she was, but now he sounded perfectly sober. Had he really been so drunk in the first place, or had he only been *pretending* to be drunk so that she would be tempted to kiss him?

"You got drunk and you kissed me," Parker went on. "Nothing else happened. It's *prom night,* for God's sake. What's the big deal?"

Sadness washed over her. She was megarich and semi-famous. She could get anything, go anywhere, meet anyone she wanted, but what she couldn't get was a do-over of the moment her first true love had found her kissing someone else.

"The big deal, Parker," she replied calmly, with all the dignity and sobriety she could muster, "is that you don't give a shit about me, but Eduardo does. He really, truly does."

Who Says Romance is Dead?

Anna and Ben walked with their arms around each other, heading away from the bonfire until its faint light was far off in the distance. They were about to spread out their beach blanket when Anna nearly tripped over something. At first she thought it was a rock. But then it groaned. A someone. She peered closely at it. *Two* someones.

Skye. Her shimmery silver dress was near her waist, revealing an equally shimmery silver G-string. She was entwined in the gangly limbs of none other than Marshall.

"Sorry!" Anna half-gasped, astonished to see that the mental-health chaperone was a closet party animal. "We didn't see you."

Skye lifted her head from Marshall's shoulder long enough to peer up at Anna and Ben. "Marshall is helping me get over Damian."

Marshall shrugged. "What the hell. I already lost my job."

"If you can't be with the one you love. . . ," Skye slurred. "However that thing goes."

"Love the one you're with?" Ben filled in helpfully.

"Yeah, whatever." She put her head back in the crook of Marshall's arm.

"Okay, well . . ." Anna had no idea what to say; it was everything she could do to keep from giggling.

"Party on," Ben suggested, peering down at them.

He pulled her away from the macking couple, and they managed to walk down the beach another hundred yards or so. Then they couldn't help themselves; they burst out laughing . . . before spreading their own blanket on the sand and giving themselves over to the moment.

At a guesthouse on Twenty-fifth Avenue in Santa Monica, Dee slept wrapped in Jack's arms. Meanwhile, he thanked whatever gods had led him to this moment and this girl. She stirred; Jack pressed her closer.

"Everything is okay," he whispered, kissing her hair. "Go back to sleep."

He couldn't say for sure that they wouldn't both wake up in the morning and give each other that who-are-you-and-what-the-hell-did-I-do? look. It had happened to him so many times; the wow-I-had-no-idea-it-was-so-late while pulling on his jeans, followed by the hey-I'll-call-you lie as he stuffed his wallet into his back pocket and made a hasty retreat.

Maybe that would happen. Maybe it wouldn't. But *this* feeling, *this* moment, had never happened to him before: He wanted to hold Dee forever. He kissed her forehead.

Shit. Maybe this was what love felt like.

After Eduardo coldly stormed away, Sam downed three cups of bitter black coffee and then took her returning lucidity and bitch of a headache to a large craggy rock by the ocean, just to think. She wasn't big on religion, but she found herself proffering deals to whatever god was in charge of these things: If he would only forgive her, she'd never be mean or petty again. She really *would* become the girl Eduardo thought she was, instead of the self-centered bitch she often allowed herself to be.

She raised her knees to her chest and encircled them with her arms, breathing in the salt air. Her perch was surrounded by the Pacific, and the constant lapping of ocean against the stone was somehow soothing. A plan. She needed a plan. What was the best way to apologize? She had to figure out how to—

"Hey, Sam."

Cammie. Dressed way down in Earl jeans and a pink paisley Imitation of Christ T-shirt; she held a large envelope in her hands.

"Have a pleasant evening?" Sam mustered all the energy she could just to ask the question. It wasn't much. She'd been sitting on the rock for a long time and hadn't even had enough will to check her watch.

Cammie didn't reply; she just motioned at the rock with a gesture that Sam interpreted by scooching to one side so her friend could settle in.

"Could you find anyplace *more* uncomfortable to sit?"

"My ass has more padding than yours does. So, you and Adam took off early in a moment of passion? That's lasted until now?"

Cammie shook her head. "Not exactly. It's been a strange night."

"Tell me about it." Sam shook her head sadly. "Where's Adam?"

"Home. I'm alone."

Okay, that *was* strange. Normally, Sam would have pressed her, but she had other things on her mind. "Guess what? You missed Eduardo. He showed up to surprise me."

"Really," Cammie replied. Her voice was uncharacteristically flat.

"He caught me kissing Parker because . . . I don't know. I was drunk."

Cammie gave the smallest of shrugs. "Shit happens."

Sam bristled. "Oh well. Thank you *so* much for all your love and support in my hour of need."

"Funny, isn't it," Cammie mused, "how something can feel like the biggest thing in the world, but then in an instant, everything can change?"

"What can be bigger than that? I just lost Eduardo—"

"I've got bigger." She fingered the large envelope in her lap.

"What are you talking about?"

Cammie pressed her lips together. "Okay, I don't

know any way to say this but to say it. It's about my mother. She didn't kill herself. I'm sure of it."

Sam put a hand to her forehead. Mental rewind. What did Cammie's mom have to do with anything?

"What are you talking about?"

Cammie tapped the envelope. "What's in here. I'd tell you to read it but it's too dark. Besides, no one in Hollywood reads, so I'll give you the coverage. Your mother was doing my father a long time ago."

"*What*? And what does that line of total bullshit have to do with any of the other bullshit that happened tonight?"

"Forget tonight, okay?" Cammie begged. "Can you just do that for one goddamn minute?"

Sam was shocked into silence. Cammie *never* begged.

"Okay," Sam agreed cautiously, though she was skeptical. "My mother. Your father. Way back when. Prove it."

Cammie hoisted the envelope. "In here is the police report about my mom's death. The papers were sealed, but Adam's parents got a hold of them. . . ." She stopped, then started again. "It's pretty goddamn clear. The night my mother died, your mother was with her. She got picked up at the Carpinteria marina and dropped off there later. Your mom told the cops she did my father on the boat."

Sam shook her head as if to clear it. "My mother was having sex with your father?"

Cammie gestured unemotionally to the papers. "It's all in here."

Sam put her palms on the boulder to steady herself. "This doesn't make sense."

"Yes it does. If they killed my mother."

Sam gasped. "That's insane."

"If it's so insane, why has it been a big secret all these years? Why did your mom leave town? She never sees you, never calls—"

Sam slapped her hands over her ears. "Stop saying that."

"Why, Sam?" Cammie pressed, loud enough so that Sam could still hear. "Why?"

Sam's hands fell to her sides. She shook her head. "You're jumping to conclusions. Sick conclusions."

"Maybe the right conclusions. That's what we have to find out."

Sam had never seen such determination in Cammie's eyes before. "What are you going to do?"

"It'll be light in a few hours. Even though it's Sunday, my compulsive father will be at the *Hermosa Beach* set by eight A.M. I'll be waiting for him. With this." She tossed the envelope up and down, like Sam had seen movie criminals do with their murder weapons.

Sam had no idea what to do or what to believe. If she read the affidavit that Cammie said was in the envelope, would it make more sense?

God, poor Cammie. She really thought that her father had—

Ugh. Clark and her mother. What a repulsive concept.

She turned to look at her friend. Cammie's hands were literally shaking. That was a first, too. The two of them had been through so much. They bitched and gossiped and fought with each other, but in the end, they knew each other better than anyone else on the planet knew them.

She took Cammie's trembling hand in her own and squeezed it.

"What's that for?" her oldest friend asked, her eyes looking out to the dark abyss of the Pacific.

"When your father shows up, we'll *both* be waiting for him."

Cammie Sheppard was a lot of things, but *grateful* was a characteristic no one had ever ascribed to her . . . not until that moment on that rock by the ocean, when Cammie squeezed Sam's hand back.